Skylark and Wallcreeper

Anne O'Brien Carelli

 YELLOW JACKET

Skylark and

Wallcreeper

Anne O'Brien Carelli

YELLOW JACKET

An imprint of Bonnier Publishing USA
251 Park Avenue South, New York, NY 10010
Copyright © 2018 by Anne O'Brien Carelli
All rights reserved, including the right of reproduction
in whole or in part in any form.
Yellow Jacket is an imprint of Bonnier Publishing USA, and
associated colophon is a trademark of Bonnier Publishing USA.
Manufactured in the United States of America   BVG 0718
First Edition   10 9 8 7 6 5 4 3 2 1
Library of Congress Cataloging-in-Publication Data is available
upon request.
ISBN 978-1-4998-0745-5
yellowjacketreads.com
bonnierpublishingusa.com

To Phoebe

Table of

Contents

Chapter 1
Three Feet

Queens, New York

October 2012—Day 1

It sounds like she's in a tunnel.

But they closed all the tunnels.

"Mom, you can't come! The water's too high."

"Can you hear me, Lily? Are you there?"

I hold my phone in front of me. "Mom! Trust me, I'm fine."

The phone buzzes, and my mom's voice breaks up, then fades away. I end the call, slip the phone into the back pocket of my jeans, and race up the metal stairs. Behind me, a heavy door holds back sloshing water that smells like dead fish and gasoline. I had just checked on the boxes we'd stacked on tables on the main floor. I hope we raised them high enough, but that water's coming in fast.

The door to the second floor slams against something hard when I push on the bar. I can see the end of a gurney blocking the way, so I give it a shove and squeeze through the opening. "Careful!" a woman in a wheelchair yells at me. "Shut that door! Keep the water out!" She's wearing a red winter coat and knit cap, even though it's October and she never goes outside.

"Sorry." I rush past her and several other people sitting quietly in wheelchairs in the long hallway. They're holding stuffed plastic bags in their laps and look at me expectantly as I race by.

I see Veronica at the end of the hall calming a group of residents who are clustered around her. "Go back to your rooms." She gently turns Mr. Michaels toward room 212. "No one's going anywhere."

"It's higher," I whisper to her as I help steer everyone toward their rooms. She stiffens and grabs the radio hanging on her hip.

"How high?" she asks as she flicks the switch.

"It's probably two feet—maybe two and a half. But it keeps coming. It's definitely not slowing down."

"This shelter in place is BS," Veronica mumbles. "Nicole?" she speaks into the radio. "Nicole?"

"On third!" Nicole responds, her voice crackly. "What's the word?"

"Lily says two feet and climbing." She steps away from two very old men who are leaning in and listening.

"Lily's still here?"

Veronica shakes her head at me and touches my cheek. "She won't leave. She's our water checker. She says maybe two and a half and still coming in."

"Better start Phase One for the second floor. I'll be right down." The green light on the radio turns red, just as the hall lights flicker. Sounds of surprise come from the rooms, and more residents start to appear at their doorways.

"Don't worry—we have a generator!" Veronica works her way up and down the hallway, stroking thin, weak arms and smiling at worried faces. "Just stay where you are so we don't have to track anyone down, okay?"

Mrs. Sidobeth, always one to raise a few questions, points her cane at me. "Why aren't you safe at home?"

"I was visiting my granny." Mrs. Sidobeth looks confused, but that could be because her dementia has taken over. "She's on the fifth floor. You know, your friend? Miss Collette?" Sometimes you can have a good conversation with Mrs. S, but then she'll repeat the entire talk the next day. She plays poker with my granny on Wednesday afternoons in the resident lounge. It's pretty funny to watch because most of them can't remember anything.

I won't be watching penny poker for a while. The resident lounge is on the first floor and almost under water.

"I'm going up," I say to Veronica, and head back to the stairwell. We've been warned that we shouldn't use the elevators in case the power goes out. The lights flicker again, and I grab the last flashlight from the supply box at the nurses' station.

The nursing home has eight floors. My granny has

4

been on four different floors since we moved her here three years ago. She says that they keep moving her up closer to the Big Pie in the Sky. I hope she stayed in her room because I really don't want to hunt for her. She tends to wander.

The fifth floor is a lot quieter than the second floor, probably because it's late in the afternoon and a lot of residents are napping. They aren't as close to the rising waters, and most won't remember that a hurricane has been banging against New York City. Some of them won't even remember they're living in Queens, right on the ocean.

I visit Granny as much as possible. She still knows who I am. I can tell her about all the weird things that happen in school. She loves hearing about Mr. Simpson, my sixth-grade science teacher, and his horrible BO, and what my best friend, Johnny, brings for lunch every day. Granny was an amazing cook and always laughs at Johnny's latest creations. His family owns a restaurant, and they let him try out recipes on the regular customers.

Yesterday he brought bright green cookies in

his lunch. They were made out of broccoli and spinach, with bacon and maple syrup frosting. I was the only one willing to try one, and they were surprisingly good.

School was canceled because of the hurricane today. Granny won't care about me missing school. She never asks about my grades or homework. I read her the stories that I write, and when she's able to focus, her suggestions always make them better. I never leave her without putting my cheek close to her face so that she can kiss me and say, "So good. You are so good, my Lilybelle."

I enter the small room that is now my granny's home. Her bed takes up most of the space, but my mom and I managed to squeeze in Granny's favorite comfy chair. On the walls are large pictures that seem to glow in the dim light. They're photos of the gardens that Granny planted all over the world. My granny's been everywhere. She tells me about her travels to places with names like Kathmandu and Bujumbura.

I haven't been anywhere outside of the city yet, but

it was Granny who helped me get my first passport. My mom wasn't too pleased, but I always keep my passport zipped into the pocket of my backpack.

When she can't remember much, Granny can still tell me about all the places she's been. On the days when she has no idea what she had for breakfast, she can still tell me the name of every flower and every person who worked beside her in those gardens.

She's sitting up in bed, dozing against a pillow covered in the bright pink pillowcase that she brought with her from her old apartment. Every time I come to see her, I'm struck by how tiny and pale she looks. I hope we don't have to evacuate the building because she doesn't look like she could stand the excitement.

She always seems to know that I've arrived because her eyes pop open, and she grins. She fusses with her short, wavy white hair, which is silly because I don't care what she looks like. "I like to look presentable," she says. "So should you."

"Hey, Granny!" I slide a chair next to her bed.

"So nobody moved me?" We both laugh. She likes

to claim that when she's sleeping they move her to another floor. Little does she know that it may happen again.

Maria appears at the door. Her normally cheerful face is grim. She's wearing an orange smock decorated with huge yellow daisies, and her wide pockets are bulging. She carries all the paraphernalia she needs to treat her residents with when she moves swiftly from room to room during her shift. A large black flashlight pokes out of one of the pockets. "Nicole needs you on the second floor," she says, gesturing for me to come. "Miss Collette, I think your Lily's going to be pretty busy for a while. Can you spare her?"

"Doing what?" Granny pulls herself up and points at the rain that's blowing sideways and beating against her small window. "Sandy's here?"

"Yep—Superstorm Sandy is right at our doorstep." Maria strides over and tries to gently help Granny lie back down, but Granny resists. I push back my chair and step out of the way. I know that nurses like Maria can be firm but kind when residents get stubborn. This time Granny wins, and her thin legs dangle off the edge of the bed, far from the floor. I want to stop everything, climb on the bed next to her, and hold her nice and steady.

Maria squats down to look at Granny eye to eye. "You need to stay in your bed and let Lily go help on the second floor. No arguments this time, okay?"

I make sure Granny's comfortable, but she waves me off. She can tell I'm anxious to find Nicole. I squeeze her gnarled hand. "I'll be back, but do as they say." She settles back down as Maria straightens her favorite pink-flowered coverlet.

The lights go out, and the room turns gray. The rain sounds more like winter sleet and pounds on the window. Granny grasps the sides of her bed and glances at her oxygen tank plugged into the socket near her bed. "We have a generator, right?" She's tough, my granny, but I can tell from her wide, bright blue eyes that she's scared.

"Count to twenty," Maria shouts down the hall. "At twenty you'll hear the generator come on!"

I grab the jean jacket I'd hung on the unused IV stand in the corner of Granny's room and work my way down the darkened hall, silently counting to twenty. There are people who normally work the night shift moving from room to room. They were here all night and stayed today, and they're not going home now. Someone has stacked the evacuation sleds along the walls, but it doesn't look like there's enough for all the residents on the floor.

The normally glowing red EXIT lights are dim. I may need my flashlight in the stairwell. I can't see anything out the window that faces the ocean—just clouds of swirling water flying by. But the lights come back on as the generator kicks in. Maria catches up with me. "Three feet of water on the first floor," she says in a low voice. "They're moving second floor to third. What a mess."

The hall abruptly goes dark. For a moment, there's complete silence on the floor. The computers at the nurses' station go down. The beeping and humming from the medical equipment stop.

Maria grabs my arm. "Oh, no. This is not good. The generator's on the first floor."

Chapter 2
Four Feet

Everyone is moving up the stairs as I slide along the cool wall to get down to the second floor. The nurses and orderlies are carrying frightened residents on short stretchers. Some of the nurses are also carrying IV bags or portable oxygen tanks, but they keep up a constant chatter.

"I knew I should've quit smoking!" one of them gasps as she lifts the end of a stretcher that holds a wiggling and moaning old man.

Another nurse chuckles, even though she's trying to drag a medicine cart up the steps. "Well, your cigarettes are soggy now!" I guess their lockers on the first floor must be under water.

There are luminescent dots scattered throughout

the dark stairwell. They're coming from glow sticks that the nurses have twisted around their necks and hung on their belts. Last year, one of the orderlies brought back hundreds of glow sticks that he bought at a concert at Madison Square Garden. "They lit up the arena," he said when he dumped the boxes at Nicole's feet. "And I figured you can't hold a flashlight while you're changing a bandage, so here you go." We laughed at him at the time. He was always preparing for emergencies we thought would never happen. Now those skinny glow sticks are lighting the way.

"Lily!" As I reach the second floor, Nicole rushes down the hallway toward me. "Go down and do a water check. But be careful—don't touch the water. We don't need you electrocuted." She spins two residents in wheelchairs at the same time and lines them up to be carried to the third floor. "Elevator's out. Hang in there, folks. Just going for a little ride."

By this time it's as black as the middle of the night both inside and out, and the wind screeches like an eighteen-wheeler slamming on its brakes. As I enter the stairwell down to the first floor, the door slams behind me. I'm all alone, and I can't hear any of the activity on the other side of the door. But somehow the distant whirring of the storm is still in the background.

I flick on my flashlight and carefully take one step at a time. The railing feels slimy. I'm glad I'm wearing my clunky black pirate boots. I hope Nicole remembers that she sent me here.

I don't really work at the nursing home. I'm just a regular visitor and probably the youngest person who comes and stays a lot. It takes two subway transfers from our apartment and my middle school, but they can always use an extra hand. They put me to work doing errands and keeping the residents occupied. But mostly I sit near my granny and read to her and tell her stuff. She's listening, even if she looks like she's not.

I'm just about to push open the door to the first floor, but the air is damp and the temperature has dropped, so I stop to zip up my thin cotton hoodie. What if the ocean is waiting there, ready to pour through the doorway and wash me away?

But I have to check—Nicole needs my report. I

reach forward to push on the bar, when the door flies open and a blinding light blasts into my face. "Anybody there?" The biggest man I've ever seen shouts up the stairwell. "National Guard! Coming up!"

I don't think he's seen me, even though I'm covered in light. I guess it would be weird to plow through floodwaters to rescue people in a nursing home and see a skinny, twelve-year-old girl with a pixie cut and freckles standing in the stairwell.

He's wearing green overalls that look like they're made of plastic. The water comes almost to his knees and would probably cover me to my waist. "Hey!" He pushes his flashlight even closer so that I wave my hand in front of my face. I almost clunk him with my own flashlight. "This is Rockaway Manor, right? The nursing home?"

"Yes it is! And they could use some help moving everyone up to the third floor. The water's climbing."

"No kidding." He turns and yells behind him. "We'll have to get 'em out this way! Let's move!"

"Out?" I can barely say the word. "You're evacuating?"

"Honey," he says as he waves people in camouflage and headlamps past me, "you ain't seen nothin' yet. That water's not going to stop. Not even for a bunch of old people." He steps by me, shouting orders.

Granny! She's on the fifth floor, but are they going to evacuate all the floors?

I scoot up the stairs, winding my way around the National Guard soldiers as they pour into the second floor. Three more flights to go.

Granny's sitting on the side of the bed, and Maria's tearing long strips of duct tape and sticking them to the bed frame. "Put your coat on and lie down, Miss Collette. Everyone has to stay in their beds."

"Don't you tape me into this bed!" Granny pushes Maria.

"Granny, listen to Maria." I come around the other side of the bed and help her slide her skinny arms into the sleeves of her wool coat. I gently pull her back, but she shakes her head and clutches my arm.

"Get a diaper cover." Maria points to Granny's small closet. "Get two. Wrap this medical record in it and seal it to Miss Collette's bed." She hands Granny's

15

thick file to me and a baggie filled with bottles of medicines. "We've run out of plastic bags, but her records have to stay dry. Attach these to her and don't let them get lost."

She grabs Granny's hand, snaps a white plastic band around her wrist, and scribbles Granny's name and room number on it. "Don't you go disappearing on me now." She moves quickly toward the door and points to the closet again. "Go, Lily. Then come help me with everyone else."

Granny's shaking when I help her settle down under her coverlet and pull the coat collar up around her neck. I stretch long pieces of duct tape and stick them across the coverlet. "This will keep the blanket on, Granny. Looks like they're going to take us someplace else, and we need to keep you warm."

She struggles to sit up. "I can walk! Let me walk!"

I can hear Maria in the hallway shouting, "In their beds. It's the only way. We don't want anyone falling." She steps in the room and hands me two glow sticks and checks the tape. I bend the glow sticks and secure them with the tape so that Granny's bed has its own lights. "Ready to roll?"

There are National Guard soldiers everywhere. They're carrying people on chairs, on their mattresses, and on the few evacuation sleds that had been hanging in the stairwells and stacked in the hallways. They try to calm Granny's neighbors, but some of the residents are screaming and grabbing anyone who rushes by.

Granny's too quiet. Her eyes are closed, but she fingers the tape across her blanket. While I stuff her slippers and some clothing into a flowered tote bag, I explain that she's going to be carried down the stairs, but I won't leave her side.

I don't tell her I have no idea how they'll get her out of the building. Or where we'll float to after that.

"Red box!" she shouts. "Red box!"

It doesn't surprise me that her mind would drift right now. She's usually pretty focused when I visit, but sometimes she says things that don't make any sense. Maria has explained to me that occasionally Granny's mind checks out for a bit. "She is eighty years old, after all," Maria commented. I know it's dementia because I've been hanging out at a nursing home.

I'm supposed to pretend that she's carrying on a normal conversation. "Yes, red box," I repeat patiently, as I check for batteries on her backup oxygen tank.

"Lily, get the red box in the closet," she says clearly, those light blue eyes of hers staring directly into my hazel ones.

I dig around in the small suitcase in her closet, but no red box. Should I tell her I already put it in the tote bag?

"Shoes. In my special shoes."

I pull out the only pair of fancy shoes that Granny's brought from her apartment. She told me they were her wedding shoes, but they look pretty beat-up. Fake crystals are sprinkled on the pointed blue silk toes. A long, red, velveteen box is in the bottom of one of them. The box is decorated with tiny gold circles around the edge.

Two National Guard soldiers enter the room and grab the sides of Granny's mattress, saying nothing as they lift her in the air. She screeches, and the female soldier smiles at her. "Don't be alarmed, dear. We've practiced this, and you'll be fine." She lifts my backpack from the bedpost and slings it over her shoulder.

"Wait!" I shove her fancy shoes into the tote bag and slide the bag under the blanket so the tape will hold it in. I give Granny the red box. "Here you go, Granny." The soldiers carry Granny to the doorway of the room as her pillow falls to the floor.

"No!" she yells back at me. "Take this, Lily!" The two soldiers press the sides of the mattress against her to squeeze through the door. I can barely see the top of her head with its wispy white hair and one frail arm in the air, clutching the thin red box.

Chapter 3
Low Tide

The hall is crowded as the National Guard soldiers carrying my granny join the line of moving mattresses. Confused residents join the pack, clutching bags and small suitcases, or just wads of clothing. Nurses are shoving them into any winter coats they can find in the back of closets. Some of the residents have white bath towels draped around their shoulders.

WM, definitely the loudest resident in the entire nursing home, stands in the hall wrapped in an orange wool poncho. She's tied a yellow-and-red-striped scarf around her neck brace. "What can I do?"

"You can sit in that wheelchair and stay there!" One of the nurse assistants, clutching a large cardboard box labeled FREEZE-DRIED COLD CUTS, kicks a wheelchair over to WM. I reach into the box and grab a plastic bag of frozen turkey slices and shove it into the front pouch of my hoodie.

WM has been here in rehab for two weeks. She named herself WM. "I'm a Walking Miracle!" she tells everyone. Her son seems to be almost as old as she is. He's always arguing with her when he visits. She broke her neck when her horse tripped, so he moved her to the city to be closer to him. He's mad that she was on a horse.

"I learned how to ride on the steppes of Siberia!" she told me. "I was a diplomat."

I had to look up what a diplomat is. I have to look up a lot of things the residents tell me about their lives. They have a million stories, and now they'll have one more to tell.

Granny's traveling mattress disappears down the stairs as I try to get Mr. Flynn's pudgy arms into the sleeves of his coat. I pull over a chair from the side of his bed and help him sit in the doorway of his room.

The soldiers are suddenly swarming the floor,

working fast. They're joined by men in yellow hard hats and glowing red jackets that say TUPPER LAKE RESCUE on the back. They've come from way up north in the mountains. They don't seem to need to talk to each other.

"That's good, Lily." Maria passes by with an armload of diaper boxes. "Do that with everyone!"

"But Granny . . ."

"And tell them we're going where there's heat, light, and bathrooms," she shouts back to me. She turns to a man in a hard hat and asks quietly, "Is that true?"

"Yes, ma'am, you're going to the Armory."

"In Brooklyn?" Maria dumps the boxes at the nurses' station. Brooklyn is right next door to Queens, but it seems like it's another country.

"There's a pool there. Bring your bikini."

Maria actually laughs as she turns and weaves her way back around the trail of loaded mattresses and plastic evacuation sleds carried by strong men patiently waiting their turn to go down the stairs.

22

The wind starts shrieking again, and instead of heightening the fear of the residents, it seems to settle them down. They know they have to go.

Maria hauls another box from the storage closet—this time bandages—and shoves it at me. The closet is usually locked and can be opened only with a secret code that the nurses know. But now it's wide open and Maria keeps pulling out supplies and stacking them at the station.

The rooms near us are now all empty. The hall is beginning to quiet down as people pour down the stairs.

"Find a cart," she snaps as she tosses medications into a metal box. "And one of those Guard dudes."

"Can't do supplies, ma'am." A short, muscular guardsman grabs a rolling office chair from the nurses' station. "People first." He pulls Mr. Flynn to his feet, then presses him gently onto the chair so that soft and round Mr. Flynn is squeezed between the armrests. The Guardsman rolls him down the hall to join the line.

But before he moves on to the next resident, the Guardsman carefully tucks a bed-sized plastic blue pad over Mr. Flynn's short legs. "Keep you dry," he says as he grabs more of the pads meant for bed wetters from Maria's stash at the nurses' station. "Waterproof!" He fist-bumps a hard-hat man as they pass around the pads.

The last person on the floor, Mr. Tennenbaum, in his matching plaid robe and slippers, is ushered through the door to the stairs. A few people wait inside the stairwell for the soldiers to help them down the four flights. One of the hard-hat men is making jokes, but the residents aren't smiling.

Now the only sounds on the floor are the roaring wind and spatters of rain pelting the windows of all the empty rooms.

I pull over a tall cart with shelves that are supposed to be stacked with food trays. It has been turned into a rolling library. I shove dozens of tattered books and magazines to the floor and stuff Maria's supplies anywhere they'll fit. The supply cart has a bum wheel and it squeaks as I walk backward and pull it to the head of the stairs. I wonder if anyone's going to carry it down. We'll need it at the Armory.

A blast of cold air comes from the stairwell, and lights flash as soldiers with headlamps move up and down the stairs. I have to get to Granny.

"This is nothing," I hear WM say to Mr. Cummings, who can't hear a word she's saying. "When I was in Bangladesh . . ."

The stairwell is crammed, but I slide by repeating, "'Scuse me, 'scuse me," until I see the pink beret that someone has pulled onto my granny's head. I'm really glad I remembered to stuff that hat into her bag of belongings. She loves that old faded thing and often wears it at night when she's sleeping.

"Still traveling?" I grab the side of her scrunched-up mattress. She doesn't look at me. Her face is pinched and pale in the dim light from an emergency lantern held up by a soldier posted at a landing. I don't want to worry about her, but I will. She'll do better if I'm nearby.

"Water's receding," the soldier says to my granny's mattress carriers. "Low tide." He lifts the lantern and spreads light on the stream of soldiers in camouflage, ponchos, and red jackets, who are holding up residents wrapped in anything that can keep them warm. I wish I had grabbed a towel to tuck into my jacket.

"Almost there, Granny," I whisper in her ear. She still doesn't look at me. She slides a shaking arm out from under the thin blanket and flops it against my chest. She's still clutching the red box. "Take this."

I start to shove the box into the pocket in the front of my hoodie, next to the packet of dried turkey. "Not there! You'll lose it!" she barks at me. Granny never yells at me. What's so important about a dumb box? She must be really scared.

The Guardswoman raises her eyebrows at me. "Tough old bird, aren't ya?"

"It's Miss Collette!" Granny snaps back. She closes her eyes but I know she's on high alert. She never really naps—just shuts her eyes until there's a new sound and then flicks them open again.

26

I shove the narrow box into the back pocket of my jeans. As we reach the bottom of the stairs, we hit a traffic jam. I lean against the wall, pull my socks up high, and retie the boot laces nice and tight. The boots are beat-up and clunky, but they make me feel strong.

I check my phone. The battery is low and there's weak service, but I manage to text my mom: Granny fine. Going to Armory Bklyn. It would really drive her over the edge if she managed to get here and we were gone. No matter when I text her, she texts right back. But this time the phone doesn't make a sound.

There's a strong smell of garbage as we step into slimy mud that's covered by a few inches of gray murky seawater. More soldiers in olive-colored rain ponchos and high rubber boots are trying to clear a path with snow shovels, but the muck slithers back. It comes up to the top of my boots, but at least it's not the swirling high water like before.

The furniture we'd lifted onto tables is soaked, and the filthy floor is littered with plastic toys from the resident recreation room. A beach ball sits oddly in the corner. Two days ago the residents had formed a circle in this room and tossed that ball around to strengthen their muscles. Granny had batted it with glee as it soared to the other side of the circle. Now it sits on a new beach on the first floor of Rockaway Manor.

We slosh through the gook, mud splashing onto the bottom of Granny's mattress. The air is bitter cold as we all move outside, but the rain has settled to a weak drizzle. I tuck the blanket around Granny's neck, but the Guardswoman touches my hand. "Time to unload," she says, and points to the street.

A row of bright gold school buses, engines rumbling and red lights flashing, are lined up, filling the entire block. "Can you sit up?" The soldier slides her arm under Granny's back.

"I'm trapped!" Granny waves at the rows of duct tape. "Get me out of here."

I pull the blanket and wrestle with the tape as Granny pushes her legs free. She's still high off the ground as the two soldiers patiently hold her mattress away from the dirty water. More people in red jackets suddenly appear and hold a long blue tarp over the shivering residents. "Just another day in Queens," one of them says as he smiles at me. I'm shaking from the cold and don't feel like smiling back.

Granny manages to wiggle free. The Guardswoman adds Granny's tote bag and my backpack to a luggage cart loaded with suitcases, duffel bags, and stuffed garbage bags. She easily scoops up Granny. "Does she need a chair?" She nods toward the beeping wheelchair lift on the side of the bus, where WM is waving to the crowd as her wheelchair is slowly raised.

"She's going to want to walk," I say at the same time that Granny mutters, "Let me walk!" The Guardswoman gently lifts Granny in her arms, carries her up the steps of the bus, and places her carefully on a bench seat in the front. The bus is almost full and strangely quiet.

I realize that no one knows where we're going.

"We're headed to heat, light, and bathrooms!" I shout to the passengers, some of whom can barely be seen over the tops of the dark green seats.

A feeble cheer answers me, the nurse assistants louder than everyone. That seems to inspire the residents to start chattering as I plunk down next to Granny. She's sitting in the corner of the seat and adjusts the collar of her coat.

"We're almost there, Granny," I say, even though Brooklyn seems far away and I'm not sure if there's overflowed ocean in the way. Where will we go if all of Queens is flooded?

"Pas de problème." She stares at me but doesn't seem to be seeing me.

"What, Granny?" I had grabbed the tape-covered coverlet before the Guard could toss it on the pile of drenched and muddy mattresses stacked up on the street. I really want to wrap the blanket around me— my jean jacket isn't warm at all—but I drape it over Granny so that her nose, glassy eyes, and pink beret are all that can be seen.

"We're in good hands," she says. Maybe she's still with me, after all. Sometimes she drifts off and then comes back. Lately she's been suddenly switching to

30

speaking French, even though she hasn't spoken it for many years. She seems to go off somewhere for a bit, then returns to English.

I know that she came to New York from France when she was a lot younger, but she never talks about it. I've tried to get her to teach me some French words, but she always manages to change the subject. I signed up for Spanish in school and wish I'd chosen French.

"Tu es en sécurité maintenant. Mais tu dois être vigilant!" She reaches out her tiny, freckled hand and pats my arm. She stretches the blanket so that it covers my legs, and gives me a tired smile.

I don't like this. She's drifting, and I don't know what she's saying.

She pokes my side. "Did you bring your bikini?" She gets a half smile out of me. Even when it seems as if she's in another world, she surprises me.

"Everybody, hold on—we're moving out!" The bus driver pulls the doors shut, and the engine roars, then settles into a rumble. "Let's get some heat in here!"

The bus beeps loudly as the driver backs it up a few

feet. He honks twice, and we're all jostled as the bus lurches forward. I scrunch closer to Granny and put my foot on the back of the seat in front of us to keep us from rocking around. The rain has started again, and it whooshes against the bus windows. Granny is still murmuring in French.

The red box pokes me, and I push it back down into my back pocket. "Granny—what's in the box, anyway?"

She snaps her legs up to her chest and wraps her arms around them. As she turns toward the rain, her head flops back against the seat.

"Granny?" The pink beret covers the wisps of her white hair. I reach out to adjust it so that I can see her wrinkled face.

"Signe ici."

"What?" I lean in closer.

"Sign here."

Chapter 4
Resist

Brume, Southern France
Winter 1944

As Collette runs down the hill on the bumpy cobblestone street, the cold sucks her breath and freezes her chest. She weaves around the people from her village who are hurrying up the hill. They're wrapped in anything they can find to keep warm. Some are hulks of many layers, and only puffs of breath can be seen as they struggle to get home quickly.

It's one of the coldest winters the village of Brume has ever seen. Collette has heard that all of France is covered in ice.

As she hurries through the village, she stays alert. German soldiers will stop and question anyone who seems suspicious, even a child like Collette, alone on the streets. As she dodges townspeople rushing to get home before dark, she wonders which ones will be plucked from the crowd by a German soldier and declared an "undesirable," never to be heard from again. She's watched the Germans round up French men to work in labor camps in Germany. Entire Jewish families have been deported.

The German soldiers own the village now. They've seized homes, railroads, and shops, or anything else they want. Elegant lampposts that dot the village, once lending soft light at night, have been snuffed out. If the soldiers need a house, they take it. If they want to eat, they raid farms of food and livestock that families have hidden away.

Over the last four years, in the midst of a world war that has spread across Europe, France lost the fight against Germany. Hitler's armies marched into Paris and occupied the northern section of the country. Now most of the southern part of France is under German control, too.

Collette's beloved Brume is in the south, just fifty

miles away from the Mediterranean Sea. Perched on a granite-and-limestone slope, the small village has changed little since medieval times. Collette makes her way through narrow, winding streets lined with solid rock churches, stately homes, and rows of stone houses and shops. She crosses open courtyards and town squares marked by high, ancient buildings and elaborate fountains where farmers' markets once flourished. Townspeople used to gather at the markets to select ingredients for the evening meal and sit in a café to gossip with neighbors.

For hundreds of years, the morning mist has settled in the olive groves and fields of lavender surrounding her town. But now a once-abundant countryside has gone empty as the war continues, and the people of Brume are forced to spend most of their time scrounging and foraging for food to survive. The fountains are silent, most shops are closed, and the markets are empty, except for the occasional long line of hungry townspeople desperately seeking rare potatoes or meat.

Collette quickly passes posters slapped up on the

sides of buildings that list new German rules that are often violently enforced. She shivers, not from the cold, but from the thought of arrest for missing curfew.

She knows to avoid the German soldiers, but she also fears that she may be stopped by the Milice. Some of the men in southern France have joined the fierce Milice, a military police force that supports the German occupation. The Milice prowl the streets and stand proudly next to German officers. They're sneaky, and she has to stay vigilant.

She ducks into alleyways and rushes by empty shops that have been abandoned by owners who escaped Brume, or were arrested and dragged away. She thinks about how her family has tried to keep their bakery going, with limited supplies and few customers. Her papa insists on making bread from whatever they can find so that his neighbors won't starve. "Someday we'll make pastries again," he often says, but Collette doesn't see that day coming anytime soon. She's seen families pack up whatever they can carry and escape in the night to Spain, across the border from southern France. Other Brume citizens suddenly disappear, taken by the Germans because they're considered suspicious or resistant.

She's well aware that the missing will never be found. She's heard the gunshots and overhears the whispers of her parents and the customers who come into the shop to use their ration cards and discuss how to survive. She watches with understanding as some townspeople cooperate with the Germans in exchange for milk for their hungry children, or protection from deportation. "We have to keep the peace," her papa has told her.

But she watches with dismay as others join forces with the Germans. "Those friends of the German soldiers are despicable *collaborators*," her papa spits. "They welcome the Germans so they can be safe and comfortable." The collaborators invite Germans into their homes and share information about their friends and neighbors. In exchange, they have full tables, fuel for their cars, and freedom to move around France.

Collette despises the Germans and fears the Milice,

but she has special hatred for the French townspeople who are friendly with both. The collaborators seem to have forgotten—or don't care—that their neighbors are hungry and hiding in the shadows.

Every day Collette sees her papa living in fear that someone—a German soldier, the Milice, or a collaborating neighbor—will decide that he, too, should be sent to Germany to work in a labor camp. "We're safe as long as we keep quiet, make the bread, and do as we're told," he often repeats to Collette.

But as she swiftly makes her way to the center of the village, she thinks about her handsome older brother, killed in Belgium fighting the Germans in battle, and her heart cracks. Her brother was so strong and funny, and determined to rescue France. She misses his cocky, crooked smile.

It pains her to watch her grieving family frightened about what might happen next. "How can we let them do this to us?" she has asked repeatedly. But her papa keeps his head down and presses hard on the dough to make new loaves, and Collette's mama looks away and says nothing.

Months ago, Collette turned to her trusted neighbor, Hélène, who listened to Collette's frustrations. Hélène kept Collette busy with chores as they furtively discussed the German occupation of Brume. "You can't show them how you feel," Hélène warned Collette. "You're angry, and the German soldiers will see that." She encouraged Collette to help her scrub her dusty floors and tend to the feeble garden behind a small shed in the back of Hélène's house. They talked of the times before the Germans had taken over the town. They planned for a life with freedom from war.

One day, after a German soldier stormed into the family's bakery and smashed the fresh loaves of bread, Collette's conversation with Hélène changed. "I can't just watch and not do anything!"

"You can resist, you know," Hélène whispered as she huddled with Collette in her sparse garden. "Many people do." She explained how a growing number of resisters were doing everything they could to sabotage the Germans and drive them out of France. They were people Collette saw every day, secretly spying and reporting on the enemy. As they innocently farmed their land, ran their shops, tended to their children, and foraged for food, they also spied on the German soldiers. They destroyed German equipment and stole their guns and ammunition. They did whatever was necessary to interfere with German victory and the takeover of France.

"As a Resistance fighter," Hélène urged Collette, "you can avenge your brother's death."

For several days, as cold weather approached, Collette cleared Hélène's garden space, dreaming of the peaceful life her family once had in Brume. She pictured her proud brother in his fresh uniform, waving confidently as he joined his friends and marched out of Brume to fight the Germans.

Her heart soon grew cold. "I want to help," she said to Hélène, pounding a small patch of dirt. "I want to resist."

Hélène knelt down and clutched Collette's dusty hands. "You're only twelve years old, but you can help us. It will be hard to do as a girl, but you can cut your hair and dress as a boy. Are you willing to do that?"

"Pretend to be a boy?"

"We'll call you Jean-Pierre. A boy traveling the streets will get little attention, as long as you stick to the dark alleys and look like you have a place to go."

Collette immediately thought of her brother's clothes, still stacked neatly in a wooden chest under her bed. "I can do that." She nodded earnestly, eager to get started.

She vigorously trimmed her hair close to her head. With Hélène's help, she cut and stitched her brother's old clothes to fit her undernourished body. She laced up the tall boots that her brother wore when he was twelve, and pulled her felt hat low over her ears.

"I'm tired of Germans whistling at me," she told her parents. Her mother touched her cheek, nodded, and looked away.

Disguised as Jean-Pierre, Collette observed German soldiers in Brume and reported back to Hélène. But tonight she has to carry out one of the more dangerous missions. She's done it before. Many times. Curfew is coming, and she has a package to deliver.

Chapter 5
Curfew

Brume
Winter 1944

The German soldiers are starting their evening formation on the Rue Grand, a wide, tree-lined street at the bottom of the hill. Somehow Collette has to move around the soldiers without being seen. A thin, ragged package is stuffed deep into her coat pocket. She has to move fast.

Tonight's mission is to deliver the package to an old house at the empty square off Rue d'Azur, where her papa used to sell his sweet calisson at the market. She can picture the tiny, diamond-shaped biscuits lined up on wooden trays, and tries to recall the taste of the sweet almond mixed with lavender honey or candied fruit, coated in sugar. She hasn't tasted sugar since the war began, and the memory is gone. Her mouth is dry.

For each mission, Hélène tells Collette where to make deliveries. By now Collette knows every street and alleyway in her town, and she slips down side streets, staying out of sight. Each "customer" answers the door if Collette knocks rapidly three times, then three times again.

Tonight when the door is opened, Collette is to say *sign here* and hand over her fountain pen and her little suede-covered notebook so that they can mark an **X**.

Collette has to follow Hélène's instructions, do exactly what she says. "Do not say *initial here*. Tonight you tell them to *sign here*." Either way, they must sign an **X** to show that they got the message.

Sign here signals that the plans of the Resistance fighters are to go ahead that night. Every time Hélène has instructed Collete to say *sign here*, then another German building mysteriously burns, supplies are stolen, or a German train explodes. There's a night of fire alarms, gunshots, and running, shouting soldiers.

But if Collette says *initial here* to the quiet people at the door, they quickly sign their X, glance around, and close their doors. They have been warned that their secret plan of resistance may have been discovered, and they need to wait for further instructions. The next day there may be extra soldiers peering at faces as people pass, stopping anyone, even mothers with babies, to check identification papers. Germans may burst into shops to check behind the counters and up the stairs, looking for hiding places, dragging out the citizens of Brume.

Collette's notebook is filled with rows of **XXXXX**, made by people with firm hands and serious faces. They usually don't look at each other after the notebook is signed, and she steps back so their doors can be closed quickly.

The package never leaves her pocket. She's only there to deliver the message and gather the Xs. She has the package just in case she is stopped and questioned. Then she has a reason for being out on the street, supposedly a young boy delivering a package for her neighbor Hélène.

The fountain pen, carefully filled with black ink, is slipped into the hem of her worn gray coat.

During the day, Collette may pass some of the people who have opened their doors to her. She may see them standing in line to collect an onion, or sitting in their shops repairing the boots of a soldier. They don't even nod to each other. The people of Brume keep their heads down and try to go about their business as if the Germans and the French police are not in charge of their daily lives. The war has made the close-knit neighbors of beautiful Brume even closer, but they don't reveal to the Germans that they know each other at all.

Sometimes when the night is freezing and she has a long list of deliveries, Collette is tempted to pull out the pen, sign the Xs, and return home to her warm bed. But the temptation is only for a moment. She knows if she doesn't deliver the message from Hélène, she could destroy a secret resistance plan that might move France closer to freedom from the Germans.

She makes sure that everyone marks an X. No names, no record of addresses. The resisters know

Hélène will check to confirm that they all signed the notebook—that the secret Resistance fighters have been informed. If Collette misses anyone—if an **X** is left out—Hélène will have to find out why. Was it too dangerous? Had there been an arrest? A French resister could die if Collette doesn't knock, speak the words that Hélène has told her to say, and hold out her pen and notebook for a written **X**.

Tonight she has six deliveries. All of them have to *sign here*. The secret plan for tonight is still on.

The German soldiers are supposed to be in tight rows by this time, lining Rue Grand. They're ordered to stand at attention to listen to speeches from large box speakers that are wired to the trees.

The townspeople are supposed to listen, too. But if they're outside, then they're risking violation of the curfew and questioning from the Germans. So they rush to get home before dark. But they can still hear the harsh German broadcasts through the shuttered windows of their homes.

The Germans have grown comfortable in their role as occupiers, so they no longer line up quietly as they used to, standing at attention with tense faces. Tonight the soldiers jostle and joke around the towering Rue Grand fountain that's decorated with elaborate statues of winged cherubs no longer spewing sprays of water. As Collette gets closer to the fountain, she cuts around the gathering soldiers. She might be able to pull off her disguise as a French boy racing home, but sometimes she's too far away from home to be able to explain why she's wandering the streets at the edge of curfew. She dreads the beginning of spring, when she'll have to remove the layers of shirts and sweaters, and there will be evidence that she's certainly not a boy.

The side streets are empty as dusk begins. She avoids the busy Rue Larouque and turns down an alley. She counts on this alley because there are many places to hide, and she's very good at hiding. She has no pattern of movement in case she's being watched.

She's sure she's just a shadow passing, but her boots seem to pound loudly on the stone street. Her mama has lined the bottoms with hay and pieces of torn wool cut from the ends of stolen German blankets to keep Collette's feet warm in the winter. But that doesn't muffle the sound as she runs and the alley echoes.

She passes her favorite fountain, where water used to pour from the mouths of stone dolphins into a circular basin sparkling with coins. She glances down a short cross street where a group of soldiers are leaning against the cold stone walls, muttering in German and smoking. They have long, heavy coats and uniform hats or round helmets, but their ears aren't covered. She can never understand why their ears don't freeze, but she guesses that they're listening for someone to give themselves away.

There are a few lights on in the homes, fuzzy yellow in the growing darkness. She needs to get farther away from the main street. She pulls her hat down around her ears. Hélène has knitted a thick black scarf that Collette has wrapped twice around her neck and tucked into her coat. She wonders where Hélène found wool to spin, since the Germans have taken all the sheep.

By running down hidden streets and cutting across alleys at the backs of buildings, Collette passes several side streets and makes it to the other side of Rue Grand. There are occasional sentries, but they're either sleeping or talking to other soldiers in low, lazy voices. It's a calm night, but she doesn't even want her breath to be seen.

The first doorway for delivery is at the top of too many stairs. She can be easily spotted. She squeezes by the side of the building through a dark, tight passageway, feeling her way along the damp walls. The worst thing she can do is get wet in the cold, and she quickly stuffs her frozen hands into her pockets.

Her heart beats faster, but she can't be nervous when she's evading soldiers. She needs to be quick and smart. When she's alone without light in the canyon between two brick buildings, and she doesn't know what's ahead of her, she lets the fear take over because it makes her more alert.

There's a small doorway at the back end of the building. Collette hopes her customer isn't waiting in the front, unable to hear her knocking. She slides the pen out through a hole in the hem of her coat.

The notebook is always in her pocket. If it's hidden

away, then it might seem important if she's searched. It's just pages of Xs so she doesn't hide it in case she's questioned. Paper is scarce in France, and the Germans have forbidden anyone to carry letters. A notebook is allowed, but suspicious. She's prepared to answer their threatening questions if she's ever stopped. She imagines a German shouting at her, jabbing at the rows of **XXXXXX**. "What does this mean?"

She's thought about what she will say. "Our family shares the bread. I write it down." Or maybe, "It's how many turnips we have left to eat." She's always ready, but so far she hasn't been questioned.

She reaches the back door of the building and knocks three times—then three times again. Within seconds the door is opened and a woman with black hair pulled into a tight swirl at the top of her head is framed by a dim light glowing behind her. "Sign here," Collette says, and reaches out to hand her the pen and notebook. The woman pulls a shawl tightly around her shoulders as an old man appears behind her. He reaches for a black coat hanging on a wooden peg, and the woman slides her arms into the sleeves. He grabs the pen and notebook, marks an **X**, and shoves it back into Collette's hand.

Collette realizes she knows this woman, from the market near her family's bakery. The woman doesn't buy anything at the market, but is always helping to rearrange the display of the few potatoes or carrots that may be available, chatting cheerfully with the people in town.

The woman briefly touches Collette's face, and they look straight at each other, eyes locking, both solemn. This never happens, and Collette quickly looks away.

A sharp voice comes from behind Collette and breaks the silence. "Qui vive?" *Who goes there?* The French words are garbled, but the shouts cut through the night and Collette spins around. "Couvre-feu!" *Curfew!*

A man in a dark double-breasted coat and sloping blue beret is gesturing from the yard behind the building. Milice! A French officer!

The officer keeps yelling a torrent of French as he rushes forward, and the only word Collette can hear clearly is "Couvre-feu!"

The man and woman in the doorway shuffle back-

51

ward and try to shut the door, but the officer is too fast. He pushes Collette aside. "Qu'est-ce qu'il se passe?" *What are you doing?*

Collette remembers Hélène's instructions, repeated many times. "Don't run unless you know for sure your life is in danger." Hélène made her repeat it. "Do not run. Especially if it's the French Milice. You have nothing to hide. You are just delivering packages from my shop to earn food for your family. If you run, the Germans and the Milice will suspect you, and your family may never see you again."

Collette forces herself to stand her ground as the officer continues to scream at the couple and wave his arms around. The woman looks at her shoes. The man in the doorway wraps his arms around the woman's waist and gently pulls her back a few steps. He has not been able to put on his coat. *He must be freezing*, Collette thinks as she, too, backs away from the irate officer. *Maybe fear is keeping him warm.*

She has to do something or the officer will soon pull out his whistle to call for other police.

"I have your package," she pulls the thin box out of her coat pocket and waves the package urgently at the old man. The officer abruptly stops his tirade. Collette adjusts her hat to make sure her face is barely visible. *I am Jean-Pierre, just delivering a package,* she reminds herself.

The officer loses his balance for a moment, and she realizes that he's probably drunk. A lot of the soldiers and French police have been drinking whatever bottles of wine they can find, now that they have destroyed the grapevines that used to line the hills around Brume.

The man steps in front of the woman and smiles at me. He looks as if he's pleased to get the package, but Collette knows he's pleased with her quick thinking.

"Yes, my package. Thank you for delivering it! Now you better get home. Curfew, you know." The old man nods at the officer and points at Collette. "He has delivered a present for my lovely wife, but he needs to get home right away." The officer steps forward and puts out his hand, but stumbles. He adjusts his large beret so that it dangles well below his ear. Collette wants to yank the hat off and toss it into the dark.

She still holds the package high. Hélène has told her that the resisters who answer the door don't really want the package from Collette's pocket. But it's the reason for carrying the notebook, and Collette should always have it with her. She has never looked in the package because Hélène said she shouldn't know what's in it. "You are just the delivery boy. If a soldier opens it, you need to be surprised."

Her feet start to sweat, when just a few minutes before she couldn't feel her toes from the cold. Her clothes feel heavy and hot. What if the package holds something that will connect them to the other Resistance fighters? *Hélène always has a plan*, she thinks, as she holds her shaking arm in the air.

"Go home, my sweet boy," the woman says. She's forcing a smile. Her eyes are frozen to Collette's and she's shivering.

The policeman lunges for the package, rips it open, and unrolls a thin, finely woven white scarf. It looks like snow falling from his hand. He beams, growls something in drunken French, winds the scarf around his neck, and tucks the ends into his long coat. Hélène has woven a thin red line along one side of the scarf. It looks like blood dripping from his neck.

He reaches over and slams a big hand on Collette's shoulder. "Va!" he shouts, and swats the side of her head. *Get going!* The couple firmly shuts the door as Collette runs across the yard, leaving the officer and the white scarf behind.

"He doesn't know anything," she keeps saying to herself as she weaves through alleyways. She pauses for a moment in a dark doorway to catch her breath in the frosty air and slide the pen back into the hem of her coat. She stuffs the notebook back into her deep coat pocket. She has five more deliveries to make, and no package. Tonight she cannot get caught again.

Chapter 6
Shelter

From Queens to Brooklyn
October 2012—Day 1

"Everyone keeps taking our food." Nicole pulls her hair back and wraps a rubber band around it. She keeps doing that. "You're going to have to go get us some. The petty cash is around here somewhere."

I can hardly hear her. The constant rumble in the Armory is like the ocean when the hurricane started. Swarms of people who have evacuated their homes are grabbing any space they can find on the huge gym floor as people yell directions, children wail, dogs bark, and frantic relatives shout out names. How did all these people get from Queens to Brooklyn?

"You've commandeered the basketball court." A

man with a Red Cross vest waves his walkie-talkie radio over the rows of blue cots lined up tightly across one end of the gym and smiles at Nicole. "Nice work. Anything I can do to help?" He drops a clean blanket on Granny's cot.

"We need to organize everyone by floor. Now. Before they go to sleep." She puts her arm around two residents who have been standing immobilized in the chaos, and steers them toward a nurse. "Let's find you good neighbors," she says.

"How is anyone going to sleep in this noise?" I sit carefully next to Granny on her skinny cot in the corner. I don't want to tip it over. We'd managed to grab cots far away from the hordes of people, but it isn't much quieter. "You should lie down, Granny." She seems smaller since we left the nursing home. Her beret has sagged across her forehead, and she doesn't bother to adjust it. "This is home for a while."

The residents are scattered among the cots, some of them still clutching their belongings. Veronica calls over the nurses and rattles off instructions, and they quickly shuffle everyone around until each resident has a cot. I watch as Maria manages to move the wanderers to the cots against the wall so that it's harder for them to escape. A few of them have been transferred to another nursing home that will keep them for a while, but most of the serious wanderers are still in the Armory. Maria's going to have her hands full.

I decide I better call my mom and let her know we've arrived safely. There's not much juice left in my phone, but if I don't call her before the phone goes completely dead, she'll probably figure out a way to swim over to Brooklyn.

I can only have a cell phone as long as I follow two rules: If my mom texts, I have to text her right back. She means right back, not ten minutes later.

And if I don't call or text to let her know where I am, then she'll take the phone away.

I try to explain to my mom that the second rule isn't all that logical. She wants me to tell her where I am, but how can I do that if she takes away the phone?

I reach her before the first ring even finishes. She asks a million questions, and I make the bus trip sound like an adventure and the Armory like a big hotel. "We have our own beds in a quiet corner and a Red Cross man is getting us blankets and pillows." I say this while watching a family unroll sleeping bags on their cots.

She wants to talk to Granny, even though we both know Granny doesn't do very well with the phone. I put it on speaker so Granny can hear better, but she insists on holding it to her ear. She smiles at me when she realizes it's my mom, and she does a lot of nodding. I'm not sure if she can understand what my mom is saying, but she seems content to hear her voice. "Lilybelle is such a good girl," she says quietly into the phone.

I lean closer and hear my mom say, "I'll get there as soon as I can, Mother." My granny nods and hands the phone back to me.

"Mom, it's me again. Granny's fine."

"Stay close to her and keep an eye on her, okay?"

She speaks rapidly and ends the question with a loud sigh. I turn away so that Granny can't listen, but she's already headed back to her cot. I wouldn't want her to know we're talking about her.

"The nurses are all here, and Granny knows what's going on. She's doing really well." I sit down at a table loaded with red-and-white first-aid kits. Some of them are stacked on a tray with packages of cookies.

I lay the phone down, put it on speaker, and tear open a package of Oreos. I peel off the top of a cookie and lick the frosting. It's the best cookie I've ever eaten, but then, I'm so hungry the packaging might taste good.

"Are you getting anything to eat, Lily?"

I almost choke on the cookie. How did she know? "As a matter of fact, I'm eating a sandwich right now."

"What kind of sandwich? Has it been sitting out? Don't eat anything with mayonnaise."

I press the cookie back together and bite it in half. "I confess. I'm eating Oreos."

"Oreos are not a meal!" She pauses. My mom loves Oreos, especially the flavored ones. "What kind? Mint?"

"Just plain old everyday Oreos. But don't worry, I'm sure they'll be feeding us something healthy soon." I grab another package of Oreos and stuff it into the pouch of my hoodie. If she ever makes it to the Armory, I'll surprise her with it.

"I just can't get there, Lily. I'm so sorry. I've tried everything, but it's impossible. The subways aren't running, the wind is crazy, there are no cabs, and it's still pouring like mad outside. I can't even get to my job. No one's allowed on the streets."

"I'll take good care of Granny, I promise."

"That's the only reason I'm not in a complete panic, honey. I know you will." She sighs again.

I look around and am glad that she can't see what's really going on. I hope she doesn't ask me to send her pictures or a video. There are people everywhere. They're emptying out duffel bags, shoving cots around, and shouting at each other across the room. A line to the restrooms weaves around the sides of the gym, and a man dressed as a clown is trying to entertain crying children by making balloon animals. The nurses never stop moving as they climb over piles of plastic bags filled with supplies and try to keep the residents together. I'm beginning to wonder if I really can take care of Granny here.

My mom is unusually quiet, but it doesn't last. "I know I've told you this before, Lily, but I wanted to name you Elizabeth."

I'm not sure why my mom is bringing this up now, but I go with it. Sometimes she drifts when she's talking, sort of like Granny. I hope my phone doesn't die or she'll think I hung up on her.

"I know, Mom. You were going to call me Lizzie."

"It seemed cute at the time."

"I'm glad you changed your mind. What's the point of having a name if you're called something else instead?"

I keep nibbling on the cookies. I wish she was sitting next to me. I'd share them with her, even though I'm starving. Granny and I had tried to eat the freeze-dried turkey that I took from Rockaway Manor, but we agreed that it tasted like sawdust.

My mom is still rambling on about my name.

"Your granny suggested I name you Lily. It's her favorite flower."

"She tells me that all the time. My favorite lily is the Stargazer."

"Your granny managed to include lilies in almost every garden that she planted around the world." Her voice softens. "And daisies, if she could get them to grow. She has such a fondness for daisies."

My mom sounds like she's less anxious now, and I realize that the knot I had in my stomach isn't so tight anymore. I didn't realize how nervous I was, but maybe I was just hungry.

"I'll find out how I can get Granny's garden photos from her room. I bet she'd like to have those back."

"You know you're her favorite flower, Lily," my mom continues, "and right now she needs you by her side. I'll get there as soon as I can."

I see Nicole rushing over to me. "I have to go, Mom. Nicole needs me. Don't worry, okay?"

"I'll try. I love you, sweetie."

I hang up, and immediately a HUG HUG HUG text

appears. I'm supposed to text back, so I send her a giant thumbs-up emoji just as Nicole hands me an envelope.

"I need you to go and get whatever food you can find," she says. "I've stashed what wasn't taken, but the Red Cross took some of our freeze-dried stuff, and the juice we had is going to little kids." She points to boxes, stacks of bottled water, and medicine carts set up as a wall around the wanderers. "We can't let anyone steal our stuff."

She leans over and pulls Granny's hat back. "How you doing, Miss Collette? Like your new home?" She gently helps Granny lie down and drapes the Red Cross blanket over her. "Close out all the noise. You're good at that."

I stand next to Nicole and we take a look around the massive gym that has been turned into a shelter. We step aside as a boy on a bicycle rides by. He's balancing a stack of beach towels on the handlebars and is tossing one on every cot. "I can't believe they've fit an entire nursing home in here and still have room for all these people. Where'd they come from?"

Two girls walk up and down the aisles pulling a wagon filled with bottled water. A man with a clipboard works his way to each cot and right behind him is a pretty woman in a pink dress and matching high heels, passing out teddy bears.

Families settle in, claiming space, shoving cots close together, spreading blankets on the floor. Fathers hold screaming babies while the mothers empty suitcases and garbage bags of belongings onto the cots, talking to new neighbors. A television hanging on the wall shows constant videos of the roaring hurricane, flooded streets and homes, and overrun shelters. They're calling it Superstorm Sandy. I'm having a hard time understanding that they're showing *us*.

Nicole has been on her feet since we first got notice that we had to evacuate—shouting directions and herding her residents on and off buses and into our precious section of the Armory. She's given me a dozen assignments, and I haven't been able to finish any of them.

I pull out the other package of Oreos and hand it to her. She gasps and holds the package close to her chest. "Where did you get these?" I'm sure my mom would understand why I didn't save them for her.

"There's a tray of cookies with the first-aid kits over on that table."

She rips open the package and pauses. "My house is gone," she says softly.

"Really? Gone?" I glance up at the television. There had been so many videos of houses under water, some even floating away in pieces. In the warm and stuffy Armory, I feel a chill. "How do you know?"

"My husband called. He's got the kids. They're all okay. House? Gone."

"You mean *gone* gone? Like washed away?"

"Sounds like it. He wants to go and check, but no one is allowed back into our neighborhood. We couldn't talk because he's taking care of the kids. He saved the family photos. He was really proud of himself. He knows that's all I care about." She reaches over and pulls me close. "He saved the pictures."

I'm used to being hugged all the time by my mom. This feels good, to be hugged in person.

Nicole points at the envelope in my hand. "Try the neighborhood stores for food. Don't worry about healthy stuff. We can't wait any longer for food to be delivered. Get a *lot* of food and try to talk them into giving it to you for free." She grabs a large duffel bag from under a cot. "I'm taking this, Mr. Feinstein! You'll get it back." She dumps it out on the end of the cot and Mr. Feinstein, always in a state of bewilderment, sorts through the odd collection of socks and hats that he had packed.

"You okay here, Granny?" She looks asleep, but I know that trick.

She reaches out and pats my leg. "Get me a Hershey bar."

I pull out the red box. "You can hang on to this now. I've got to walk around a lot, and it keeps popping out of my pocket. Put it under your pillow."

She lifts her head. "Open it."

I sit on the floor, eye level with Granny's worn out face. "What's in it?"

The box is long and thin and doesn't weigh much.

I lift the top, not sure what to expect. Maybe a watch? A bracelet?

"It's a very special pen." Granny's eyes are brighter now. "A Montblanc fountain pen. Solid-gold tip—see?"

I try to hide my disappointment by scooping the pen out of the indentation in the red velvet lining, and examining it. I had thought it would be something fancier—maybe a valuable necklace made of shimmering jewels, or an expensive, shiny gold watch.

But a pen? All this time I've had a pen stuck in my pocket?

Granny holds the box while I pull off the long top of the pen. It does seem to have a gold tip. It feels heavy in my hand. A closer look shows that it appears as if it's made out of blue marble. The side is engraved with a gold **F**. A teeny **4810** is etched on the gold point.

Granny strokes the side of the pen, carefully puts it back in the box, and then places it in my hands. "Put it away."

I guess she's worried that someone will steal her precious pen, so I quickly pack it away and stuff the box under her pillow. It may be pretty, but it's just a pen.

"You have to take care," she says, and I realize that there are tears in her eyes.

"Granny? What's wrong? Don't worry, it's only Brooklyn. I'll be back with the Hershey bar and some food really fast, I promise."

"Lilybelle, I'm not that hungry. Keep the pen with you. Someone could take it when I'm sleeping. That happens in shelters. Trust me, I know this." She quickly wipes her eyes. "You need to take care of it, ma chérie."

I'm not used to Granny's tears. And now she's back to French again.

I reach under her pillow and show her I have the red box. "When I get back, I want to catch you sleeping." As I lean in so she can kiss me on the cheek, I realize that I've just said what my mom says to me every night. Even though I'm twelve, my mom still checks on me, and I've gotten pretty good at pretending I'm asleep.

I turn and shove the box into the pouch of my

hoodie. I grab the duffel bag, and as I leave the Armory, I pass a phone-charging station set up by some volunteer high school boys. I send Johnny a quick text. At Brooklyn Armory. Where R U? I get an instant response. Restaurant. No power. Big mess. Armory??!!?? My phone beeps a low-battery warning. Yeah, more later! I text, and hand over the phone. The boys give me a receipt. I'll text my mom after I bring back food.

I'm in unfamiliar territory, even though Brooklyn is only a few miles away from Queens. It's evening, but the streets are busy. The flooding never reached this far, and the rain seems to have let up. It looks like everyone in Brooklyn just kept right on moving. Do they know that there was a hurricane and the Armory is filled with homeless people? I look in the windows of packed coffee shops, but the food is mostly huge chunks of coffee cake lined up on the counters. They'll never part with those; they look expensive. Isn't there a bodega or a corner grocery store?

I plunk down on a black metal chair outside a

restaurant. It seems too chilly for anyone to eat outside, but some people are still sitting at the tables with piles of food in front of them. I'll never convince anyone to hand over free food.

I wish I had a warm coat. I'd even wear a hat.

"Can I help you?" A woman with a black down vest approaches my table. Her name tag has *Tanya* scrolled in gold letters on it. She has a notepad, and I realize that she thinks I'm there to order something. I start to get up, but she puts her hand on my shoulder. "How about some soup?"

"Soup?" It sounds wonderful, but I can't use the petty cash to buy myself something to eat.

Tanya gives me a kind smile. "On the house, honey."

I don't know what that means. "That's okay," I say. "But do you have something else?"

She looks startled. "Ha! Looking a gift horse in the mouth, are you? Soup is what I can offer, and even then I'm not supposed to."

"It's not for me." I decide it's worth a shot. "My

granny and the others are in the Armory over there." I point down the street to the giant stone building that takes up an entire block. "We had to evacuate because of the flood. And I'm supposed to find food."

She sits down next to me. "Really? I knew they put a lot of people there, but I had no idea. It's so weird because we didn't have power for a while, but that was it. No flooding here." She looks at my duffel bag, and I can tell that she's beginning to think I'm pulling a fast one. "Seriously?"

"Seriously. We brought some food from the nursing home, but the Red Cross took it."

Now other people are listening, so I go on. "I mean, the Red Cross needed it because there are little kids there. And they said that food is coming, but I need to bring some back." I show her the envelope. "I can pay for it, but I'm supposed to try to get some for free."

I hadn't planned on getting food this way, but it seems to be working. One woman puts down her glass of wine and reaches for her purse.

"Nursing home?" A man turns from his plate

that's piled with lettuce. "There's a nursing home in the Armory?"

Now I realize that I'm getting somewhere. "Yes, tons of old people. We had to be evacuated because of the flooding. Some of them have dementia and have no idea where they are. And my granny is eighty and she's sleeping on a cot. And we need lots of food."

That does it. They jump into action. I'm pretty pleased with myself, and am actually smiling as they announce to the restaurant that there's no more food for customers—it's all going to the Armory. The chef and servers load up carts and boxes and march down the street, with customers helping to carry.

"What's your name?" Tanya shouts to me over the chattering of the restaurant crowd moving down the street.

"Lily . . . but my granny calls me Lilybelle."

"Follow Lilybelle!" She puts her hand out to stop a taxi as we all cross the street and flow into the Armory.

"Arugula?" laughs Nicole as we deposit the collection of food on the floor in the middle of the rows of cots. "Artichokes?" Now she's getting hysterical. "Wine!" she shouts, and the nurses suddenly gather around her and grab a box filled with bottles.

"Hey, it's food." I was so proud a moment ago. Now she's laughing at me.

"No—no, it's great!" Nicole hugs me again. "Lily, look! There's cans of pears here, and fresh tomatoes. And who couldn't use some mozzarella? It's a feast!"

She pulls the restaurant chef aside and starts talking about digestion and special diets. I head back over to Granny, realizing that I never got her a Hershey bar. I almost turn around to go back out to find one when I see that she's sound asleep. This time, she's really asleep.

WM, still in her neck brace, leans back in a lawn chair she's placed right next to Granny's feet. She gives me a silent salute.

Mrs. Sidobeth, always nosy, inspects the pile of food, commenting on how she hasn't eaten in days. A nurse reassures her that she just had a peanut butter sandwich, but soon there will be more to eat.

I settle down on the empty cot that's next to Granny and pull the beach towel around my shoulders to try to get warm. I just want to lie down, just for a minute. I pull off the boots, one by one, and flop down on my stomach.

My hoodie is bunched up, and I pull down the front to get comfortable. And then I realize—the red box is gone.

Chapter 7
Noah's Ark

Brume
Winter 1944

"Jean-Pierre . . . pssst . . . viens ici!" Collette can hear Hélène whispering for her to come, but can't see where she is.

It had been another long night of deliveries. It seemed as if there were clusters of Germans everywhere. They weren't paying attention to anything but their cigarettes and joking comrades, so Collette could dodge them easily. It was the French police, the Milice, she feared the most. Their dark coats can't be seen as easily, and they don't roam the streets in groups, like the Germans. Many times she's had to press against a wall or duck into an alley as a solitary Milice would saunter by. She's ready for her bed in her family's little stone house.

"Jean-Pierre!"

Collette finally spots Hélène in the doorway of the shed behind her house. The shed once stored bags of wool and mordants for dyeing. Now it's empty—or at least it appears to be. Collette steps inside, and Hélène quickly shuts the door and slides the lock.

It's so dark that Collette can't see her own hand. She can hear Hélène breathing softly. "Shhh . . . wait," Hélène whispers, before Collette can ask what they're doing there. She smells sweat, but it's not Hélène's.

"So this is Jean-Pierre?" A man's deep voice comes from below Collette in the pitch-black. "Let me see if what they say is true."

He lights a match, and she gets a glimpse of him squatting on the floor near her dirty boots.

Hélène quickly stuffs an empty feed sack along the bottom of the door. "No lights yet!"

He shakes out the match, but lights another one.

There is something about him that reminds Collette

of a rat. She only sees him in a quick flash, but he has a thin mustache and is crouched low to the ground. She half expects to see a tail.

"Is it true that you can hide anywhere?" he asks, holding the match higher. "Come over here so I can look at you."

Collette looks for Hélène's reaction but can't see her at all. She leans over, and he lights another match close to her face. She jerks back, but he grabs her coat and pulls her closer to him. She tries to pull away, but his grip is tight. Hélène clears her throat.

"I have to get home. Curfew," Collette says as calmly as she can, even though she wants to escape. She's used to staying alert and being on guard, and this man is too close—she doesn't trust him. She tries to picture where the bolt on the door is located.

"You'll be late tonight." He keeps pulling until she's forced to sit on the cold dirt floor, close to his smelly body. "Are you strong? Can you carry something small, but heavy?"

"Of course I can," she says without hesitation. For

several weeks she's been gathering Xs, limited to the town of Brume. Maybe this will be her chance to do more for the Resistance fighters.

"Of course Jean-Pierre can." Hélène flicks on a flashlight and aims it at the floor. The light is weak, but it's so much better than the solid black. "It's not too far, and he's proven that he can go anywhere. All he has to do is climb the wall and leave the package at the top."

"Wall?" Collette pictures the brick-and-stone walls marking off many areas of the village. But there are also the cliffs in the hills around Brume that look like steep rock walls.

The man pulls a small burlap sack out of the deep pocket of his coat. It's tied with string and looks like it holds flour or sugar.

Could he really have sugar? she thinks, covering her mouth to hide a gasp. What her parents could do with a bag of sugar—or real flour!

"Jean-Pierre." Hélène sits next to Collette on the floor and points the flashlight at the bag in the man's hand. "Can you carry this in your coat and climb a wall? Without falling? Or dropping it?"

"I think so . . ." she says. "But why?"

The man lifts Collette's arm up and places the bag on the palm of her hand. "Feel how heavy," he says solemnly. The bag feels soft, but there's something in the center as solid and heavy as a jar of jam.

"Jean-Pierre," Hélène continues. "This is Panther. He trusts you."

Panther! Collette thinks, feeling a rush of excitement. *The famous Panther is next to me!*

Panther is one of the best-known Resistance fighters in the Alliance, a strong bond of hundreds of French people who are secretly resisting the German occupation. The Alliance fighters are fiercely loyal to their beloved country and determined to drive the German soldiers out of France. No one's supposed to know who's in the Alliance. But everyone knows about Panther.

The Germans have started to call the Alliance Noah's Ark because everyone in the Alliance has a secret animal name. Panther is one of the fiercest Resistance fighters in southern France and one of the strongest leaders of Noah's Ark.

Collette is no longer tired. "What do you want me to do?"

"Just as Hélène said," Panther says calmly. "Several miles before Mont Saint-Victoire begins, there are chains of low, steep hills."

"I know those hills. I've climbed them many times before the war." Collette pictures the sharp hills that lead to the gray limestone mountains across France, where Resistance fighters are known to hide in pockets and deep caves. She knows that they scale the vertical cliffs like beetles, always scrambling to squirrel away weapons, radios, and explosives.

"You'll climb the rock wall at the edge of the Laurent family farm."

"Tonight?" Collette is familiar with the once-beautiful farm. The Laurents used to grow lavender and sunflowers at the foot of a steep hill before the Germans came. Now the fields are barren, and not just because of winter. At the end of the empty fields are rough chunks of stones mixed with shrubs and low trees, abruptly changing to a steep wall of sheer rock.

She's never climbed those hills at night, and certainly not the steep side of a mountain. She's not even sure it's possible without a bright moon. But if there's too much moonlight, she could easily be seen.

"Go to the far side of the farm and climb straight up the mountain wall. Leave the bag in the empty tree stump at the top. Go down the other side." The man gently slides the bag into her coat pocket and helps her stand up.

Hélène shines the light on Collette. She makes sure Collette's thick scarf is tight, and the coat buttons are fastened. Then she presses the package farther down in Collette's pocket. "Don't hit this pocket on any rocks," she says. As she looks at Panther, the flashlight reveals her worried face.

Collette freezes. *This is not a mountain climb for a routine night delivery*, she thinks, her mind buzzing.

She slides her hand down to feel the edges of the bag. It seems to be jammed tightly in her pocket. "What is it?"

Hélène grabs Collette's arm and faces her. "Be very careful. It's a bottle of nitric acid from Marseille, protected by fleece. Don't inhale it. And if it spills, it can burn you badly." Panther snaps his head around, astonished that Hélène has told Collette what she's carrying. The Resistance fighters share as little information as possible. Then if they are tortured, they'll have nothing to tell.

"It's safe if you are safe." Panther makes an attempt to smile, which makes him look even more like a rat.

But instead of being afraid, Collette feels flushed with determination. She'd heard whispers that nitric acid can be mixed with other chemicals to blow up German trains. She'd heard how the chemical has been sprinkled on food supplies on the German freight trains, poisoning the troops. And now she's been charged with secretly delivering this dangerous tool for the resisters. "Of course I'll be safe."

Hélène unlocks the door. "Do your best hiding." She motions for Collette to leave the shed.

Panther follows her and laughs softly. "We're hunted down like animals." He scans the street and steps out into the alley. "But they don't know that Wallcreeper is among us." He gently pushes Collette forward. "Now go, Wallcreeper." Before she can ask any questions, he's gone. She walks quickly along the cobblestones, staying close to the sides of buildings.

Wallcreeper—he called her Wallcreeper! She's an official member of the Noah's Ark network, with her own secret animal name. *It's a good name*, she thinks proudly. She's watched the wallcreeper birds in the cliffs near her town. They are quiet, grayish birds that build nests high in the mountains around Brume. They silently duck and hide, whistling only when something comes too close. Sometimes they show a flash of red under their wings.

She is a wallcreeper—taking roundabout routes to the nest, mostly silent, staying hidden.

She reaches the edge of the village quickly, but not

without evading soldiers who are eagerly searching for strays. She stays bundled up against the harsh cold, but sweats under heavy layers of clothing when she hears the stomping and chatter of the Germans. She has to resist patting her pocket to make sure the bottle is still secure in the soft fleece wrapping.

There's just enough light so that she can make out the brush and rock croppings along the Laurent farm and the steep cliff that juts out of the sloping hillside. She passes the stone cottage, keeping her distance so that the sleeping Laurent family isn't awakened by skittering rocks and footsteps in the night.

She crosses the vacant fields, stumbling over clumps of frozen mud. The rocky soil had been plowed under, ready for spring seeds that never came.

As Collette starts up the slope of the hill, at first she can follow an overgrown footpath and scramble over flat rocks. Then the ground changes to sharp rocks laid out like uneven steps, and finally, a steep mountain wall with crevices just wide enough for her boots. She can barely see a row of scraggly bushes at the top. *If I climb steadily,* she thinks, *I can reach the drop spot in less than two hours, just after midnight.*

The wind starts up and burns her face and ears. Her hands are numb from the cold, but she needs her fingers free of gloves so that she can hold on tightly as she steadily pulls herself up the rough limestone wall. She can climb quickly if she can find toeholds and grab bushes that somehow grow in the thin cracks. She makes fast progress at first, focusing on the wall and not on the danger.

"Halt!"

Instantly she flattens against the wall, her arms and legs spread out like an X. Her feet are stuck in crevices, and she grips pieces of rock that can break off at any moment. She can't look around and risk losing her balance and falling.

"Halt!" Again, the sound of the sharp voice smacks against the wall.

Collette sucks in her breath and holds it. Frozen against the wall, she listens to see where the sound is coming from. She's holding the rocks so tightly that her arms begin to shake. *Will they shoot me?* she frantically wonders, her heart pounding.

There's more shouting, gunfire, then louder yelling. Her foot slips and broken pebbles tumble down the side of the rock wall. She concentrates on how she'll protect the bottle of nitric acid if she falls. Should she toss it below right now?

The voices continue nearby, but they're not shouting at her. As she clings to the side of the rocks, she realizes that the sounds are echoes from the village, off in the distance.

Letting out her breath, she carefully lifts her right foot to find the next crack in the wall that can sustain her, and pulls her body up. The wall may be high, but now she knows for sure that she'll make it to the top.

Step by step she sticks her foot into a hole in the sheet of gray, drags herself up, and moves the other foot. All she can think about is the next foothold, the next place to grab. She is determined not to slip.

"I am Wallcreeper," she whispers to the wall.

Finally she is able to clutch a juniper branch and

pull herself over the top of the cliff. The tree stump is visible a few feet away. It rests on the side of the cliff, almost as if someone has moved it there. It seems to be waiting for her—a Noah's Ark drop spot that no one would ever expect.

Most drops that the Resistance fighters use are hidden spots behind fence posts and under benches. This one is part of nature, hollowed out as a mailbox. Will anyone ever know that it was Wallcreeper who dropped off the package, sent there by Panther?

Collette scans the area and gently places the bag in the bottom of the stump. She doesn't ever want to be seen, but especially now, at the top of the ridge. *I'm a perfect target*, she thinks as she crawls across the cliff to the other side. *I can't call attention to Noah's Ark.*

Climbing down takes longer. It's hard to see footholds, and her strength begins to wane. Just before the sun rises over the mountains near Brume, she slinks under the thin quilts on her bed. She keeps her coat on. She has to be ready. Panther may need her again.

Chapter 8
The News

Brooklyn
October 2012—Day 2

How will I ever find my granny's special pen? I figure if I retrace my steps—I hadn't gone very far—it could be on the ground somewhere. Maybe under the table outside the restaurant.

But when I'm finally able to escape the Armory late the next afternoon, the pen isn't there. It isn't anywhere.

The restaurant where I got the food is closed, but I can see there's someone inside. I bang on the front window, but the man moving furniture is listening to music and dancing with the chairs. I remember his black dreadlocks with the yellow tips. He was the one pushing a cart to the Armory that was loaded with loaves of fresh bread and boxes of butter.

I race down a thin alleyway to the back of the restaurant and spot a door propped open. The kitchen is gleaming, everything shiny stainless steel, no food in sight. No one is cooking.

"Hello?" I cut through the vacant kitchen and step into the dining area.

The man jumps in surprise and pulls out an ear-bud. "Sorry, we're closed!"

I scan the floor of the empty restaurant, hoping I'll see Granny's little red box shoved in a corner, or maybe hidden under one of the wooden tables. On the top of the long bar is an arrangement of glass mugs catching the sunlight, but no red box. No pen.

"Oh, hey, it's the Armory girl!" He finishes shoving chairs under the tables. "What's up? Sorry, we're all out of food, so can't help you there. Maybe you'd like some crème brûlée? I saved some—got to eat it before it goes bad."

I've never heard of crème brûlée, but at this point

I'm so hungry that I'll eat anything, even if it's gone bad. Everyone at the Armory had feasted on peanut butter and jelly sandwiches while I was gone, and was probably eating pears and mozzarella right now. "Sure—but that's not why I'm here."

I follow him to the kitchen, and he yanks open a large steel door to a walk-in freezer. The shelves are empty except for big tubs labeled SHERBET and stacked trays of what looks like empty cupcake shells made out of chocolate.

"Cupboard's pretty bare," he says as he reaches behind the tubs and grabs two small flat-bottomed bowls and shoves the door closed with his foot. "You wiped us out. But deliveries are coming later. We'll be ready for the breakfast crowd. It's all good." He pulls out two spoons from a small crock on the counter filled with silverware and hands one to me. "Go for it."

We sit on high stools at the kitchen counter and share the best thing I've ever eaten. It looks like vanilla pudding with cinnamon on top, but tastes a lot better than those plastic cups of pudding my mom stacks on the kitchen counter. She tries to buy super-healthy stuff, but there's always a stash of junk food, like Oreos, chips, and Jell-O cups. I'm all for that, although I'm suspicious of food that's supposed to be cold but can survive outside the refrigerator.

I tell him about my friend Johnny and how he works in a restaurant, inventing new recipes. "What is this again?" I'm so glad to be eating something, especially something this delicious, that for a moment I forget about my mission.

"Crème brûlée. It's French. Come back another time and we'll have chocolate mousse, or an éclair. I'm a pastry chef, but right now I'm slinging hash." He plucks a giant spatula from a container on the counter and starts to play it like a guitar. "Life is good in the neighborhood . . . !" he sings. He has big white teeth and seems to like to smile. "So why are you here?"

"I had a box in my pocket, and when I went out looking for food, I lost it. I thought I might have dropped it here."

The man puts the spatula back in the container and

jumps off the stool. "Let's hunt—what's it look like?" I describe the box, and we scour the restaurant, even the big plastic garbage can.

I lean my forehead on the front window and look out at the street, wishing that the box would magically appear in the gutter or on a potted plant next to the front door. I don't even realize that I must have sighed, because the man stands next to me and says quietly, "Pretty important box? Was it the one thing you were able to save?"

I realize he must think that I rescued the box when I escaped the flood, so I tell him the whole story. "It's just a pen, but for some reason it's important to my granny. I've got to find it or she'll be sad. And she's never sad."

"Can't you just get her another one?" I describe the pen—the blue marble, the engraved **F**, how heavy it is.

"Sounds expensive," he says, then looks at the expression on my face and backtracks. "But probably not. Let's see if we can find a replacement. You might have to say good-bye to that particular pen, but this is

New York City, and André"—he points at himself—"will find you another one just like it."

He reaches into a khaki messenger bag and pulls out his laptop. Within seconds he's located a couple of places in the city that specialize in pens.

He points to a website that has pictures of hundreds of fancy pens. "Fountain Pen Emporium! The biggest collection of fountain pens in the world!" He scrolls down the site. "It looks like it's right across the river from Brooklyn, in Manhattan. Who knew?" He writes down the address. "New York City really does have everything."

I still have the cash that Nicole gave me. Maybe I can use that to buy another pen, and talk to Nicole about paying her back. "I should call, but my phone is charging back at the Armory." I'm getting nervous about leaving Granny alone for so long, but I have to come back with that pen. "What subway would I take to get there?"

"Normally you'd take the 2, 4, or 5 train to Wall Street—or you could take the F train. You'd be there in a flash. But nothing's running because of the hurricane."

"Nothing's running? No subways?"

"All flooded. Lower Manhattan still has tons of water and no power. Haven't you watched the news?"

I slump down in a chair. "I *am* the news."

"Can't you wait a few days? They're pumping out the tunnels and subways. They'll be up and running soon."

For the first time since the waters started to rise, my chest tightens and my chin begins to wobble. I hardly ever cry, but this is too much. I couldn't stand it if I disappointed my granny. "I can't tell Granny I lost that stupid pen. I just can't." I drop my head to hide the tears.

"Whoa, kid, don't cry." He closes his laptop. "Look, there are some junk stores a few blocks from here, and a few antique stores. Maybe you should start there. Find a replacement."

"But she'll know if it's not exactly the same. It seems like it's a pretty special pen."

"Well, you can always walk across the Brooklyn Bridge to Manhattan. Lots of people are planning on doing that tomorrow, to get into the city."

I pull nervously on the strings of my hoodie. "I've walked it before, with my class. It's high over the river, but it's not too far to walk. Is everything in Manhattan all shut down?"

"Just for a few blocks. It's crazy town. The bottom part of Manhattan island is pitch-black. The rest of it . . . business as usual."

"Do you think the Pen Emporium will be open?"

"It's in the section of town that might have electricity. You could be their first customer tomorrow if you walk over the bridge and it's open."

"I could do that. Do you think I could do that?"

André is nodding so hard his dreads are bouncing around. "You can call, but it might be much better if you go there and tell them your story. Can you shed a tear or two? That might help. They'll replace that pen, I guarantee it. Probably engrave it, too." He grins at me again. He makes me feel like I can definitely do this. Granny will never need to know.

It's already getting dark outside, even though the huge clock over the bar says it's not even 6:00. I snap the buttons on my jean jacket and turn to head out the kitchen door. "I've got to get back. I'll keep Granny busy so she doesn't ask me about the box."

"Wait!" André disappears into the restaurant and comes back carrying a small glass bowl. He pulls my pocket open and fills it with peanuts and mints. "From the bar." He pats the pocket. He unwraps his red-and-black knit scarf and winds it slowly around my neck. "Go forth into the big city, my little refugee, and bring back that pen!"

Then he opens the freezer, plucks a few chocolate cups from the muffin pan, stacks them up, and hands them to me. "For your granny," he says as I gently slide them into my other pocket.

As he locks up the back door of the restaurant, I walk around a dumpster to get back to the alley. Behind two beat-up garbage cans I spot a bicycle. It has rusty white fenders, thick tires, and a big, wide front basket that's decorated with colorful plastic flowers. I stop and point as André comes up behind me. "Is that yours?" I grab the handlebars, straighten the bike, and check out the tires. It looks old, but solid.

"That's used for our neighborhood deliveries. We've got a few regulars."

I roll the bike forward and look up at him, hoping I don't have to beg.

He nods.

Pushing the bike quickly through the alley, I hop on when I reach the street and aim for the Armory. No school tomorrow. I have a bridge to cross.

Chapter 9
Worst Dressed

Brooklyn Armory
November 2012—Day 5

I've been stuck helping out in the Armory and haven't been able to sneak out and get to the Brooklyn Bridge. I spend a lot of time rounding up the wanderers and sometimes take groups of residents for walks around the blocks of Brooklyn. If you could call it walks.

Venturing outside consists of herding small groups up the block and back again, very slowly. Some of the residents take off, and we have to send a nurse's assistant after them. But mostly the residents gaze at every store window and make loud comments about the displays, or stop in the middle of the sidewalk and greet the people rushing by.

I miss being able to talk to Johnny all the time,

but he's busy helping his family. I laugh a lot, which is quite surprising since there's not much about our situation that's funny. Granny complains about how her back hurts from sleeping on the cot, and she's tired of the constant noise. We sit on her cot and watch people like they're in an armory reality show.

Some of the family drama is quite entertaining, and Granny seems to follow the story lines. She's especially interested in what's going to happen to the young couple across from us who are always arguing. She pokes me late at night when I'm trying to sleep. "They're fighting again," she giggles.

My mom texts constantly and calls in the evening. She spends the first few minutes telling me what's going on with the city cleanup and how impossible it is to get anywhere. I tell her funny stories about the Armory to calm her down, and keep reminding her that someone has to look out for Granny until the move back to Rockaway Manor. I make it sound like we're staying at a comfy resort because my mom is convinced the Armory's like the Superdome after Hurricane Katrina.

She says school's still canceled because of Sandy, but she misses me and worries about me and Granny.

"Mom, Granny's enjoying herself for the first time since we moved her to the nursing home. She has a lot of new friends, and the food is great." I look at Granny inspecting those weird bright orange crackers with peanut butter in the middle. She tentatively takes a tiny bite and offers one to WM, who seems to have adopted Granny. They speak French together when Granny can focus. Mrs. Sidobeth joins in and pretends to understand what they're talking about.

"I'm not happy with this," my mom says. "I love you, sweetheart. But you need to be in your own bed. As soon as they clear out the subways and get them running again, I'm coming to see for myself."

I repeat, "I'm fine, really I am."

She finally says good-bye, then texts me her three hugs: HUG HUG HUG. I text back a smiley face and scan the world of chaos that has become my new home.

My cot is pretty comfortable, now that I've spread towels and blankets on it. I did the same thing for

Granny, to form a sort of mattress. Granny complains about her cot, but she seems to be sleeping better than ever. I think the activity during the day wears her out.

The noise doesn't die down much at night. It's just a different kind of noise. Babies cry a lot, and it seems like every adult snores. There are dads sitting in corners in little groups, and moms on cots with sniffling children.

Every couple of hours during the day there's an uproar somewhere in the Armory. People get on each other's nerves, or sometimes a family will start to cry and shout if they get news, good or bad. Some of the parents have organized a play area for their kids, and volunteers come in and try to teach some school.

Granny's not interested in exploring the gym, and she doesn't wander much. She's fascinated as she sits in an aluminum beach chair and watches all the action. I bet she misses her comfy chair from her room at Rockaway Manor.

It's strange to step outside and see that people on the street have no idea what's going on with all the displaced people in the Armory. I want to invite them in to see our world, but at the same time I don't want them to look at us like animals in a zoo.

When I take residents outside in the crisp October air, they're glad to get some sunshine after being in the smelly, crowded Armory. It's chilly and we have to bundle them up, but it's a lot better than tossing beach balls on the first floor of the nursing home for exercise.

Everyone in Brooklyn seems to think that the residents are cute, and some even stop to chat. They talk to the residents as if they're children. Maybe they haven't seen hordes of old people on the street before. I guess once you're ancient in Brooklyn, you move out.

Nicole and I corral some of the walkers and steer them back inside after a slow shuffle down the street and back. "And to think it was my dream to have a house near the ocean," Nicole says wearily.

"You still haven't gone home to look?" I slap the handicap button that's on the wall so the door will swing open for the wheelchairs to go through.

"Can't do it. My husband sent pictures. It's nothing

but a pile of rubble. I keep thinking that he's playing a joke on me."

"Did he find anything you can keep?" I spot two men from our group stuck in the revolving door, and go over to free them. I realize they've been doing it on purpose and are having fun trapping each other. Nicole and I exchange a look and burst out laughing as we move everyone back into the Armory. It's good to see that she can laugh.

"He found our big plastic toy box. It ended up on the top of a pile of debris in our street, and everything was still in it. My husband said that when he brought it back to my kids they completely changed. No more crying. They just wanted their toys."

"Don't you have to get home?" We stand and take in the picture in front of us. All the cots are still full. People are lined up at tables of volunteers who pass out supplies and help people fill out piles of forms. A group of boys have made a ball out of old shirts tied together and are tossing it around, annoying women who are trying to set up a reading corner.

The nurses in our part of the Armory look tired and bedraggled, but we can hear them cheerfully talking to the residents as they pass out today's lunch. Most of the nurses have been here since we evacuated. Some can't go home because there's no place to go.

Nicole sighs. "This is home for now. My family's staying with my in-laws, and, frankly, I've got the better deal!" She puts her arm around my shoulders. "And what about you?"

"My mom wants me to come home, but she's also worried about Granny. She's always texting to check on both of us." I hold up my phone and point to the stream of texts that go back and forth between my mom and me.

"She's just being a mom, honey. And Miss Collette is very lucky. Some of these residents don't have anyone. You tell your mom that." She grabs the arm of a man walking by with a box full of subs from a nearby deli. "Who are those for?"

He smiles and hands her two sandwiches. "For you, sweetie."

"I'll be your sweetie if you pass those out to the nurses over there." She points at her crew distributing plastic cups of applesauce. "I'd kill for a hot meal right about now."

We don't have a food shortage anymore. I have no excuse to duck out to look for the next meal, so I can't hunt for the pen. Granny's been so busy chatting with her new neighbors and napping that she seems to have forgotten about it. But she does keep asking for something different to sleep in besides the same old nightie and her winter coat.

There's a huge mound of used clothing forming in the corner of the gym. Everyone in Brooklyn seems to be using the hurricane as an excuse to clean out their closets. There are things in that pile that no one would wear even under the worst of circumstances. I spend time with some of the younger kids, sorting through the clothing and tossing out the gross stained pants, extra-wide shirts, even underwear. The kids like to climb to the top of the pile and slide down, unearthing prom dresses, hundreds of worn T-shirts, and stretched-out pajama bottoms.

Nicole makes me wear latex gloves when I dig for clothing. "Nasty," was the only thing she said when she looked at the pile. But she was pleased when I dug out some football jerseys donated by a high school in Connecticut. The men in the nursing home are all wearing green-and-yellow jerseys with big numbers and somebody else's name on the back. They're very proud of their new team, and even Mr. Tennenbaum wears one over his plaid robe, which he has yet to take off. It makes it easier to keep track of them as they explore the gym.

I take a picture of them and send it to Johnny. Team Armory. He sends back a picture of his father and brother, both wearing dirty aprons and hair nets, washing dishes in their restaurant kitchen. Team Dirty Dishes! I wish we could talk more, but he's helping his family. I have so much to tell him. Maybe soon he can bring us some takeout from the restaurant.

The food is generally okay here. Deliveries come by the truckload. There's a lot of PB&Js and ham sandwiches on gooey white bread, pull-top cans of fruit cup, and these strange crispy potato sticks.

There's a lot of pudding, which makes me wish for more of that crème brûlée, and crates of bottled juice drinks that taste like gritty water. We try shaking them to see if that helps stir them up, but the sandy-looking stuff just settles on the bottom.

I stick to bottled water. There's a plastic mountain of it in the hallway. I was making regular water deliveries around the floor with my bicycle, but Nicole asked me to stop giving the residents so much water. She's running low on adult diapers and bed pads, and taking the residents to the bathrooms is a nightmare. They seem to like the adventure, but she just wants to load the residents on the bus and take them back home.

It seems as if we've been here for a lot more than a few days. Nicole thinks it could be at least another week before the residents get moved out. "The first floor of Rockaway Manor is a wreck, but the building stayed solid," she reports. "They're doing a closer inspection now that the water's cleared out." She keeps checking her phone. "Last message said the residents could be sent to different nursing homes around the city. We just don't know yet." I've never seen Nicole cry about her own house, but when she talks about the possibility of breaking up her residents, her eyes well up.

Where will my granny go? I wonder. I can't look at Nicole when she starts talking about splitting everyone up, or I'll cry, too. Poor Granny's always getting moved around.

Maria comes up behind me and puts her arms around my waist. "When are you ever going to go back to school? We all love you here, but you're going to get suspended!"

"School's still closed. Johnny says they had some damage from the storm and won't reopen for a while." I walk away from my granny so she can't hear us. "I got everything covered."

"You got everything covered all right, but you're living in an armory with a bunch of strangers and old people." Maria puts her hands on her hips and tries to look tough, but I don't think she really means it.

She knows that she can rely on me more than some of the adult volunteers. A lot of the Brooklyn volunteers don't stay very long and just get in the way.

"Johnny texted me that a lot of kids have water damage or no power and had to find someplace else to live for a while." I show her some of the texts from Johnny:

Samuel's family still in a shelter. Water's in basement and now there's mold.

No power or heat at Carrie's apt. Staying with cousins up north. Not happy.

"Or he says they're helping out relatives," I add.

"Like you."

"Like me." I start gathering up magazines that have been passed out to the residents. I don't know why anyone would think they would want to read *Glamour* or *Golf*, but piles of them keep coming in. I read *People* magazine out loud to Granny and her friends. They're fascinated, even though they have no idea who I'm talking about. They especially like the Worst Dressed section, so I have to go to that first.

I like looking at the stories in the magazines that describe the hurricane. I missed a lot, even though I was right in the middle of it. I realize I've developed a whole new routine in this new home.

"Well, look who's here!" Maria jerks her head toward the Armory entrance, and there's my mom, swooping across the gym.

Chapter 10
The Tour

My mom has raised her arms so she looks like she's flying. She's carrying two Macy's shopping bags high in the air.

My mom always seems to add sparks to a room. Her shiny brown hair, trimmed perfectly just below her ears, swings back and forth as she weaves around the cots and tables. She spots us and strides right toward us. I wonder what's in the bags. I hope it's my clothes. I've picked out a couple of lame T-shirts from the clothing pile, but nothing else looked appealing. If I'd known she was coming, I would have told her exactly what to bring.

If she went shopping, I'm in trouble. She tends to choose things for me that match the color of my eyes.

Since my eyes are hazel, I have a lot of brown and green sweaters tossed on the floor of my closet.

She pulls me in and squeezes, smacking my back with the Macy's bags. "I brought you a change of clothes. I hope to God you've been washing out your underwear." She's wide and soft, and it feels like I'm deep in a sleeping bag on a chilly day. I didn't realize how much I missed my mom's wraparound hugs.

She steps back, drops the shopping bags, and strokes the top of my head like a puppy. "Granny's doing good," I say, pointing to our corner of cots.

I peek into the shopping bags, surprised at how much she managed to squeeze into just two bags. "This is great, Mom!" It occurs to me that the amount of clothing might be a sign that she's decided I can stay at the Armory a little longer. I hope so—I need the time to track down Granny's pen. "Would you like a tour?" I wave my arm around with a flourish, as if she's a guest in a museum. She doesn't answer, but makes a beeline for Granny.

My mom is not a small woman, and it's hard to believe that tiny Granny is her mother. Granny grips the side of the cot, preparing for one of her daughter's enthusiastic embraces. My mom plunks herself down next to Granny, tipping the cot so that Granny looks like she's trying to stay seated in a rowboat.

Maria runs over to steady the ship. I'm right behind her, but my mom has already pulled Granny close to her and says, "Lily says you're fine, Mother. Is that true?"

I start unloading cases of bottled water from a nearby shopping cart, heaving them onto a table.

"Of course it's true!" Granny clasps her hands and drops them in her lap.

"Thank you, Granny," I mutter, glad that this is a time when Granny's focusing.

"Lily's doing a wonderful job looking after her," Maria adds. "I don't think we could survive in this place without Lily."

This is not necessarily the best strategy to take with my mom. Last night on the phone she started fretting about how long I'd been at the Armory. "You don't need to be so responsible, Lily. You need to be a kid."

"But Granny wants me here," I'd said. I thought that would help convince her to let me stay, but she obviously needed to check everything out for herself, now that she could get here. She surprised me with this visit. She scans the gym, corner to corner.

"Nicole says we'll be out of here any day now. Then I can come home." I scoop up half a dozen water bottles and hand them to Maria so she can deliver them to the nurses. "Did you bring me some dry socks?"

This gets her going. She slides over the Macy's bags and pulls out clothes that had been scattered all over my bedroom. "I didn't know what you wanted, so I grabbed everything I could. It's a nightmare shopping in Manhattan right now, so I couldn't get you anything new." She digs into the bottom of one of the shopping bags and pulls out a clean towel and packages of underwear and socks. "They had these at CVS and I grabbed them." Drugstore underwear and ugly white socks look perfect right now.

I take off my jean jacket and hoodie that I've been wearing for days. I dig through one of the shopping bags and pull a clean but well-worn hoodie out of one of the bags. It feels so familiar and comfortable—like home. "Thanks, Mom."

My mom looks pleased that she got it right. "Let me talk to your granny and then you can show me around." I sit across from them on my cot.

"Can you stay?" Granny leans against my mom. "I'm sure Lily can get you a cot and a blanket."

My mom wraps her arm around Granny's narrow shoulders. "Do you need me to stay?"

"If you make Lily go back home, who will sleep next to me and tell silly jokes? Who'll grab me a slice of free pizza before it's all gone?"

Granny's hands are fluttering, and I start to get worried. That's one of the first signs that she's getting upset.

"You eat pizza?" My mom grabs Granny's hands. "Don't you get heartburn?"

She seems to be missing the point, so I jump in. "It's okay, Granny. I'm not going anywhere. Right, Mom?"

Granny looks first at my mom, then at me. "I would

love it if you'd *both* stay." She gives me a sly look and I realize she's actually quite calm. "Of course, I could always come home with you."

My poor mom looks stricken. We've had this conversation with Granny so many times, but it's never easy.

"Granny," I step in again. "You want to go out in that rain? It's still such a mess out there!" I point to the television where the same weatherman has been waving his arms around a map for days.

A nurse walks by and asks Granny if she'd like a cup of yogurt. Granny curls her lip and asks if there's any chocolate pudding left. "Hang on, Miss Collette, I'll get you some. Sit tight."

"Lily, why don't you give me a tour while your granny has a snack." My mother heaves herself off the cot and kisses her mother on the forehead. "We'll be right back."

We spend the next hour wandering around the gym, and I introduce her to some of the volunteers. My mom examines every square inch of the Armory, including each stall of the restrooms. She tries every exit door, even though they've been inspected by the fire chief, police, and lots of other important people carrying clipboards.

She greets every resident as she tests the cots, studies each can of food, and goes through Granny's medical file with Nicole. "She's searching this place like a bloodhound," Maria says as my mother shakes out a stack of sheets, checking for bedbugs.

"This place smells like sweat, but it's clean," my mom finally announces, putting her arm around my shoulders. Her closeness is comforting, but I'm still not sure what she's decided.

"Granny needs to take a nap, Mom. She likes me to sit with her."

She gestures toward the glowing television. "I saw Rockaway Manor on the news last night."

"I know. Everyone here cheered because it's still standing. Do you think Granny will be able to go back?"

"They told us they'd cleared out the first floor and

they're doing repairs." Her voice seems to catch for a second and she briefly rubs my back. "But I'm only giving this a few more days, and then we need to do something else about your granny."

"Can't she just come live with us?"

I already know the answer to this question. We've discussed it many times before. Mom works, I go to school, and Granny can't ever be alone.

"Honey, she needs twenty-four-hour care. I know you love her and I'm so proud of how you've stayed by her side, but pretty soon we're going to have to get her settled somewhere else." She points to the garbage bag under Granny's bed and sighs. "She doesn't even have a place to put whatever she has left."

"She has her wedding shoes."

My mom gives a little smile. "And that ratty old pink beret. I've tried to toss that a million times, but she gets very upset."

"Mom, she showed me her pen." I want to see if my mom can explain the history of my granny's special pen.

"What pen?" My mom takes a packet of tissues out of her pocket and wipes off a nearby table.

"The blue one with the letter **F** on it. Granny says it's from France."

"Your granny never talks about France. I've tried over the years to find out about her childhood, but it was during the war and it must've been pretty tough." She inspects the tissue to check for dirt and tosses it in the garbage. "But aside from slipping into French every once in a while, you'd never know she grew up there. She doesn't even have an accent."

We both watch Granny as she sits on the edge of her cot and chats with Mrs. Sidobeth. She has a little color in her cheeks and looks comfortable. "Maybe she'll talk to you about France," my mom continues. "I've always wondered, but whenever I've asked, she's changed the subject. I finally left it alone."

We're silent for a moment. I want to tell her so much, but it's not the time. I have to first finish my mission to find the pen.

As Mrs. Sidobeth wanders off, my mom goes to the

table near our cots, grabs two packets of Oreos, and pulls up a lawn chair next to Granny. I watch as they talk quietly while munching on the cookies. Granny inspects each Oreo, opens the tops carefully, and licks every bit of frosting. My mom pops them into her mouth and chomps away, gesturing with the next cookie in her hand as she speaks. They finish all the cookies and brush the crumbs from their hands.

She helps Granny settle down on the cot and points to the shopping bags. "In one of those bags are clean pillowcases." Together we arrange fresh pillows for Granny. My mom sits back down in the chair, touches Granny's wispy hair, and tucks the blanket around her shoulders. Granny reaches out, and they hold hands.

Sometimes I forget that my granny belongs to my mom, too.

Granny closes her eyes, but I suspect she'll be awake for a while.

My mom stands up, turns toward me, and puts her hands on her wide hips. "What am I going to do with you, sweetie?"

She always says that with affection—and a touch of worry.

"I'm fine, Mom. Really." Maybe one more time will finally reassure her.

She motions for me to move away from Granny's cot, and we lean against the cool wall of the Armory, facing each other. I'm not prepared for her tears. I've only seen my mom cry once. It was after we took my granny to Rockaway Manor.

"Mom," I say, "I'm taking good care of Granny. And Nicole and Maria are taking good care of *me*."

"Your granny has made it very clear that she wants you to stay here. She reminded me that you actually may be enjoying yourself."

I cheer silently, thankful that my granny always seems to understand me.

My mom continues. "I'm a little more comfortable with the idea now. My office has reopened, and I have to go back to work." She dabs her cheeks with a tissue. "But if you don't text me, I'll be back in a flash and haul you home." She tries to look severe, but she's a giant hugger and I think I see one coming.

But she surprises me. She pulls up to her full height and lifts her chin like she's a queen regarding one of her subjects. "You're a wise young woman, my Lily. A little too independent sometimes—but you get that from my mother." She glances over at Granny, a tiny bundle of blankets. "You may stay for now."

This time it's my turn to go in for the hug.

I walk her toward the entrance, past the residents. She points at the group of men in their hand-me-down football jerseys and gives me a questioning look. We both smile. "Now, Lily, the textbooks I found on your desk are in the bottom of one of those bags. Keep up with your schoolwork, okay?"

For a fleeting moment, I want to pick up the Macy's bags and follow her out the door. I wish she'd brought some food from Johnny's restaurant, or maybe my favorite pillow.

She gives me one last hug. "I love you, Mom," I say as she releases me.

"Me too, honey." She seems to shiver a bit. "Listen to Nicole and wash your hands a lot." Her forehead has a sheen that wasn't there when she arrived.

"And please don't go out on the street alone. It's Brooklyn, remember."

She pulls a miniature bottle of hand sanitizer out of her pants pocket and tucks it into the pouch of my hoodie. Then she pulls out three twenty-dollar bills and rolls them into a slim tube. "Here, take this money for emergencies." She presses it in my hand. "Hide it in your shoe."

I can't help but smile to myself. It seems as if I've been hiding a lot of things lately.

She steps into the revolving door, gives me a little wave, and disappears into the rain.

Chapter 11
Rabbit

Brume
Nearly Spring 1944

"Tonight's delivery is going to be more dangerous than usual." Hélène pulls gently on Collette's thick black scarf and stands close, her sad brown eyes staring directly into Collette's bright blue ones. "If you don't get there quickly, you'll be in a nest of Germans and French police. They'll be arriving to dine with a wealthy French family in one of the fancy mansions on the Rue des Fleurs."

She goes on to explain that Collette is supposed to move past the front gates of the house on the Rue des Fleurs, sneak to the back, and peek through the kitchen window. Inside, Collette should be able to see a woman cooking for the German and French collaborators.

That woman has to sign the notebook.

"She'll have on a flowered scarf to hold back her long black hair. Get her attention through the window, and she'll come outside and shake the crumbs out of a tablecloth."

Collette tucks her pants into her boots and starts to calculate her route to the other side of the village. She'll have to hurry. This time the package has to be delivered to a home where the enemy will soon be gathering.

When she straightens up, Hélène is still staring at her. "Tell the woman to *initial here*. Hand her the notebook and pen so she can mark her **X**, but be sure she knows the message."

"Initial here," Collette repeats impatiently. "I've got it."

Initial here means *not tonight—but wait, it will be soon.* The woman in the flowered scarf will know that she has to be more alert than ever. The Germans suspect that the Resistance fighters have something planned. They do—soon Noah's Ark will strike, but not tonight.

Hélène signals Collette to step into the shed. "He's back," she says with reverence. "He wants to speak to you."

Collette carefully steps into the dark shed. It's hard to see anyone, but she knows that Panther is there. Again, he stays close to the floor, but this time she quickly sits down next to him. She can smell tobacco and sweat. His breath is foul, but she doesn't turn away.

His growl is so low she can hardly hear him. She leans closer. "Tonight, after you deliver the package for Hélène, you're going to take a count at the bridge on the Route de Ruisseau, on the edge of town. In a few days, we're destroying that bridge because we need to keep the Germans from moving easily in that part of the village."

Collette knows the short wooden bridge but doesn't know what he means by taking a count.

"Your job is to count the number of Germans at the

post," he continues. "Are there four? Five? Do they stay together?"

Now she understands. The soldiers could be anywhere. She needs to count them all so that Noah's Ark can be well prepared. "Both sides of the bridge?"

"It's not a long bridge. It's not a wide stream."

"Alone?" Collette asks, quickly regretting the question. She doesn't want to show Panther that she's afraid, but this night is turning out to be full of danger and she wonders if anyone will be protecting her. For the first time, she wants to say, "But I'm only twelve!"

"Yes, you go alone! Tonight. After you deliver the package to the house on the Rue des Fleurs, go and count soldiers. Then we'll know for sure." The door creaks briefly as he steps into the alley and disappears.

Hélène steps forward and pulls Collette toward the door. She cracks it open a bit so that they can see each other in the gray dusk. "You have a busy night ahead of you, my dear. Your missions are even riskier than scaling the mountain. You'll be close to the fire." She grabs Collette's cap and pulls it down hard. "Don't get burned."

A light snow is falling, even though signs of spring are beginning to peek through the frozen ground. It's easier for Collette to get quickly to the right street because the German soldiers are huddled inside the cafés and houses they've stolen from their owners. They stay close to warm fireplaces and hardly ever venture out. It's rare for snow to fall in Brume, and they're tired of this brutal winter. Everyone is.

Collette sticks close to the sides of buildings. She occasionally backtracks so that her footprints in the thin layer of snow will confuse anyone who might be following her. She stealthily approaches the magnificent house on the Rue des Fleurs, a street that's lined with tall, slender cypress trees, elegant mansions, and imposing stone churches. Her heart races as she gets closer, and she anxiously seeks places to hide. This street feels too open. She needs to be smart.

The looming house, three stories of stone trimmed with marble sills and steps, is lit up. Lanterns hang on a black wrought iron fence at the edge of a cobblestone drive. She counts two dark, sleek cars idling in the circular drive in front of the massive mansion, and another car is rumbling in place on the street. All have bright headlights piercing the twilight. The drivers are waiting in the cars, ready to transport passengers at any time.

Terrified that she'll be seen, Collette ducks behind a giant stone urn filled with dirt. Nazi flags, lit up by the headlights, are stuck in the dirt. She peeks around the urn as car doors are slammed. A tall man in an ankle-length black overcoat is laughing with a short German officer. They pause and light cigarettes.

As they walk slowly in Collette's direction, she pulls her body into a tight ball. She desperately wants to run but remembers the terrifying *Halt!* when she was clinging to the side of the mountain, and stays still. She imagines the crack of the gunshots, only this time they would be just a few feet away. She's far enough back in the shadows but presses her hands against the urn to stay steady. The stone is frigid.

The guests turn up the drive and climb the marble steps into the grand house, speaking a mixture of French and German. Collette backs up quietly, staying low.

She sees that a black iron fence stretches around the front of the huge house, but then it turns into a low wall a few feet away that she can easily climb over. As she searches for a spot that will be out of sight, she hears singing.

It's not soldiers singing, which often happens when the Germans have sloshed their way through bottles of French wine.

A girl is singing. In German.

Standing next to a car on the drive is a young girl wrapped in fur. She has a pale pink fur hat that's tied under her chin. Her wine-colored velvet coat is trimmed at the bottom with a wide band of more light pink fur. Her hands are in a fat pink fur muff.

She's standing stiffly as she sings, facing two short German men in uniform, and an even shorter man in a knee-length dark coat, who is clapping delightedly.

The ends of her long, dark hair are picked up by the brisk wind and she falters a bit, but continues her song. The men burst into applause, and the short man shouts, "Brava!" He gestures for the other Germans to follow him inside, leaving the girl in the cold.

Collette stands up without realizing it and moves closer to the drive. The girl seems to be about her age, but Collette's never seen her before. School had continued off and on during the war, relocated to an old barn at the edge of the village, but Collette hardly ever went. She certainly had never seen this girl there.

Suddenly the girl walks toward Collette and peers into the darkness. Before Collette can run, the girl pulls her hand out of the muff and holds up two fingers. V—for victory—the symbol for winning the war against the Germans that is recognized around the world. Collette gasps as the girl flashes the V, rushes up the marble steps, and disappears into the house.

Collette runs back to the low stone wall, quickly climbs over it, and races to the back of the house. She can see several people in the bright glow of the kitchen against the approaching nightfall. The woman in the flowered scarf is constantly moving. She stacks platters with food and hands them to women who go in and out of the kitchen. Every once in a while, she steps toward the window and glances out, but never stops to take a long look.

Collette waits until the woman comes close to the window again, then briefly steps into the light, and back out again. She's not sure if she's been seen, but she knows to wait.

The back door flies open, and the woman steps out, shaking a white tablecloth. Collette runs over and hands her the notebook and pen. "Initial here." The woman drapes the tablecloth over her arm, kicks the door closed behind her, and scans the grounds behind Collette. She marks a wobbly **X**.

Collette is surprised to see that the woman is young but as wrinkled and grim as Collette's own mama. The woman shakes the cloth again, glances furtively at Collette, and rushes back inside to warm her hands at the woodstove in the corner of the kitchen.

"Where are you going next?" Collette jumps at the sound of a girl's voice and peers around the side of the house.

Standing under the kitchen window is the same girl

in fur, but now she's wearing worn-out pants, brown leather boots, and what must be her father's coat. "I'm coming with you," she says. She's abandoned the fur hat and has replaced it with the blue beret worn by the Milice. Her long hair is tucked into the beret, but she still doesn't look like a boy. She grabs Collette's arm and pulls her to the side of the house. "You're not very good at this, are you? You're standing in the light."

Collette pulls away from her, but the girl won't let go of the coat. Collette frantically scans the area, but the only activity is the gentle snow falling on the ground.

She sticks to the deception. "I have to get back. I was just delivering a package, but it's almost curfew and I have to leave."

"Let me come. I promise I won't talk and I'll stay out of sight. Better than you do."

"Let go of my coat." Collette glares at the girl and jerks her arm away. "I'm going home."

"No, you're not." She points up at the window. "You just delivered a message. You have more to do tonight, I know that. And I'm coming with you to help."

Collette remembers Hélène's instructions about what to do if someone stops her. "I am just delivering packages for a shop—for food, for my family."

"Well, if you are going home, then show me where you live." She drops her hand from Collette's coat, makes a dash to the low wall and jumps over it before Collette can move. She pops up and waves at Collette to join her. "You definitely don't want to stay where you are," she says, loudly enough for anyone nearby to hear.

Collette leaps the wall and squats down behind it. "*Shhhhh!* You're not coming with me. If we are caught after curfew, they could take us away somewhere— even kill us."

The girl reaches into her pocket and pulls out an apple and a buttered biscuit.

"My father buys fruit from the market in Marseille." She thrusts the food toward Collette and says slowly and deliberately, "He buys fruit. In Marseille."

Collette studies her, weighing the words. Marseille, south of Brume on the Mediterranean Sea, is one of the places where the orders for the French Resistance come from. Where the nitric acid came from. Where people in Noah's Ark are hidden, and rescued, and supplied with what they need, to secretly fight the Germans in the village.

Collette slowly takes the apple and relishes the feel of its smooth, round shape. An apple! She drops it into her pocket while shoving the biscuit into her mouth. It tastes like honey.

The girl leans her face close so that Collette can see milky-white skin and deep brown eyes fringed by thick eyelashes. The girl speaks slowly, "He goes often to the market in Marseille. I've been with him. Now, am I coming with you?"

Collette continues to chew the soft biscuit as she considers this girl. She knows that there are people in Brume who take the biggest risk of all, by hiding families from the Germans and helping them escape. Others spend time in the company of Germans and Milice, pretending to be on their side but gathering information for the Resistance fighters. They appear to be collaborators, but they're actually spies.

Maybe that's what this girl's father is doing in his fancy house filled with well-fed Germans. He gathers information at Marseille, spends time with the enemy, then reports information to the French Resistance. Maybe he's just pretending to be a collaborator. Is that what this girl is trying to tell Collette?

But this girl is too risky. "Go home," Collette says to the strange girl who sings to Germans while dressed in pink fur. "Go inside, into your warm house."

The girl pulls out another apple and stuffs it into Collette's coat pocket. "The girl in the kitchen? That's Rabbit." She slides in another biscuit next to the apple. "Not because she can cook rabbit so well. But because she's fast. She can run like a rabbit."

Collette wants to be rid of this spoiled girl who knows too much. It's time to move, and Panther said she has to do this mission alone. She can lose the girl in the streets as they make their way out of town toward the bridge.

"Don't talk," Collette says as she swallows the rest

of the biscuit. "And don't sing, either."

The girl smiles. "I sing so that I won't throw up," she says, and the smile fades.

They sneak across the yard and over the wall near the front fence. A man in front of the house speaks loudly in German, and a woman giggles in response. Collette and the girl run up the street, away from the lanterns, Nazi flags, and headlights. Even as they flee, Collette is careful to hide in doorways, creep along the sides of stone walls, and cover her tracks.

She keeps glancing back to see if she's alone.

Chapter 12
Skylark

Brume
Nearly Spring 1944

"Stay low!" Collette can't believe the girl is still with her. She's tried everything to lose her, but every time she looks back, there she is, close behind. The people in town have closed their drapes and shuttered the windows. As Collette cuts through side streets and gardens, dodging anything in the way, she feels like a panther sneaking through the night. She wonders if that's how Panther got his name, only this panther has a cub that won't let go.

Collette has to admit the girl's instincts are good. Whenever they hear voices, whether in French or in German, the girl ducks into a doorway or flattens herself against a wall in the dark. Her black coat, dark hair, and navy beret help her blend in to the night.

The cobblestone Route de Ruisseau at the edge of the village turns into a rough, unpaved road that's a mixture of frozen wheel tracks and puddles covered with thin layers of ice. Houses stop, and stunted oak and juniper trees begin. Collette decides to take a risk and stay on the road because it's much faster than stumbling through the woods. They have at least a mile to cover before they reach the bridge.

The only sound is the crunching of their boots, and it seems so loud. There are no birds at night, no voices echoing from the village. Collette picks up speed and hopes there's no one around to hear them jogging down the rugged road.

There's a slight moon and a scattering of stars in the slate-colored sky, but sometimes they're covered by wispy clouds. Collette doesn't notice stars any- more. She used to study them through the window of her home, wondering how far away they were. Now she rarely looks up unless she's looking for German planes.

As the road narrows and disappears into a close crop of oak trees, she slows to listen. The girl stops, too. Then she taps Collette's shoulder and points.

There's a tiny red spot of light in the woods.

Collette pulls the girl down next to her. The light moves and then goes out. The faint smell of cigarette smoke drifts by.

Collette holds tightly to the girl's coat, hoping that she understands that she's to freeze in place and not make a sound.

The girl doesn't flinch. They are just two boulders on the edge of the road.

There's a rustling in the woods, then the sound of a man relieving himself, followed by a grunt. A lone soldier tramples branches as he makes his way back to the road. He shouts a flood of German words, but his back is turned and he walks hesitantly away from them. An answering shout, followed by laughter, pierces the night. The soldier shouts something back and walks faster up the road.

"Idiot was lost," the girl mutters.

Collette claps her hand over the girl's mouth. But

the soldier has picked up the pace and is no longer visible. She drops her hand and glares at the girl, only to be met with a grin on that pale face. "Now what?" the girl says.

Does she think this is all a game? Collette wonders, glaring back at her. She quickly moves to the edge of the woods and squats down, the girl right behind her. "I have to count," Collette whispers. "Count the number of soldiers on both sides of the bridge."

The girl doesn't ask why, just nods. "Far side first?"

Collette shakes her head and adjusts her hat, pulling it down tightly around her ears. "You stay here—or go back home. I don't want to have to worry about whether you're going to get us caught."

"Let's split up," the girl continues. She draws two vertical lines in the dusting of snow on the ground, followed by an arrow circling around the lines. "You go around to the right and check on the far side of the bridge. I'll take the left and count soldiers on this side."

"Did you hear me? You have to get out of here."

The girl continues to ignore Collette and draws a wavy line, leading away from the two lines in the snow. "Down the stream is a place to cross. Your feet will get soaked, but there are rocks to make it easier."

"How do you know this?" Collette tries to keep her voice down, but she wants to yell at this annoying girl who is taking over the mission.

"I come with my father on this road. He visits the soldiers and brings fruits and vegetables from the market in Marseille. Last summer, I played on those rocks, but they shouted at me because they were storing ammunition there."

Collette suddenly feels the bitter wind stinging her face. Her entire body is ice cold. Her shoulders and knees ache from crouching and hiding. Her legs can't seem to support her, and she sits down hard on the cold ground. This girl has been to this bridge with the Germans. If she leaves, she might tell about the mission. If she stays, she'll get them caught. "What are you doing here?" she manages to ask.

"I'm doing exactly what my father does. Counting

soldiers." The girl turns and strides up the road toward the bridge.

Collette is left sitting on the ground for a moment. She starts to call out but realizes that if the girl gets herself in trouble, it doesn't mean that the soldiers will know that Collette is there, too. *Let her go,* she thinks. *The job for Panther comes first.* She jogs up the road until she hears the bubbling stream, then cuts back into the woods, bearing to the right as the girl had drawn in the snow. The moon lights her way for a while, as she scrambles over logs and shoves aside branches that have brand-new leaves. She stays low, stopping once to listen.

As she emerges, she can see the lights of a German outpost on the other side of the water, upstream, at the end of the short, rickety bridge. A wooden shed stands directly across from her. Next to the shed is a large square space surrounded by sandbags, stacked like a stone wall. The rocks in the stream are in front of her, just as the girl described. The ammunition is stored on the other side, just as she said.

Collette steps behind a scraggly oak to stop and think. Is she walking into a trap? The girl knows too much. And now she knows the mission.

The voices of the German soldiers are muffled by the running water, but Collette can see that they have a campfire going on the other side, near the bridge. Two soldiers are sitting on a log wearing their round-topped helmets, warming their hands. They stretch out their feet and try to knock each other off the log. The third soldier paces up and down the road that continues beyond the bridge through acres of fields. He repeatedly stops, swings around, and aims his gun at the sky, making machine-gun noises.

She glances to make sure the soldiers are occupied, pulls her heavy gray coat up around her waist, and plunges into the fast waters to reach the first large, flat rock. The water is just deep enough to slow her down as she struggles to get to the other side. Her legs feel sluggish as the cold grips her and drenches her boots and the soft blanket linings. She slips off the rocks, sinking up to her knees in the icy water, flinging out her arms to stay balanced. The bottom of her coat drops and gets soaked, dragging her down as she struggles to plow through the stream. Gradually she's able to lug her feet from the silt and rocks at the bottom and push herself onto the high, muddy bank of the stream. Her wet pants and coat cling to her, seeping cold deep into her bones. She crawls over the edge of the bank, staying low.

Her boots are heavy, and she can't feel her feet. The soldiers laugh and whistle as they soak up the heat of the fire. Collette lies flat on the frozen ground.

Such a narrow stream and a small, short bridge that's so important. If the bridge is gone, the soldiers will have to do what Collette just did. And when the ice begins to melt and rushing water fills the stream to the top of the bank, the Germans will need to build a new bridge to get their trucks full of soldiers back and forth to Brume.

If she can help take that bridge down, she'll do it.

Collette pulls her body forward using her elbows and shoving with her feet. She remembers her brave brother telling her about fighting the war in Belgium. He had come home briefly before returning to battle and described the hours he spent hunched over in wet, muddy trenches as bullets rained down. He pulled himself through fields, flat on his stomach, rifle in hand. She remembers that he's still there, only now he's underground, buried in the middle of a battlefield.

She's wearing his beat-up old boots and will use them just as he used his boots as a soldier. Only she plans on making it home so she can report to Panther.

On this side of the stream, she no longer has the cover of the woods. She sprints to hide behind the shed and cuts through a field to spy on the soldiers from behind. Her boots are cumbersome because the blanket lining is now soaked and squishy, but they don't slow her down. A cluster of juniper shrubs is her only protection, but now she can see across the bridge to where she and the girl had been hiding in the trees.

She still counts only three soldiers, two dark forms visible against the fire and the one lone soldier still aiming at the dark sky.

Collette searches desperately for the girl but can't see her on the other side of the bridge. She hopes the girl has gone back home.

Suddenly the soldiers at the campfire all stand up. Rushing across the bridge are three additional soldiers, waving rifles and shouting in German. Ahead of them is the girl, her oversized black coat dragging, her hair falling out from under her blue beret.

The Germans gather around the girl, noisily jostling each other. One of them pulls off her beret and puts it on his head, dancing around the fire. The others point and laugh.

And the girl is laughing, too. She's laughing!

Collette has to cover her mouth to keep from crying out in dismay. The girl looks tiny in her father's coat, surrounded by hulking German soldiers. But she doesn't seem afraid.

The girl pulls something out of her coat pocket, glances around dramatically, and puts her finger on her lips. *"Shhh . . ."* Her high-pitched giggle can be heard through their deep laughter.

One by one, she hands them each a bar of chocolate.

They tear open the wrappers and devour the candy bars.

"Singen!" they shout, still grinning as they munch on the chocolate. The girl snatches back her hat, stuffs her hair underneath, stands tall and straight, arms at her sides, and sings in German. The men are quiet. Her voice wavers, but it still soars through the woods and she never hesitates.

The soldier who had been shooting at imaginary aircraft joins the group, his rifle slung across the front of his uniform. He starts to sing along, drowning out the sweet tones of the girl. The other men try to hush him, and he reaches for the girl and yanks her coat. She pulls back, but he keeps tugging, singing loudly.

Collette grabs a handful of the branches to keep herself from running toward the fire. Should she help this stupid girl who foolishly thought she could give candy to the Germans and get away free? But Collette can't get caught, or all of Noah's Ark will be in danger. As she holds her breath and watches as the scene plays out in front of her, she can feel anger building. She had always felt brave and important. Panther is counting on her. But this girl has caused Collette to be fearful. This girl has caused trouble, and Collette will not put the Resistance fighters at risk.

She peers around the shrubs, anxious to leave, but now uncertain about abandoning the girl. For a moment, she's numb with terror, but she brushes away the fear and frantically searches the ground for something to throw. If she can toss something near them, she might be able to divert their attention and the girl can get away. "Stupid girl," Collette mutters to herself as she looks around for rocks.

The singing soldier picks up a stick from the fire. The end is glowing, and he pokes it at the girl. "Tanzen!" he yells, and waves the stick around while he pulls the back collar of her coat, throwing her off balance. The girl looks bewildered and shuffles her feet in place. "Tanz!" another soldier shouts, and she dances more vigorously. They all join their comrade in teasing her as he threatens her with the burning stick.

The soldier isn't satisfied with the girl's dancing. He roughly pulls her coat collar down, but this time he pokes her once on her back with the hot stick. She cries out and stumbles, but keeps moving her feet as he circles her.

Just as Collette reaches for a large rock, a German officer bursts out of the old wooden shed behind her, shouting and gesturing. He has no coat. His uniform is covered with ribbons and medals. Collette ducks down. He takes long strides toward the campfire, passing Collette so closely she can see that his boots are untied.

The soldiers instantly pick up their rifles and spread out, three of them dashing across the bridge, back to where they came from. The girl also races across the bridge and cuts into the woods, away from the soldiers.

Collette doesn't wait to see what the screaming officer does next. This time she makes it across the stream without floundering in the icy waters and disappears into the woods. Branches snap her face and her soggy coat catches on brambles, but she keeps going, vaulting over fallen logs and dodging trees.

When she can no longer hear the officer and can't run one more step, she emerges from the woods onto the edge of the road. She leans against the trunk of a tall plane tree to catch her breath and listen for the pounding of footsteps. The soldiers seem to have returned to their posts. To her surprise, the girl steps out from behind a nearby tree, looking bedraggled as she fights with her father's coat. She covers her mouth to muffle her cries as the coat slides over the burn spot on her back.

Without saying a word, Collette steps behind the girl and gently pulls down the coat's collar. She carefully peels away the burned wool shirt from the raw red wound at the top of the girl's back, scoops up snow, and pats it on the girl's skin. The girl gasps but holds still.

"Believe it or not, you can use vinegar to soothe the pain," Collette says. "My mama taught me that."

The girl buttons the coat up to the top, grimacing as

it rubs against her back. She roughly brushes tears off her ashen face, leaving streaks of dirt across her cheeks. "I was just trying to help you count. My father walks right up to the soldiers! He's brought me along before, to sing a song for them. He gives them chocolate."

Her hands shake as she pulls out the last chocolate bar and hands it to Collette. At first Collette drops it into her pocket with the apple and the roll, but she can't resist and pulls it back out again. She quickly unwraps it and slides a chunk of chocolate onto her tongue. She moves it around slowly in her mouth, letting it soften, savoring the first candy she's tasted in years. It's so much better than she had imagined.

She offers a piece to the girl. "You keep it." The girl waves it away. "My father can get me more."

Collette takes one more bite and carefully wraps the rest to save for her mama and papa. She knows they'll wonder how she managed to get chocolate when they are surviving on so little, but they won't ask.

"Who *are* you?" Collette asks the girl, remembering that this girl is from a house where enemies visit freely.

The girl breathes in a deep breath of the frigid air and blows it out slowly. She still has tears. "My name is Marguerite. And you have to admit, I did draw out the Germans so you could count them all."

Suddenly she whisks Collette's hat off her head, revealing the ragged, short hair. "And you are certainly not Jean-Pierre. Let's get out of here." She turns and runs swiftly up the road toward the village. For a second, Collette freezes. Who is this Marguerite? She races after the girl, who seems to know so much. This time Collette has to catch up.

They run side by side, breathing hard. As they reach the streets of Brume, they pause to rest, and press their backs against the cold stone blocks of a high church wall. The girl winces in pain and pulls away from the wall. She has deep shadows under her eyes. "We're on the same side, you know."

Collette quickly decides to take a risk. "I'm not really Jean-Pierre. My name is Collette."

"I know," Marguerite says solemnly, handing Collette her hat, "and Panther is waiting for you."

Collette moves away from the wall with a flash of fear, itching to run. *How does this girl know about Panther?*

Marguerite backs up and gives a slight wave. "Tell Panther that Skylark and Wallcreeper saw seven soldiers tonight. Not six."

She ducks into a dark alley and is gone.

Chapter 13
Keepsakes

Brooklyn

November 2012—Day 6

A parade of National Guard soldiers rolls shopping carts overflowing with belongings through the gym. They've finally brought everything from the closets of Rockaway Manor that hadn't been flooded. Plastic bags labeled with room numbers are dumped in the middle of the rows of cots. The nurses quickly sort the bags by floor, and I help with deliveries.

I find Granny's room number right away. She sits on the edge of her cot and reaches out to pull the bag toward her. I help her sort through what the soldiers managed to retrieve. "Here's your special pink pillow, Granny." I shake it out and place in on her bed. "It fell off the bed when they moved you." She scoops it up and clutches it to her chest.

She holds every item and pets it like a kitten. Her button-down sweaters, nightgowns, and clean underwear are treated like old friends. She pulls out a shiny patent leather handbag and struggles to unclip the gold clasp. She shakes her hands impatiently. I open it and pull out a brush filled with gray hairs, a lipstick tube, and a stack of letters that are held together with a thin blue rubber band.

"Where's my pen?" She snatches the collection of letters. "Do you still have my pen?"

I keep plowing through the bag, hoping that her dementia will suddenly kick in and she'll forget that she asked.

"Put these with the pen." She pushes the letters against my chest. "Read them. And take that pen back. It needs to go back." I drop the letters on her bed and keep pulling items out of the plastic bag.

"Go back where, Granny?" I keep my nose in the bag. I want to steer clear of the subject, but she's beginning to get agitated again. Something about that pen gets her upset.

"Broom!" She's raising her voice and tugging on my arm.

"Granny, calm down. Just tell me what you want me to do." She's shouting, "Broom," again and not making any sense. I hope my mom's visit didn't get her confused.

"Do you want me to get a broom and clean up our part of the Armory?" I neatly stack her things in a cardboard box, stow it under her cot, and tidy the rumpled covers on my own cot. "I can straighten everything up, but right now you should go and change into your red sweater. You can sleep in it tonight. It's your favorite, isn't it?" I sit down gently next to her on the cot. She seems so distraught and I can't seem to calm her down. Her face is pink and her light blue eyes are filled with tears. How am I ever going to tell her that I lost her precious pen?

She taps the pile of letters next to her. "Please—take the pen to Marguerite."

"Marguerite?" I hand Granny a clean nightgown and her worn red sweater with the fake pearl buttons and help her stand up. She shuffles away from me and disappears behind the coatracks that Nicole set up as a private changing room. "Granny, who's Marguerite? Are these letters from her?"

I remake her cot with the Red Cross blankets and toss the letters into my backpack. She and I can look at them once she's had a chance to rest. Maybe then she'll make more sense.

In a few minutes, she reappears wearing her pink beret and red sweater and settles down on her cot. "Je suis fatiguée, Lilybelle." Her pale yellow nightgown barely covers her thin legs.

"I know you're tired, Granny." I slide my new white socks on her feet and tuck her in for a nap. I grab the scarf André gave me and signal to Maria that I'm going outside. She salutes. She'll keep an eye on Granny.

It's a dreary day, and a brisk wind scatters litter around the sidewalk. I'd stored the bicycle in the lobby near the phone-charging station, but I have to walk it once I get outside. There are too many people and I don't dare try the busy bike lane in the street.

I have no idea where I'm going. André had said that there were stores nearby that might have a pen that looks like my granny's, but in what direction? And if I ever find the pen, who is this Marguerite I'm supposed to deliver it to? I keep walking, wheeling the bike around squares of dirt in the sidewalk where skinny trees have been planted.

The lights of restaurants and shops come on, one by one, and I think of Johnny. But I'd better not text him right now. He's probably passing out menus to customers and serving up pie and coffee. His favorite time of day is when the lunch crowd fills up the family's restaurant.

I sit on a stoop and check my phone to see if I can find information about stores in the area that might have fountain pens. There seems to be a row of antique shops a few blocks away.

It's beginning to rain, and I loop the scarf around

my neck a couple of times. Next to me, stacked against a brick building, is abandoned, broken furniture, including pieces of a bed. Someone else must have been displaced.

It'd be nice to actually have a mattress again, I think as people rush by, probably to a real bed and their own television. They may have neighbors who play music too loudly or cook weird-smelling food, but at least they don't have hundreds of people in their home.

From my bed in our apartment, I have a view of the building right next to us, and sometimes I can see a man in his underwear eating out of a cereal box while he yells at the television. It's crazy, but I miss that.

I grab the handlebars and decide to risk running over pedestrians so that I can beat the rain and get to one of the antique stores. As I round a corner, I swerve to avoid a large stroller that takes up the entire sidewalk. The mom pushing the stroller sails on by as I struggle to keep the bike steady on the uneven sidewalk. A man with a huge black umbrella curses at me as we almost crash into each other. Less than a block later, I give up and realize that riding a bike on the sidewalks of Brooklyn, especially in the rain, is probably not a good idea.

I roll the bike under an awning that covers the entrance to an apartment building. A doorman immediately joins me. "Just what we need—more rain." He buttons up his black raincoat all the way to his neck. "Those poor people."

I must look confused because he continues. "You know, all those people who were under water a few days ago. Sandy did a real number on this city. Been here all my life and never seen anything like it."

I'm tempted to burst out my story. "I'm one of those people! My granny's living in an armory!" But I don't say anything. I couldn't possibly explain why I'm out in the rain looking for a fountain pen, instead of inside a warm building, taking care of my grandmother.

The doorman motions for me to move on, so I keep walking the bike, looking for any store that might seem promising. The rain's getting misty and it's hard to see. The streets begin to empty, and I pass by a restaurant that's packed. The aroma of spaghetti sauce is torture.

"I'll try three shops, then I'll go back," I vow to myself. I don't want to give up, but it's looking like the Pen Emporium on the other side of the Brooklyn Bridge might be my only hope.

After a few blocks, I steer past the entrance to the basement of a brownstone, when I notice that at the bottom of the stairs is a window with KEEPSAKES scrolled across in fancy gold letters. There's a lamp in the window that has a glowing green glass shade pouring light onto rows of sheet music laid out like a fan.

The street is empty and the shop looks like it's a possibility, so I decide to risk leaving the bike for a few minutes and check out the store. There's no way they would have my granny's pen, but maybe I could find something similar. At least I could dry off a bit and ask if they know where I can look for fountain pens in Brooklyn.

The shop is dimly lit, and at first I'm not even sure

it's open. A bell jingles when I push hard on the door, but the entrance is almost blocked by a huge rolltop desk that's filled with little drawers and cubbies. Stacked on the desk are musty old books and a row of animal figurines made out of what looks like silver, connected by cobwebs.

I squeeze by the desk to take a quick look around. If there aren't any pens in sight, I'm out of there. It's hard to identify anything in the faint light, but it seems to be one room lined with bookshelves. There's a strong smell of mildew.

Beyond the desk is a round table that looks like the one in my King Arthur book. At least a dozen chairs, some with high backs covered in red velvet, surround the table. Shiny plates with faded pictures of pink and yellow peaches sit in the center of lace place mats. Gold forks and spoons rest in an X across the plates and a gold knife is lined up at the top of each place mat.

I recognize crystal wineglasses almost like the ones that Granny gave to us when we emptied out her apartment. These have the initials ES etched on the side, and gold trim around the rim. A large china bowl, decorated with orange-and-black goldfish, sits in the middle of the table. It holds at least a hundred peppermint candy sticks, stuck upright.

"Want one of those, don't you?" A tiny woman wearing a blue velvet hat with a fluttering peacock feather, steps out from behind a tall bookcase. "Well, you can't have one. They're for my guests." She's wearing an apron with bright red cherries on it, over a fur coat. I stifle a laugh and immediately think about Johnny and how he'd be trying not to laugh, too.

Her voice is scratchy and high-pitched, and she's peering at me through huge red-framed glasses that cover most of her face. "I don't remember you," she says. "But if someone sent you, then sit down."

She darts toward me and I back away, but she's really fast and manages to scoot around me and the big desk and lock the door. "Now sit. We'll wait for the others."

I have to move deeper into the shop to get away

from her. I'm used to conversations that don't always make sense, and I'm sure I could push her out of the way and escape. But I don't want to hurt her.

"I'm a customer." I give her a fake friendly smile. "I saw the sign and decided to stop in."

"Do you eat veal?" The woman locks two more locks on the door and then slides in a safety chain. My smile fades as I realize that unless there's a back door, I'm completely trapped. Nobody has any idea where I am. In fact, I'm not sure where I am. Maybe André would eventually spot the bicycle, but if I don't get out of here soon I might as well say good-bye to the unlocked bike. I reach for my phone.

"Goldfish?" The woman pulls a handful of goldfish crackers out of the pocket of the apron and throws them at me. Then she picks up a spoon and heaves it my way, followed by a fork. I duck behind one of the tall chairs and frantically look around for another exit. "SIT DOWN!" she screams.

I've watched Nicole calm down residents who get upset, especially when they aren't completely in the real world. I know what to do. "Okay." I stand up slowly. "Where would you like me to sit?"

This approach seems to work because she points to a low stool opposite her. "There." She arranges herself on the tall chair nearest the door, spreads out her fur coat, and reaches for a peppermint stick. "So, how was the play?" She calmly sucks on the candy, smearing the red lipstick that outlines her lips.

I can see her face better as we sit across from each other. She's a mass of wrinkles, and I recognize the glazed look of someone who lives only in her own mind. I hope Granny never gets this lost. Nicole's warned me that it could happen any day.

"It was a wonderful play. It was about a pen." I casually stand and ease my way around the store, scanning to see if perhaps there are any pens buried under the dust. The bookshelves are mostly empty, with an occasional figurine or damaged book. "Do you have any old pens?"

She studies the wrapper of the candy stick, peeling it carefully, licking the plastic.

Just as I sneak past her toward the door, she picks up a wineglass and heaves it at me. She misses by a mile, but then she grabs a plate and throws that, too, coming awfully close. Another plate follows, and the rest of the silverware is next. "SIT DOWN!" She keeps screaming at me, and no longer does she seem amusing. This is when residents are handled by nurses and orderlies, but I can't ring a buzzer or call for help. Who would hear me? And who would I call? I'm not supposed to be here!

As objects crash around me, I'm able to pull the chain aside and start on the locks. My hands are shaking and I almost drop my phone. A spoon thumps against my arm. The locks keep getting stuck. "Stop it!" I yell back, and the tears finally break loose. What am I doing here?

As she pelts me with handfuls of goldfish crackers, the door is finally free. Rain is pouring in sheets, but I'm relieved to be in fresh air and see that the bike is still there. I jump on and take off with no idea if I'm going the right way. The streets are empty, so I'm able to pump fast for two blocks and around the corner, anxious to get back to the warmth of the Armory.

But I get twisted around, and the rows of Brooklyn stoops start to look the same on every block. Where's the abandoned bed and the grouchy doorman?

I pedal frantically until I realize that twice I've passed a dry cleaning store with a blue velvet tuxedo hanging limply in the window. I hit a chunk of sidewalk, the bike slips as I brake, and I tip over, banging against a wrought iron railing. No one is around, but I'm not so sure they'd help me anyway. It's too wet to take out my phone. I have to find someplace dry.

As I check the bike and retie the laces on one of my boots, I spot the green awning that I'd ducked under before. It's across the street. I jump on the bike and pick up speed, holding tight, barely able to see in the rain. By the time I roll the bicycle into the gym, I'm completely soaked and breathing hard. But I'm home.

"Where have you been?" Maria starts to hug me, but then steps back. "Honey, you're drenched to the bone! Dry off and then get over to that pile and find something to change into." She points to the stack of clothes that's built up high again. I'm so anxious to wear dry clothes that I actually consider grabbing a pair of extra-wide pajama pants and somebody's old sweater.

The hum of the Armory surrounds me, by now a familiar sound. I can detect the occasional family squabble, or the whine of a child who's sick of being cooped up. Some of the residents of Rockaway Manor are playing cards and giggling, probably because they don't really know where they are. Others keep calling for a nurse—I could name most of those residents by now.

I don't care how grungy that pile of clothing is. I want to disappear into the mound of soft cloth and sleep until everything is back to normal again.

"Must be raining!" one of the nurses says as she races by with a pile of blankets. "You can't tell the weather in here. You have to go into the lobby where there are windows!"

I drag one of the Macy's bags out from under my

cot and pull out a flannel shirt and leggings that my mom had folded neatly on the top. By the time I've changed and brushed my teeth, the lights in the gym have been dimmed, and snores have already begun. Nicole ushers Mrs. Sidobeth back to her cot. "You can talk to Miss Collette in the morning, sweetheart. She's sleeping now."

I'd shoved my phone back in my pocket so it wouldn't get wet, and it buzzes. It's a text from Johnny: Power on! Restaurant full!!! It's not the time to catch him up on how I had to dodge flying forks and goldfish or battle Brooklyn in the rain just to find an old pen.

But I do text my mom. I'd missed her evening call that was followed by a series of texts, so I let her know that I was busy and couldn't answer. She calls me immediately. "I'm tired, Mom. Busy day."

She presses me for more information because she's my mom. What did I eat today? Is there enough heat? Is Granny sleeping well? As I listen, I want to give in and say, "I need you, Mom." But not yet.

The tears are too close and she'd know, so I say good night.

I grab my blanket and gently curl up next to Granny on her narrow cot. It sinks a bit and wobbles until I can get comfortable. She's tiny and doesn't take up too much room, but the edge of the cot still digs into my back. I don't mind.

She reaches her hand over her shoulder and pats my arm. "Ma douce," she says lovingly. I know what that means. *My sweet.*

I can't disappoint her.

Chapter 14
The Code

Brume
Nearly Spring 1944

Monsieur Ruse knocks twice on the thick oak door of Marguerite's elegant home in Brume and walks boldly into the house. Marguerite and Collette race to the front hall. Their tutor has arrived.

Without breaking stride, Monsieur Ruse brushes past them. His tweed coat smells of garlic and hangs loosely down to his knees. He has a hacking cough, and he whips out a gray rag and spits a glob of phlegm into it. Marguerite's father opens his office door and holds out a bottle of wine. Monsieur Ruse grabs the bottle, enters the office, and kicks the door shut.

"The tutor is here!" Marguerite announces, just in

case household workers are cleaning nearby, while her mother delivers worn clothing to village families.

None of the workers know that Monsieur Ruse can't read or write. He's not a tutor at all. He's a resister who brings messages from Marseille to Marguerite's father. To explain his weekly visits, he pretends to be Monsieur Ruse, a schoolteacher hired to be a tutor. Marguerite's father has arranged for Collette to join Marguerite on the days that Monsieur Ruse pays a visit.

It took a while for Collette to feel comfortable around Marguerite. But after a few missions, she found that she felt safer if Marguerite was by her side. They pretended to be two friends on bicycles, a boy in a cap, and a girl with long, brown hair and a blue beret. They made deliveries, spied on Germans, and reported back to Panther. He never thanked them, never commented on their friendship, but he always had something else for them to do.

They take the front hall stairs two at a time to the library on the second floor. Sleet taps on the windows and scatters frozen pellets on the grounds. Collette sinks into a chair that's close to a low-burning fire in the massive fireplace. "I hope we don't have to go out in this weather. It's so cozy in here."

"This bad weather won't stop the Germans," Marguerite remarks as she picks up a book from an old rolltop desk and shoves a heavy chair next to Collette. She drapes a soft red plaid blanket over both of them. They kick off their boots and extend their toes closer to the fire.

The room is wall-to-wall books. The two girls have already worked their way through the bookshelves as they have waited for Monsieur Ruse to finish his meetings. They've flipped through tomes about the history of France, or journals about farming or manufacturing.

When the war first started, before the Germans occupied Brume, Marguerite's father had quickly gone through his extensive collection of books and removed almost half of them. The Germans had been destroying books and disapproved of so many titles and authors. It was not worth the risk to display them on his shelves or hide them away. When Marguerite asked where he had taken them, he flushed and rested his hand on her shoulder. "They are in the sea, my love. The French do not burn their books."

Marguerite had helped him reorganize the rows of bookshelves so that they still looked packed. To fill an empty shelf, she spread out her seashell collection from trips to the Côte d'Azur that her family had taken before the war. She propped up a few books to show off their elaborate dustcovers, even though the titles were tedious. *Insects and Grapes* and *Plowing in Sandy Soil* were prominently displayed on metal stands.

Her father added to the shelves the pottery he'd collected in Provence, as well as inkwells, cut-glass paperweights, and Chinese porcelain jars. He hung claret-colored velvet curtains to block the window.

The result is a cluttered array to make the room appear to be a comfortable sanctuary.

But there are no radios, no newspapers or maps, and no personal papers ever in plain sight. Marguerite knows that her father has them somewhere. She's seen her father studying the silk maps and underground newspapers that Monsieur Ruse brings when he can get them.

But none of these things are in the library, where dinner guests often wander in to explore the shelves and smoke pungent cigarettes. The smoke from the fireplace and the cigarettes soaks into the pages of the old books.

Marguerite has grown used to the smell. Her father often reeks of cigarettes and hair pomade, and she doesn't mind at all. She hands the book from the desk to Collette. "This week's book is about growing sugar beets. It was delivered yesterday."

Collette opens the book and scans the fuzzy black-and-white photographs of fields of beets, and detailed, colored drawings of the fat yellow root with crinkly leaves. Most of the words are too technical for her to understand, but she's able to pick out the names of places like Paris, Germany, Russia, and Ukraine. For some reason, a chapter is devoted to Napoleon

Bonaparte. She imitates a picture of him with his hand tucked in his vest.

Her stomach starts to rumble as she looks at pictures of the sweet purple sugar beet syrup. She longs for a chunk of fresh bread with a slice of peppery Gaperon cheese or perhaps a handful of tangy green olives. She finds every opportunity to visit Marguerite's kitchen and stuffs her pockets to take food back to her family. Marguerite's kitchen larder has less to offer this winter, but Collette's family cupboard is frequently empty.

Marguerite sighs. "I hate waiting." She flips her legs over the side of the comfortable chair, leans back, and counts the beams in the ceiling. "I wish my father still had the big globe we could spin, or his typewriter. But the Germans took those away a long time ago. I wonder if we'll ever get them back."

Collette points at a sketch of a giant sugar beet. "This might be a way for France to have sugar again."

She's interrupted by Monsieur Ruse, who slowly climbs the stairs, sneezing loudly. He enters the room dabbing at his wide nose, leaving a string of green goop stuck to his mustache. His spectacles, low on his nose, are crooked, and his black hair hangs in clumps. He wears the glasses to look more like a teacher, but Collette and Marguerite know he doesn't need them. The second he enters, he stuffs them into his pocket and takes in the room with rheumy eyes.

Collette pictures actually being tutored by him and tries to make herself invisible in the chair.

"Why are you sitting there doing nothing?" His voice is raspy as he shouts his question into the hallway, slams the door, and says urgently, "It's a short one today. Get busy." He hands Collette a piece of butcher paper used once for wrapping raw meat. She doesn't hesitate to grab it from him, even though the paper is smeared with blood spots and grime.

The two girls scramble out of their chairs and Monsieur Ruse claims the one closest to the fire. Before they can settle at the big desk, he has pulled out a footstool and rested his filthy boots on it. He tugs the blanket over himself, closes his eyes, and wheezes in a steady rhythm.

The girls go to work. Collette lays the book down

179

in front of her on the desk and Marguerite picks up a stubby pencil. They are ready to decode.

Marguerite reads the first set of numbers on the scrap of butcher paper, "Twenty-one, two fourteen." Quickly, Collette finds page twenty-one, runs her finger down to the second paragraph, and over to the first letter of the fourteenth word. "P."

Marguerite records the letter, then reads the next batch of numbers, "Thirty-four, thirty-seven." Collette finds page thirty-four, the third paragraph, seventh word, first letter. "A."

They rapidly complete the first line. "Hmm, pas de citrons," Marguerite reads, puzzled.

Collette taps the paper. "Pas de citrons!" *No lemons!*

Within minutes, they've figured out the entire message, even though they have no idea what it means. Marguerite reads aloud, "Pas de citrons. Pas de poires. Les fraises de Bessan sont en avance." *No lemons. No pears. Bessan strawberries are early.*

Monsieur Ruse pops up. "Early?" He tosses the blanket aside and drops his boots to the floor, leaving a smear of mud on the braided rug.

Marguerite reads the message to him.

"Go!" Monsieur Ruse picks up their boots in front of the fireplace, tosses them at the girls, and has a coughing fit. He doubles over to catch his breath. "Go tell . . . your . . . father," he wheezes.

Collette grabs the boots while Marguerite tears the butcher paper into tiny pieces.

"I'll do that!" Monsieur Ruse slumps in the chair and waves them toward the door. He wipes his face with the rag, already soaked with fluids. "I'll burn the scraps. Now go! Vite! Vite!"

As the girls dash down the stairs, Marguerite's father steps out of his office. "Your tutoring is over so soon?" he asks loudly. He ushers them in and firmly closes the door. "Where's Monsieur Ruse?"

"He told us to tell you the message. He's very sick, Papa."

"No lemons, no pears," Collette reports as she slides on her big boots. "And Bessan strawberries are early."

Marguerite's father flings the door open and calls up the stairs. "Monsieur Ruse, come here, please."

Monsieur Ruse shuffles to the top of the stairs and abruptly sits down on the top step. "I cannot." When Marguerite's father growls at him, he grabs the railing and pulls himself up. He wavers for a moment and stumbles down the steps clinging to the handrail, coughing so that droplets fly about. "I am too slow."

Marguerite's father pulls him into the office. "The strawberries are early! We must get him to Spain!" Collette has never seen Marguerite's father so frantic.

Monsieur Ruse slumps into a chair and moans.

"Papa!" Marguerite pulls on her father's arm. "Who has to get to Spain?"

Both men slowly turn toward Marguerite.

Collette freezes. She knows he can't answer her, but she can sense what's coming. Monsieur Ruse stops his groaning and leans in as Marguerite's father tucks his finger under Marguerite's chin and stares into her eyes. "You two are going to have to deliver this message as quickly as you can."

Marguerite's eyes widen, but she doesn't flinch. "Where?"

"The drop spot is a log in front of Madame Monette's. But skip that. You have to deliver the message to her personally."

"Madame Monette!" Marguerite exclaims. "She's an old lady!"

Collette double-ties her boot laces. "We're ready." She knows that Madame Monette is a very old woman, but if two young girls can play a part in resisting, so can old Madame Monette, living alone in the country.

"Make sure," Monsieur Ruse says to them through his grubby rag, "Madame Monette understands that Bessan strawberries are coming early. She'll know that Bessan is near the border of Spain."

"Tell her no lemons, no pears," Marguerite's father repeats, as if they might forget. "Give her the whole message. Say that the greengrocer thought she'd like to know that Bessan strawberries will be early."

Marguerite decodes the message as she listens. Something is happening sooner than expected—a lot sooner—and it isn't about lemons, pears, or strawberries.

Marguerite's father gives his daughter a quick hug.
"Get your coats. Be safe. Go fast."

"You can trust us, Papa."

"I know I can. But this is . . ."

"More dangerous?"

He pauses and rubs his forehead. "It's . . . it's very important. He has to get out of Brume and go south to Spain. I hope it's not too late."

Chapter 15
Invisible

Brume
Nearly Spring, 1944

"Wait!"

The girls press back on the pedals so that both their bicycles come to a halt and slide on the gravel of the drive. It's another wet and windy day. Collette pulls her cap down to cover her ears and tightens the thick black scarf around her neck. She looks back to see Marguerite's father standing on the porch. He's not wearing a coat, and sleet splatters down on him. He's holding up a basket and three skinny carrots by the greens and waving them. "Take these carrots to Madame Monette!"

"He's really making a big show out of carrots,"

Marguerite mutters to Collette as he scurries down the steps and walks briskly across the drive. A swirl of brisk wind scatters dead leaves at his feet.

He places the wicker basket in Marguerite's bicycle basket and shows her that under the cloth cover is a potato. He adds the carrots, folding the greens over and replacing the cover. "We don't want Madame to go hungry." He adjusts Marguerite's coat collar and turns back, crossing his arms against the cold.

The girls resume their trek through the village streets to the outskirts of town. They don't try to hide, but they take side streets, as usual. Not many people, including soldiers, are willing to go outside and fight with a frosty wind that bites at their cheeks.

Collette's hands freeze on the handlebars, and she pulls down her coat sleeves to serve as gloves. It doesn't take long to navigate the streets, and they hardly say a word to each other as they aim toward Madame's home, less than a mile from a road that circles the village. Soon they leave the protection of stone houses and brick walls and make their way into the countryside, barely able to stay upright on their bicycles as the wind pushes against them.

They pass woodlands on both sides, and try to skirt the frozen ruts of the narrow dirt road.

"There!" Collette points over to a small stone house with a thatched roof, set way back from the road next to an abandoned olive grove. Smoke puffs from the chimney, but no lights inside the house can be seen. An outhouse stands crookedly behind the house.

Collette spots the log at the end of the drive—the drop spot. She rides past it, up to the blue wooden door. She props her bike against a stack of firewood that's covered in snow. Marguerite pulls up beside her as Collette knocks on the door.

"Madame Monette?" Marguerite calls. "We have some vegetables for you."

Collette can smell the sweet smoke of a brushwood fire.

The door opens a crack, and Madame's large nose appears before the rest of her lined, droopy face. She's wearing a blue kerchief around her head, with tiny red flowers. "Ah, Marguerite. Come in."

The house is one small room, sparsely furnished

with a rough wooden table and a wide hutch that has peeling green paint and a shiny ceramic counter. Rows of glass jars are lined up neatly. When spring finally arrives, they will hold Madame's famous lilac-and-wild-berry jam.

A skinny bed, covered with a worn, gray blanket, has been shoved into the corner next to an empty coal bin. Stairs made of tree limbs lead to a narrow loft above their heads. Embroidered hand towels, hung neatly on the backs of the chairs, are the only decoration.

The room is plain but warm from a fire of burning sticks. Marguerite unbuttons her coat and Collette removes her heavy scarf and hat.

"My apologies," Madame fusses with her dirty apron. "I have no light. We're not allowed candles, and my lantern and flashlight were taken away."

Marguerite plunks the basket down on the table. "You can still see what we brought." She smiles at Madame. "Some carrots and a potato."

Madame's brown eyes soften, but she makes no

move to peer under the cloth cover. She doesn't invite her visitors to sit and glances nervously at Collette, who's quietly looking around the room, peering into dark corners and stepping back to look up into the loft.

"I thought you'd like to know," Marguerite says to Madame, "we've talked to the greengrocer. There are no lemons, no pears . . . and the strawberries from Bessan are early."

Madame makes no effort to hide her dismay. "The strawberries will be early?!" She paces the room, grabs a whisk broom, and vigorously sweeps the hearth, then busily straightens the glass jars that are already lined up perfectly.

Marguerite guides Madame over to a chair while Collette takes the potato and carrots out of the basket and places them on the table. Madame adjusts her kerchief and reaches under the table for a tin pot containing a wooden spoon and a sharp knife. "He has to go!" She centers the pot in front of her. "Now!"

"Who is *he*?" Marguerite asks.

Collette is surprised that Marguerite asks her the

question. There are strict rules about identifying anyone who might be working with resisters.

Madame glances at the door and the small, dirty window and whispers, "All I know is that a lieutenant from British Intelligence was dropped near here last night."

"A British spy?" Collette knew that British soldiers were not only helping resisters by dropping supplies and weapons, but now they were also joining the resisters on the ground. There were even rumors that American soldiers were also in France, spying against the Germans.

"He's coming to teach us a new code. The one we're using can be broken too easily."

"You mean page, paragraph, word?" Marguerite asks. "We've been using that for too long. We do need a better code."

"But what happened to the lieutenant?" Collette scans the house again, looking for loose floorboards or hidden doors.

"I haven't seen him." Madame fingers the precious

carrots and potato. "But I know he's hiding in the out-house." She stands up and begins chopping a carrot and the greens into pieces. "I left an onion and a chunk of bread in a bucket. When I looked this morning, the food was gone."

"You mean he's still in the outhouse?" Most of the village houses have indoor toilets, but many farms still have outhouses. Collette can't imagine hiding in one. The smell!

"Ewww!" Marguerite holds her nose. "How long has he been in there?"

"He spent last night in someone's barn, but at dawn he was supposed to find his way to my storage bin attached to the back of the outhouse. I kept my flower pots and gardening tools in the bin." She cuts the potato into chunks.

"Didn't you look to see if he's in there?"

"I didn't want anyone to see me lift the lid of the bin. You never know if Germans are around in the woods."

"He must be frozen solid."

"I covered the bottom with straw and tossed an old quilt in there." Madame rapidly slices a carrot. "I tried tapping on the wall inside the outhouse. I thought he might tap back. But there was silence. I couldn't even hear anyone breathing."

"Maybe he's already gone."

"He's supposed to wait for nightfall and go to the next stop in the village."

Collette suspects that the next stop will be Hélène's shed, where Panther meets with spies and resisters.

Madame pauses in her chopping and rests the knife on the table. She looks at the girls with weary eyes. "'The strawberries are coming early' means that the Germans are doing a house-by-house search. We knew it was going to happen, but it's sooner than expected."

Collette's immediately on her feet. "We need to warn the lieutenant. Get him out of that bin."

Marguerite buttons her coat and heads for the door. "Do you know his code name?"

Madame sweeps pieces of potato into the pot. "All I know is he's a British Intelligence operative. They call him the lieutenant. He'll pretend to be French, and he's supposed to be a genius at codes. That's more than you should know!" She picks up the last carrot to chop, hesitates, and hands it to Marguerite. "If he's still there, he'll be hungry." Marguerite stuffs it into her pocket as Madame continues. "Use the password or he won't answer. Tell him 'Soon the lilacs will be back.'"

The girls emerge from the dark house to discover that midday sunlight is beginning to appear and the sleet has moved on, but the wind is still brisk. Collette looks up and down the road and scans the overgrown olive grove and the woods.

The outhouse is made of a few worn boards and leans to the right. There's one door in the front, with a carved wooden handle and rusty hinges. Collette can now see the extra space extending from the back.

She opens the crooked door and ducks inside the outhouse, as Marguerite stands guard outside. Collette breathes through her mouth but can still smell the stench. She can barely stand up in the small space but has no desire to sit on the crude wooden seat. She doesn't look down, for fear of what she might see piled up in the hole below.

"Hello?" she says to the inner wall that separates the outhouse from the storage bin. "Lieutenant?"

Silence. *Perhaps he's no longer hiding*, she thinks.

Marguerite peeks in the door. "Use the password."

"Soon the lilacs will be back." Collette slowly enunciates the French words, still speaking to the inner wall. "Can you hear me? Soon the lilacs will be back."

She hears a soft rustling on the other side of the wall. A muffled voice says in flawless French, "They will fill the fields."

"He's still in there!" Collette bolts out of the outhouse and joins Marguerite at the storage bin. She looks around again, remembering Madame's comment about Germans in the woods. They grab the lid, push it up, and prop it against the outhouse. As Collette leans over to look in the bin, a hand in a brown leather glove grips the side.

The lieutenant stands up. Both girls gasp.

"You're a woman!" Collette steps back as the lieutenant climbs out and reaches down into the bin and pulls out a small canvas rucksack.

"Bonjour." The lieutenant brushes her uneven bangs away from her face, runs in place for a few seconds, and swings her arms around. She's wearing bright red lipstick, a tiny bit smeared at the upper lip, and she has circles of pink rouge on her pale cheeks. Pencil lines run along the arch of her eyebrows. "I don't think I could take one more minute in there. And I've been in a lot of tight spots."

Collette knows there are supposed to be very few words exchanged between resisters in the middle of a mission, especially with British agents who parachute into France to deliver supplies and assist with the fight. The wrong word, the wrong expression, can be deadly.

This time she doesn't have to try to keep her mouth shut because she can't think of what to say. She's certainly seen female spies before—after all, she speaks to Rabbit and Hélène often. But this tall, thin lieutenant with long, wavy brown hair is totally unexpected.

She realizes that's probably part of the plan.

"So you know the password!" The lieutenant straightens the thick navy cable-knit sweater that hangs over a dark turtleneck sweater and khaki overalls. She brushes off bits of straw and adjusts her leather aviator cap so that the flaps fit tightly over her ears. "Who are you?" She squats down to unbuckle the straps on the rucksack. "And why'd you let me come out in the daylight?"

Her French is rapid, with an extra guttural growl.

Marguerite is first to find her voice. "Marg . . . I mean, Skylark." She can't seem to take her eyes off the lieutenant. "And this is Wallcreeper."

"Skylark and Wallcreeper!" The lieutenant pokes around in the rucksack, shoving aside cotton under-wear and black wool socks. Collette spots a pink wool beret mixed in with boxes of powdered coffee, women's black shoes, ration tickets, and a small silver compact.

The lieutenant pulls out a pencil case. "Well, it seems to me you deserve a reward for releasing me. If you get me to the next drop safely, I'll give you some more tools of the trade." She pops open the long case and holds up a pencil.

Collette almost hands it back. "We're not little children," she says.

"It's actually a dagger." The lieutenant points to the sharp metal tip of the pencil. "Don't stick it in your back pocket. I did that once. Not a good idea."

She continues to rummage around in the rucksack and pulls out a wide scarf in green-and-black paisley. She tosses the aviator cap into the rucksack and ties the scarf around her head like Madame Monette's kerchief. Her shiny brown hair flows out from underneath in all directions.

She points to one of the flaps of the aviator cap. "Message hidden in the flap. But you probably already figured that out."

"Our tutor hides notes in the lining of his hat," Marguerite volunteers. Collette nods but wonders if the hiding place is a bit obvious. How long has this odd woman been a spy?

"Don't worry," the lieutenant says, giving Collette

a sly grin. "The message is written in invisible ink and both flaps are stuffed with crumpled paper. As long as nobody pees on the message, it can't be seen."

She reaches into a pocket on the outside of the rucksack and pulls out a small box. She pops open the lid and reveals a petite bottle of perfume labeled BEAU PARIS. "The Germans use fancy chemicals, but we know how to hide invisible ink in perfume." She pretends to dab a little behind each ear. "But lemon juice and urine work just as well."

She seems awfully silly for an intelligence operative, Collette thinks as she watches the lieutenant pull the compact out of the knapsack and inspect her lipstick in the mirror.

"We have to get moving," Collette snaps. The last thing she wants is to be caught with a British agent.

Suddenly the lieutenant is all business. She chucks the compact into the rucksack and quickly buckles up the straps. She picks it up, ready to go. "Do we have bicycles, or do we cut through the woods over there?"

Just as she points to the clump of trees across from

the house, a faint, high-pitched whine can be heard in the distance. "That's a car! They're coming!" Collette grabs the lieutenant's arm. "We need to go."

"Look!" Marguerite points at Madame Monette riding on a bicycle on the path away from her house, pushing down hard on the pedals. Madame turns at the road and races away from the sound of a rapidly moving automobile.

"They're not going to drive by!" Collette pulls on the lieutenant's jacket. "They're searching houses!"

The lieutenant shakes off Collette's grip and reaches into a pocket hidden under the flap of the rucksack. She pulls out a slim brass case about the size of a man's wallet and holds it gingerly on the palm of her gloved hand. "This is a cigarette case. Don't ever open it."

Collette steps back. She knows the case is probably booby-trapped with explosives.

"If I have to," the lieutenant continues, "I'll offer the Germans a cigarette. If you hear an explosion, run for the olive grove faster than you've ever run in your life." She gently slides the battered case into the pocket of her overall pants. She gives Collette a wink. "I'm a lot smarter than I look."

"They'll surely see us if we try to get away now." Marguerite's voice is shaky.

The lieutenant puts her hands on Marguerite's shoulders. "I promise you, we're almost done with this war. Soon you'll be saying your real name and wearing pretty dresses again. In the future when there's a knock on the door, you'll fling it open instead of fearing for your life."

The car seems to be getting closer.

The lieutenant points to a metal button that holds the giant sweater closed. "Don't worry about what happens to me. This button is also a compass. I'll head south to Spain."

Collette's not sure the lieutenant will have the chance. When the Germans search a house, they do it thoroughly.

The lieutenant shoves Collette toward the bin. "But for now we have to hide! You—get in." Collette doesn't dare look at Marguerite's face. They've both been in danger before—after all, Marguerite was caught in the middle of Germans, who turned on her. But they'd never been right next to a British spy who might be caught in the middle of a mission. Collette steps over the side of the wooden bin.

Marguerite climbs in after her, and they wriggle around until their knees are bent and they can fit in the cramped space. Marguerite's legs start to shake and Collette reaches out and grabs her knees to hold her steady. Marguerite places her hands over Collette's and grips them tightly. They don't look at each other.

The cover is slammed shut, but there are gaps between the warped boards. Some sunlight comes through, along with drafts of winter cold. Marguerite makes a noise that sounds like a cry.

Collette thinks of her family, sitting by their warm fire, wondering why she never came home. She presses her back against the thin wall of the storage bin. The driver of the car grinds the gears and spins out at the turn, toward Madame's house.

Collette drops her head to her knees. She can feel

her bowels shift and can't believe she's just inches away from an outhouse and can't use it.

A watchdog never sleeps. She sucks in her breath as she remembers Hélène's motto. *We wasted time, Marguerite,* she thinks. *We let our guard down.* Her eyes fill with tears.

The lieutenant speaks clearly to us through the inner wall of the outhouse. "If they come back here, you two stay hidden. I'll come out of the outhouse and distract them." Collette taps the wall in response. The lieutenant continues. "Stay until you hear the car drive away, or . . ."

"What if they find us?" Marguerite's voice is trembling.

"You tell them you were on your bicycles and stopped to use the outhouse. They frightened you, so you hid. That's all."

"But that's not all!" Collette wants to shout. This lieutenant doesn't seem to understand what it's been like to live in Brume. More resisters in Noah's Ark have gone missing every day. A few come back with tales of torture and labor camps, but mostly they don't come back.

She hopes the lieutenant isn't foolish enough to have radio parts in her knapsack. Getting caught with a radio or replacement parts means certain death. The Germans might even shoot them on the spot.

Collette closes her eyes to the sun rays streaming through the cracks in the cupboard, and lifts her face to absorb the light. She can hear the Germans pounding on Madame's door. They don't wait to see if she opens it. Collette hears the hutch crash to the floor and glass is smashed against the walls. The men shout at each other in German.

Collette pictures the table with the carrot and potato pieces. She hopes Madame was able to fill her apron pockets before she fled.

There are more shouts, and the car engine starts up again. But one man calls out, and the engine stops. Collette signals to Marguerite to stay quiet.

It sounds as if the two men, laughing and talking, are coming toward the outhouse.

Collette hears shuffling, and the door to the out-house creaks open. The lieutenant speaks quickly in French, explaining to the soldiers that she was hiding because they frightened her.

She switches to a few words in halting German. Collette recognizes *bitte* (please) and *meine papiere* (my papers). She's heard those words many times since the Germans moved into Brume.

The German responses are harsh and impatient. One man keeps yelling out orders, right outside the storage bin. *Move away, move away,* Collette prays. She presses her lips together to keep from making a sound. She hopes Marguerite is doing the same.

The lieutenant seems to hear Collette's thoughts and keeps talking as she moves away toward the house. The soldiers argue with each other briefly, and there's a scuffle. Their voices fade as they move around to the front of the house. Collette can no longer hear the lieutenant.

She realizes she's been holding her breath. She lets air out slowly, terrified that even that soft sound will bring the Germans back. A draft of cold whistling air suddenly blows through the cracks of the storage bin.

A loud explosion blends with the screaming wind.

The girls burst out from their hiding place. By the time they are halfway to the olive grove, the lieutenant is already on the other side, frantically waving at Collette and Marguerite to run even faster.

Chapter 16
A Bridge to Cross

Brooklyn to Manhattan
November 2012—Day 8

By looking at a map on the wall of the Armory, I've been able to figure out how to avoid busy roads to get to the Brooklyn Bridge. I bicycle along side streets and cut through neighborhood parks, where giant uprooted trees often block the path. They're splintered and splayed out, sometimes piled on top of other trees that had been torn apart by the hurricane. Branches are scattered everywhere, even strewn across paved playgrounds, as if Sandy ripped them off the trees and carried them far away before letting go. Thousands of autumn leaves, still fresh, are spread across green picnic areas and piled against chain-link fences.

Police officers wave me on. "Go home, kid!" But I keep going, sometimes lifting my bike over tree trunks that have crashed to the pavement. I finally spot the bridge ahead of me.

A line already winds around several blocks, as people in Brooklyn wait for the extra buses to Manhattan. After a rain-soaked weekend, they seem determined to go to work, even though the subways are closed and the tip of Manhattan still doesn't have any power.

I guess everyone had the same idea to get in line right after the sun came up. They're all bundled up, sipping coffee and checking their phones. There's a low hum from the line as conversations start up and they slowly move forward to board the special buses. But mostly the crowd is subdued and cold.

I figure the restaurant wants their bicycle back, but I'm going to keep it one more day and get over the Brooklyn Bridge to the city. I have to get to the Pen Emporium to find a replacement pen so I never have to tell Granny that I lost the original.

I've been texting Johnny about my plans to go to Manhattan, but it's too hard to explain the whole story in a text. I'm dying to tell him everything that's been going on over the last few days, but as long as school is out, he's spending all of his time at his family's restaurant. The story will have to wait.

My mom called before she left for work, as usual. My school is still closed, but teachers have emailed assignments. I promised to do my homework and described a busy day at the Armory, including plans for Johnny and me to take Granny for a walk. She reminded me that Granny tires easily but was pleased that Johnny will be with me. My mom wasn't too sure about Johnny when she first met him, especially because he was only eleven and had a pierced eyebrow. But once she saw him working in his family's restaurant, she started to like him more. He's been around for over a year now, and she's used to him. It helps that he brings us leftovers from the restaurant's kitchen.

At the end of the call, she seemed reassured that all is well in Brooklyn.

I bike easily past the long line and work my way over side streets to the beginning of the bridge. There's a small crowd of people there, but they stretch out over the walkway and keep moving over the river to Manhattan.

Here I go, I text Johnny as I pull my bike up to a handful of people gathered around dancers in black tights and gray T-shirts that say NYC DANCE COMPANY. While one of the dancers makes a beat with "uh-uh-uh San-DY," the rest hip-hop dance in unison. They're serious and never look up. They're working hard, but they still must be feeling the cold. I guess everyone in this city has to find a different way to cope with Sandy.

I just want to get to the pen store and back again before I run out of money, and before Granny starts to figure out that something isn't right.

"Lily!" I think I hear Johnny's voice. Was it just wishful thinking? "Breakfast!" He rolls his bike in front of mine and grins. He's shorter than I am—in fact, he's shorter than most kids, but he always seems older and taller.

Last time I saw him, his wild, fuzzy brown hair

had a pink streak. Today it's tipped in bright blue, and I have to smile. I can count on Johnny to do the unexpected, and now he's right next to me. I had seen him right before the storm, but it seems like ages ago.

"What are you doing here?" I pull my bike over to the side against the high steel fence, to get out of the way of the walkers on the bridge. Traffic roars below us as a steady stream of buses makes its way up the ramp to go over the bridge to the city.

"Classy bike." He rubs his fingerless gloves over the edge of the basket. I've plunked my backpack into the basket, and added a bottle of water, a box of cheese crackers, and some pudding cups. Johnny shoves over the crackers and places a brown paper bag in the basket. "Doughnuts. Girl needs to eat."

Johnny loves to get people to try his newest recipes. There's no way Johnny had made plain old doughnuts. He can't even make a pancake without adding squash for color and raisins for a sweet surprise. Someday he's going to have his own cooking show, I just know it.

I peer into the bag and, of course, the doughnuts are unusual shapes and colors. He pulls one out. "This one is stuffed with popcorn and pretzels if you want something crunchy." I shake my head, so he pulls out a fat orange doughnut. "Made with sweet potatoes and marshmallows. Very filling!"

I pull off a gooey piece and am not surprised that it's quite tasty. "What else?"

He shows me one with peanut butter and jelly leaking out the center, but the one I choose has pieces of Oreo cookies blended into the doughnut. I can't resist eating all of it, even though I've already had a breakfast of potato sticks and fruit cup. "Yum. This is a keeper."

"What's the big hurry to get to Manhattan?"

I usually tell Johnny everything, but it suddenly feels weird if I tell him that I have to get to a fountain pen store as fast as possible. He'll think that my brain got soaked in the flood. "I'm picking some things up for people at the Armory." I hate to lie to him, but it's an explanation that he might buy.

"You can't get anything in the city. There's no power at all in Lower Manhattan. You're better off in Brooklyn. What do you have to get?"

"It's a long story." I should have known that Johnny wasn't going to accept my answer. He reaches into his backpack and pulls out a black knit hat, zips up his fleece vest, and starts walking his bike along the bridge.

"So tell me," he says, motioning for me to follow him. "I can get to the restaurant late. Something's going on, and I want to know what it is."

So I tell him. In fact, I don't stop talking for the full thirty minutes it takes to walk the bridge. At one point, I climb on my bike to try to pick up the pace, but he insists that we walk. "Too many people. Keep talking."

I love talking to Johnny about it all. It's the first time I've been able to describe everything to anyone—from measuring the floodwaters, to delivering mozzarella and canned pears, to losing the pen. I describe my visit to Keepsakes as an adventure, but I know he understands. He says all the right things. At least he makes the right noises at the right times. "Cool." "So wrong." "Unreal."

And he asks about Granny. He gets why I don't want her to be sad. "So what's the deal with your granny and this pen? And who's Marguerite?"

"The pen must belong to Marguerite. Except that it has an **F** engraved on it, so maybe that's Marguerite's last name. I really have no idea." We wind around a couple who stop to take pictures. "And I don't want to ask Granny until I know I've got the pen. Or at least one like it that will hopefully fool her."

"And the 4810? Is that some sort of code or something?"

"It has to have a special meaning, but I haven't been able to figure it out. Since I lost the pen, I've been avoiding the subject. All I know is that Granny really wants me to give that pen to someone named Marguerite."

"Maybe your granny stole the pen and she wants to give it back before she dies."

I stop my bike. Even though I've been wondering the same thing, I didn't like to hear anyone say it out loud. Even Johnny. "She's not dying. And she doesn't steal."

Johnny climbs on his bike as we reach the end of the bridge. "Well, maybe Marguerite is her long-lost granddaughter and there's a check for a million dollars rolled up inside the pen. And she wants you to deliver it—and all you'll get is her pink hat."

"Funny. Really funny." I pull out ahead of him, and we work our way through a flow of people filling the sidewalks, pouring from the bridge into the bottom tip of Manhattan. The narrow streets are lined with tall office buildings and the occasional shop or restaurant, all closed and dark because they still have a power outage. Traffic is light, mostly taxis. Loud machines pump water down the sewer drains, and the police have rolled out yellow tape to mark off sections of the street, deep puddles, and piles of debris.

One street has a power line down, and sparks are flying as it wiggles around on the pavement. Cops and city workers are everywhere, keeping people away.

We watch for a while, like tourists, as a man in a long dark coat argues with a cop, gesturing up at the building near the sparking wire. He finally gives up, flings a duffel bag over his shoulder, and walks away. "I just want to get my stuff!" he yells one more time.

The police attempt to direct the small amount of traffic, but no one seems to be paying much attention. Cars jockey for space, jerking around wooden barriers and parked trucks that have giant buzzing generators. "Typical New York," one police officer yells to another. "Life goes on." He blows a whistle at a taxi and bangs on the hood. "Move!"

We don't have far to go, but we end up mostly walking our bikes instead of riding them. It looks like everyone stayed home again today, except for those who are determined to get to work, and others who just want to take pictures.

Superstorm Sandy left its mark everywhere, but the few people on the street keep acting as if nothing has changed. They step around anything that's in the way. Mud mixed with garbage has piled up against the curb. Standing water fills any spot where the pavement dips. Sawhorses have been set up around manholes and open gutters. There are stacks of soggy junk shoved up against the buildings.

"Looks like people are already starting to clear out the flooded buildings," Johnny says quietly as we wheel our bikes around mounds of broken pieces of wood, torn plastic, tree branches, and silt-covered lawn chairs.

"This is what came in with the ocean, honey," a woman standing in a store doorway says to Johnny. "It's all from somebody else's house." She grabs a wide broom and starts pushing piles of soaked trash into the gutter.

It's a gray day. By now the lights would be on in the buildings and neon glowing in some of the windows. But the only source of bright light is yellow flashers, set up on top of metal barrels. As we work our way farther from the bridge, it seems as if most of the stores are shut tight. I start to get a little nervous that this trip will have been a waste of time. "I hope the pen store is open. The website said they're closed only on Sunday and Monday, so we should be okay if they have power."

We zigzag across an intersection, avoiding a gushing pipe and roaring machines near a subway entrance. Men in bright orange-and-yellow vests are shouting, "Three levels! At least another week!" as they ramp up the equipment to pump water from the subway tunnel.

"Over there!" Johnny points across the street, but all I see is a bar with a giant shamrock over the door. On the same block are stores with crisscross metal gates covering the plate-glass windows.

Then I see it—on the corner a hidden doorway. FOUNTAIN PEN EMPORIUM is in peeling gold ink on the rippled glass on the door. It looks closed.

Chapter 17
Standing Order

Manhattan

November 2012—Day 8

I try the door handle of the Fountain Pen Emporium and knock on the window while Johnny locks our bikes together and leans them against the building.

I pull out my phone and check the time. "It's too early. They're not open yet."

"Or maybe they're not going to open at all. This block looks sort of dead. Doesn't seem like they've got power here."

"WHAT?" A man jerks the door open, and I jump back, stumbling into Johnny. "You need a place to stay? Is that it? No lights, no heat, so now you're homeless? Bah!"

The man is the same height as Johnny and has a giant piece of greasy hair stretched over the top of his bald head. His glasses are greasy, too.

We all stare at each other for a moment. I realize that people who live in the Armory are considered homeless, but how could he know where I've come from? "Actually, I'm here to buy a pen." I peer over his shoulder and see a narrow store about as big as Granny's room at Rockaway Manor. There are pens crammed everywhere—stuck upright in jars, laid out in display cases, and mounted on boards hanging on the back wall.

"Well, why didn't you say so!" He steps aside and waves us in. "All day it's people looking for a place to sleep until they can get back into their apartments. Just because I have electricity. Do I look like a hotel?"

"Not really," Johnny mutters in my ear. "Looks like a prison cell."

"I heard that!" the man barks at Johnny. "This is my piece of heaven, I'll have you know."

The store is warm and stuffy. Johnny shoves his

hat and gloves into his backpack. Stacked way up high on the sides of the cramped store are shelves filled with plastic boxes. At the end of the room is a high counter with a magnifying glass on a long, bendable stand. The man climbs onto a tall stool behind the counter and holds up a bright red fountain pen with a gold tip. "Feel that," he says, handing it to Johnny. "Heavy, huh?"

As Johnny weighs the pen with his hand, I close the door and look around. At the very top of the loaded shelves are rows of photos. All around the room are hundreds of overlapping pictures of famous people, all with elaborate signatures.

I tug on Johnny's shirt and point up. "Jay-Z?"

"Loves my pens," the man says. "Never signs a contract without one." He points around the room, rattling off names. "Frank Sinatra, but you probably don't even know who that is. This place opened in 1946, and Frank was one of the first customers. I sell to Bruce Springsteen, that country guy Tim McGraw, even Woody Allen has a few. There's senators, mayors, even Bill Clinton. You probably don't know who he is, either."

We crane our necks and turn slowly to inspect the photos. "Look." Johnny points over in the corner. "Madonna! Seriously?"

"Big-time collector. How about that one, huh?" The man points with his thumb behind him. "This red one's for her." We move to see, but he's blocking the photo. "The one who dressed in meat. You know, Lady Gaga."

"Lady Gaga buys your pens?" I start to giggle and am so glad that I'm not alone. No one would believe this.

"So does Johnny Depp." Johnny points at a note pinned to the wall straight ahead of us, and reads the signature. *To Henry—see you next time I'm in New York, JD.*

"That's me. I'm Henry." He collapses the lamp and swings it against the wall. "So what do you kids want? If you want a ballpoint, those are not pens, they're sticks, and I don't sell them. You need to write something down; is that why you stopped here?"

"It's a little more complicated than that," I start to say, but Henry interrupts.

"Do you even know what a fountain pen is? Know how it works?"

Before we can answer, he demonstrates. He shows how very old pens were dipped in a bottle of ink or an inkwell, blotted on a rag or special paper, and then drawn across a heavy sheet of stationery. He writes his own name in angles with deep blue ink, asks for my name, and writes it like medieval letters in green and gold ink. For Johnny he writes in big, elegant loops, "Like Hancock scrawled on the Declaration of Independence."

From the shelves, he pulls out boxes of ink bottles and ink cartridges that slide into newer fountain pens and shows us his collection of old, elaborate inkwells.

"So which one do you like the best? If you had all the money in the world, which pen would you buy?" He lays out a dozen pens on the high counter. Most of them are dark blue or black, but some are rich colors in dark red, emerald and gold, or shiny silver. Some have jewels embedded in the side, or tiny colored sketches of the Beatles, Snow White, or famous paintings. The autographs of the One Direction singers are featured on a set of multicolored pens in an elaborate case.

He makes us lift each pen to see how it feels in our hands, and write the word *pen* several different ways. "Too light? Does it fit your hand?"

One has a tiny diamond at the end of the pen cap. "There's more diamonds on the nib." He touches the point used for writing. I like that one the best, but Johnny likes a big, thick black pen with a fat gold nib engraved with someone's initials.

For several minutes I forget why we're here. I like the quiet closet-like store, away from the noise of the street, where just writing the word *pen* takes concentration.

Johnny takes Henry's writing assignment seriously and asks a million questions. Henry seems pleased that someone cares, and pulls out more and more pens from the plastic boxes. "This is one that Bill bought for Hillary for Christmas in 2001. I'm hoping Obama will order one for Michelle. This one was used to sign the contract for building the new Freedom Tower. The Supreme Court buys the same ones every year—those people have no imagination."

He keeps handing Johnny pens. "And here's one that was given to all the Brooklyn Dodgers when they beat the Yankees in the World Series in 1955."

Johnny exclaims at every one. He pulls off the caps, waves them in the air, and pretends to write.

"We can engrave them with anything you like." I perk up when I hear this. If we can locate a blue marble pen like Granny's, maybe he can add the letter F on the side.

"This one here costs over ten thousand dollars," Henry says, putting his palm out and displaying a thin silver-and-blue pen dotted with tiny pearls. "Owned by a movie star. Someone you'd know, but I'm not talking. Had to buy it back. She's going broke. Want to buy it?"

Johnny reaches for a dark red pen with the number 5 etched in gold on the side.

"Maroon 5." Henry snickers. "Get it?"

I realize this can go on all day. "I'm interested in a very particular pen."

Henry looks up as if he, too, realizes that he could go on forever about his pens. "Well, why didn't you say so?"

I don't bother to mention that he'd been talking nonstop, so I couldn't really tell him why I was there. Besides, it's interesting to hear about the role the pens had played in so many people's lives. Apparently even Oscar winners looked forward to getting a fountain pen in their gift bags.

But I'm in a hurry. I describe my granny's pen to him. I wish I'd taken a picture of it so I could show Henry, but I never thought that I would lose it. I didn't even think it was important enough to photograph.

"That's strange." He steps back behind the counter. "Blue marble, gold tip with **4810**, engraved with an F?" He carefully gathers up loose pens scattered on the counter and places them on a tray lined with red velvet.

Johnny stops scribbling with a guitar-shaped pen and looks up.

"That's right." I watch Henry's pale face closely. He looks perplexed. Maybe he has a pen just like it but doesn't know where to look for it? Just because he knows a lot about his pens doesn't mean he knows where they are in his jam-packed store.

"That pen was here in the store two days ago." He shuffles through a pile of papers in a shoebox on the counter. "We were only open for a couple of hours, but I remember it. Beautiful Montblanc pen, obviously a special order, probably made in Germany in the thirties."

I'm not sure if I'm hearing him right. "Two days ago?"

Johnny puts his hand on Henry's arm to get him to stop rustling papers. "Well, where is it now?"

"Oh, I sold it." He pulls his arm away and looks up in surprise.

"Wait," I say, leaning over the counter, trying to get Henry to focus. "You sold it already?"

Henry jerks back as he realizes that we are both within a few inches of his face. "One of my dealers came in with it."

"Dealers?" I'm confused and immediately think he's talking about drugs. I back away. Johnny reaches for his backpack that he had dropped on a low shelf. What are we getting ourselves into?

"*Antique* dealer. In Brooklyn," Henry continues. "Antique dealers know that if they get an interesting fountain pen, they get it to me right away. Dealers send me pens from all over the world. Some of these pens are worth a lot of money. Like these." He holds up one that is fat and gold, and another that is plain white but child-sized. "I don't take most of them, but the good ones I can always sell. It's actually a pretty brisk business, believe it or not. I don't need much room, live upstairs . . ."

I can see that he's going to go off topic again, so I interrupt him. "Wait—an antique dealer brought you a pen from Brooklyn that sounds like my pen?" I turn to Johnny. "But I just lost it a few days ago!"

"Somebody must've found it on the street and brought it to an antique store." Johnny points to the ten-thousand-dollar pen. "It probably looked valuable."

Suddenly Henry seems to lose his willingness to talk. He starts packing up the pens into the plastic boxes and shoves them back on the shelves. "The dealer couldn't bring it here until two days ago. I don't know how he got it, and I don't want to know." He covers the shoebox and slides it under the counter. "I'm closing now. Nobody's around—no need to stay open. You kids have to move on."

My shoulders sag and all of a sudden I feel worn out. Potato sticks, pudding, and Johnny's doughnut are sloshing around in my stomach, and the early bike ride didn't help. I've lied to my mom and walked a bicycle around piles of trash from the hurricane—for what? It's all getting to be too much. "I'm not even sure what I'm doing here," I say with a sigh. This is all happening too fast, and it's just about a silly pen. But I can't seem to let it go.

Johnny pulls me next to him. It's what he does now

and then, always at the right time, but not usually in front of anyone else. "Henry," he says. "Please tell Lily what happened to her pen."

Henry stops moving around and sits back down on the stool. "I've had a standing order for that pen for many, many years." He rests his hands on the table. "Every year she calls to see if anyone has found that pen. And then, in the middle of the flood, it appears. Like magic. From Brooklyn, of all places. So I didn't waste a moment. I contacted her and shipped it to her right away."

"Shipped it?" Johnny asks. "In the storm?"

"Sure. The first thing they did was clear the roads to be able to bring in supplies like generators. I shipped the pen on a delivery truck, overnight express."

I try to make sense of his words, but I'm having trouble following him. "She? Who is *she*?"

Johnny jumps in. "Shipped it? Where?"

"To a woman named Marguerite. She's French, but now she lives up the coast a couple of hours from here. She's probably writing with it right now."

Chapter 18
Fearless

"Marguerite?" Johnny and I both blast Henry so that he draws back, startled.

"Granny's Marguerite!" I lean closer to Henry, and he holds up his hand.

"That's all I know. What's so important about this Marguerite?"

I try to gather my thoughts to explain to the owner of a pen store why the name of a French woman is so exciting, but my brain is racing. Johnny makes an attempt. "Lily and her grandmother are living at the Brooklyn Armory."

Henry takes off his dirty glasses and rubs his eyes. It looks like he's about to ask a question, when my cell buzzes. I pull the phone out of my pocket and signal Henry to wait.

"It's Nicole," I say to Johnny, pointing at the number. "Hope Granny's okay." I put the phone on speaker. Nicole speaks fast, whispering, "Lily? Where are you? Your mom's here at the Armory, and she's making a scene. She wants to know where you are. Didn't you say you were going for a walk with your friend Johnny? You better get over here." I start to tell her that I'm in Manhattan, but she keeps talking. I can barely hear her with the noise of the Armory in the background. "And Miss Collette? I'm getting worried about her. She keeps talking to me in French. She's really getting agitated."

My hand tightens around the phone. "I don't want to talk to my mom. She'll just make me come home."

"She's worried sick, but I keep telling her that you're a godsend and you're taking care of your granny. But, Lily, I can't keep covering for you. Your mother's a basket case."

"But I texted her and told her Johnny was with me and she seemed cool with that." I don't mention that I hadn't told my mom how far I was going—across the bridge to Manhattan on a bicycle.

"She keeps saying that you are very independent, but when I said you are very brave, that seemed to send her over the edge."

"Oh, don't tell her that I'm brave! She doesn't want me in a situation where I have to be brave!"

"Wait—your mom just went into the restroom. Here, talk to your granny. See if you can calm her down. Miss Collette, Lily's on the phone. I'll hold it—talk right into it. That's right, she's on speaker."

I don't want the entire Armory to hear me, but Granny's hearing isn't the best on the phone, so I speak loudly into my phone. "Granny? How're you doing? Guess what! I found Marguerite."

"Who is this?"

"Granny, it's me. Lily. You can relax now. I'll tell you all about it when I get back to the Armory."

"Who is this?" I get that familiar feeling of frustration mixed with sadness. Granny is in one of her memory loss phases, and the phone is making things more confusing for her.

Then she rallies. "Do you have my pen?" She's

getting louder and I can hear Nicole trying to quiet her, but Granny persists. "Lily? Is that you?"

I thought I was used to her sudden changes in focus, but I feel so helpless. Henry comes around the counter and leans in to listen. "Yes, Granny," I try to speak soothingly, "everything's going to be fine."

"Did you find Marguerite? Did you see her? Tell me about her!" I look at Johnny for help—what can I tell my granny?

Nicole interrupts Granny's pleas. "Uh-oh. Your mother's coming over."

"Lily! Where are you?" My mom's voice comes on the phone, and she sounds more than just worried. I know she loves me, but it seems as if recently the only conversations we have are about my location, my plans, and dangers lurking everywhere.

"I'm doing errands with Johnny, Mom. *Chill!*"

"Don't tell me to chill! Your granny is as tough as nails, and she'll be fine. It's you I'm worried about. Taking off like that was not part of the agreement."

"Mom, you seriously do not need to worry about

me," I say firmly. "I just went out for a walk with Johnny. As soon as they move Granny back to Rockaway Manor, I'll come home."

It's too quiet on the other end of the phone. I look helplessly at Johnny, and he takes the phone from me. "Hey—this is Johnny. Lily's annoying, but she really is okay."

I'm not sure that's going to help, and snatch the phone back. "Mom, I've told you, I have a bed and food at the Armory, and I'm surrounded by nurses."

Johnny pats my shoulder and smiles. "Nurses—nice touch."

"Who's Marguerite?" my mom asks. "Your granny keeps talking about somebody named Marguerite, and she gets pretty agitated. Nicole says it's not anyone from the nursing home." She doesn't wait for me to respond. "Years ago, I'm pretty sure she mentioned an old friend named Marguerite—someone in France. But she didn't want to talk about her. Do you know if that's who she's talking about now?"

"I don't know. Granny doesn't always make sense." I hate saying that about my granny, but my head is spinning from talking to so many people at once. "You can go home, Mom. I'm fine!"

"I do feel better that you're with Johnny, but you need to get back here. Are you close?" She sounds a little calmer. Luckily, she doesn't give me time to answer. "Text me. A *lot*."

Nicole comes back on the phone, her voice hushed. "Your mom's putting on her coat, so you've satisfied her for now. But stop putting me in this position! Your granny's resting. Call me later, okay?" The phone goes dead.

Henry returns to his stool behind the counter. "Wow, you ought to work in an emergency room doing triage. What's the deal with your mom? Are you a runaway or something?"

I explain about the evacuation. He seems impressed that I'm still living in the Armory with my granny. "I can see why your mom worries," he says. "But you seem like a kid who can handle herself."

"She says I've been independent since the day I was born. I guess I'm just like my granny."

"Your granny must be pretty interesting."

"Granny was always traveling, going to dangerous places. My mom spent her entire childhood waiting at home, wondering if her mother would come back hurt, or worse. . . ." I stop and think for a minute. "I guess that's why my mom understands me but still freaks out."

Henry pulls out a soft cloth and lines up the pens on the velvet-covered tray. I want to go back to talking about Marguerite, but he asks, "Was your grand-mother in the military? A spy or something?"

Johnny and I laugh. "Nope... she was a gardener!" I tell Henry how my granny believed that peace could be accomplished by people working together to create a park or a community garden. "She's been everywhere—Lebanon, Palestine, Colombia—sometimes for weeks at a time."

"Ah." Henry shines each pen and straightens them so they are lined up neatly. "Maybe you're also like your father? Is he the adventurous type?"

Johnny glances at me, and I turn away. "Her father's never been in the picture," Johnny explains.

"He was in the army and was killed before Lily was born."

"Really? Killed in action?"

Johnny knows that I don't like talking about my father, mainly because I don't have much to say. My mom says he was strong. She felt safe when he was around. But she won't say much more than that.

My granny says he was fearless.

There are a few pictures of him, but I can't really tell if I look like him. He seems very serious in his army picture, but my mom insists there's a twinkle in his eye.

"He re-upped before he knew about Lily." Johnny seems hesitant to continue.

"Re-upped?" Henry looks confused.

This I know about. I'm used to reciting the answer whenever anyone asked about my father. "He was in Iraq, and he volunteered to go back." I face Henry. "He promised my mom he wouldn't do that because she was so worried about him, but he did it anyway. She was waiting to tell him that she was pregnant with me, but he died before he ever found out." I slide out of my backpack and plop it on the counter. I don't like where this conversation is going. I have enough things to think about.

"Wow, that's tough for both of you." Henry keeps polishing the pens.

Johnny jumps in. "Lily's cool about it." He knows what happens when I ask questions about my dad and don't get any answers. My mom always says she made a mistake and fell for a man who wanted to see the world, and then she changes the subject.

I believe if my dad had known about me back then, we'd know each other now. He would have come home.

Henry nods again. "Lots of bravery in the genes," he says as he carefully places the tray on a shelf.

I like Henry's conclusion. I *am* brave, and I want to prove it even more. "How do I get to Marguerite's?"

Chapter 19
Bonjour! Bonjour!

"Lily, what are you talking about?" Johnny's voice is sharper than usual.

Henry grabs a stack of pens from a jar and tosses them on his counter. They roll in different directions, and Johnny snatches one before it falls on the floor.

"To get to Marguerite's, you'll have to take a train," Henry says quietly. He sorts the pens in a neat row.

I rummage around in my backpack, looking for the envelope of money that Nicole had given me. She didn't know the restaurant food was free, and I forgot to return the money to her. Should I use it and pay her back later? I have a little bit in a savings account.

"How much do you think the train will cost?" I empty the backpack onto the counter—the bag of doughnuts, a sweatshirt, a half-empty bottle of water, and the stack of old letters that Granny had given me.

Johnny touches my arm. "Lily, you'll have to leave the city."

I feel the envelope of cash, deep in the bottom of the pack.

Henry picks up the letters and gently removes the rubber band. "Do you mind?" He doesn't wait for an answer and carefully examines each envelope, sometimes holding them up to the light. "These look like they were written with a Parker 51. Why do you have these?"

I explain how I'd found them in my granny's belongings when we evacuated. "I'd never seen them before, but she wanted me to save them." Henry leafs through the letters. The top envelope is yellowed and worn, torn open at the top, and the ink is faded. In place of a stamp someone had written *Free* in the corner.

The envelope is addressed to my granny in Brume, France, but it's her maiden name before she married my grandpa. The edges are marked in red, white, and blue dashes, and *1944* is stamped in a circle over the address.

The return address shows it's from Marguerite, in Spain. I pause for a moment. Why was this mysterious Marguerite, who now lives a couple of hours away, writing my granny from Spain in 1944?

"Too bad these are written in French." Johnny presses open one of the letters. "Lily, these might be clues about your granny and Marguerite."

I stuff the envelope of cash into the pocket of my sweatshirt and shove everything but the letters back into the pack. I have to keep busy to hide the flush of tears that seem to suddenly want to appear. I have no idea what I'm doing. One minute I'm out to find Marguerite; the next I want to forget this entire mission. My voice catches as I mumble, "I'm not a detective, Johnny. I just want to see my granny smile when she sees her pen."

As I start to pull up my hoodie, Henry reaches under the counter and pulls out a wrench. Johnny and I jump back as Henry bangs the wrench loudly on a radiator in the corner: CLANG CLANG CLANG! He shouts into a vent in the wall, "Rosie, wake up!" CLANG CLANG!

We freeze as he holds the wrench in the air, ready to bang it again. "Rosie!"

"Whaaaaat?" comes a voice from above us. "I'm sleeping!"

"Get down here!"

"Why? Leave me alone."

Henry bangs again as Rosie, her voice high-pitched, yells, "All right already! I'm coming!"

Henry calmly replaces the wrench and climbs back on his stool. "My daughter can help you. She lived in Paris for a couple of years. She wanted to be a famous artist."

Johnny perks up. "Is she famous?"

Henry rolls his bloodshot eyes. "Can't draw a straight line. But she speaks pretty good French."

"Excellent!" Johnny grins at me, but I'm not so sure. This quest to help Granny is turning into a crazy reality show with a new character called Rosie.

"Now my daughter wants to be a Broadway star," Henry continues. "I've called her Rosie since she was a kid, but she insists on being called Rose." He laughs so that spit flies out and lands on the counter. "It would help her new career if she could sing or dance." He chuckles again and winks at me. Johnny laughs with him as Henry adds, "She's sleeping on my couch until her apartment's declared safe. Her building got hit pretty bad by the hurricane."

I can feel my spirits lift immediately. Rosie sounds like someone who could understand what my life has been like over the last week.

The door to the shop flies open, and all I can think of is my third-grade teacher who always burst into our classroom all disheveled, just when the bell rang. Rosie commands the same attention. She fills the doorway wearing a pink shiny robe with gigantic flowers and is holding a pair of pink slippers with fluffy pom-poms. I recognize the robe as a kimono because Granny gave me her old one when she cleaned out her closet before going to the nursing home. This kimono is loosely wrapped around Rosie, tied around her ample waist. Green-striped pajamas peek out from under the robe.

She stands in the doorway and purses her pouffed lips as she peers into the shop. She runs her fingers through thick, curly hair piled on her head. The color of her hair is a vibrant shade of red I've never seen on another person, and I've been out on the streets of Brooklyn.

"What?" she asks again, and slides her feet into the slippers. Her toenails match her fingernails— glittery pink.

"Nice of you to join the land of the living," Henry comes from around the counter and shuts the door behind her. The small shop is now overloaded with pens and people, and feels damp and steamy. There's a new smell that I can't place until Johnny whispers, "Coconut. She smells like coconut." He looks around the store in every direction, but his eyes keep gliding over Rosie in her robe. She lowers her eyes at him, pulls the robe tighter, and says playfully, "Hello there, boys and girls."

Henry returns to his stool behind the high counter. "My daughter is the understudy for the chorus of an off-Broadway play. She sits in the theater all night waiting for someone to sprain their ankle, and then she sleeps all day."

Rosie scowls, but she doesn't look like she's actually annoyed. "At least I'm not trapped in a room with fountain pens all day."

They seem to be enjoying each other, even though the words are tough. I think of conversations with my mom when I get impatient with her. Two hours later, I'll miss her voice.

Henry holds up the letters. "We need a translator. How's your French?"

Rosie wiggles by Johnny and me and scoops up the letters. "It was pretty rusty, but there's a French guy in the show and we talk every night in the dressing room. I've been getting a lot of practice. He misses home." She opens the first one. It's neatly written in black ink on thin, yellowing paper. We gather closer around the counter. She flips through the rest of the letters. "It looks like the last one was written in 1950." She looks up, puzzled.

"My granny gave those letters to me to keep. I have no idea what they say."

"Well, let's find out." She extends her hand. "I'm Rose, but I guess as long as I'm stuck living under my father's roof, I'm called Rosie." We introduce ourselves as she vigorously shakes our hands and says, "Bonjour! Bonjour!"

Rosie starts to read aloud in a surprisingly soft voice, rarely hesitating as she translates.

Chapter 20
The Letters

As Rosie reads the first letter, she keeps stopping to ask me questions. But I can't answer them. All I know is that the letters were written by Marguerite to my granny Collette, a long time ago. "Keep reading."

I watch her run her finger along each line.

November 1944
Madrid, Spain
Dear Collette,

By the time you receive this letter, I hope I will still be in Spain and you can write me back. Send letters to the French Embassy in Madrid. My mama says they will find us because my papa had to register with the embassy.

I am sorry that I could not say good-bye, and I hope you are safe. In August, right before the Americans landed in Marseille (freedom!), Rabbit told us that we had to leave Brume in the middle of the night. There were too many people in town who thought that my father had helped the Germans and we were in danger.

At first we were told we could take one suitcase and meet by the fountain on the Rue Grand in the morning. But Rabbit said that was a trick and we were going to be deported. So we took what we could carry and left in the dark. I wish I could have told you, but we had no time.

I still don't know if I can tell anyone that my father was in the French Resistance, spying on the Germans and French Milice when they came to our home. In fact, I'm afraid to write that in this letter because it's hard to figure out who to trust. So many collaborators have been killed or deported. I hope my father can tell his story so everyone knows the truth. He was not a collaborator! Monsieur de Gaulle should help him!

Wallcreeper—we have so much we could tell, don't we?

I am also sorry that my mother packed our suitcases many months before we escaped, so my clothes are all too small! You probably have to dress like a girl now. I'm sure you are very uncomfortable.

Can you check to see who is living in our house in Brume? I know that you can climb over the wall and get inside. My papa says he's heard it's empty—everything is gone—and no one wants to live there, but please take a broom to it and take care of it for us until we can return.

Please write back,

Marguerite (Skylark)

"I don't know the word *wallcreeper*," Rosie says, pointing at the word. "What does it mean?"

I pull out my phone and look it up. "A wallcreeper is a bird that lives in cliffs in southern France. I have no idea what she's talking about."

"And *skylark*?"

"Skylark . . ." I search and find a description. "It's a bird that lives across Europe. It sings when it's in flight." I play the recording of the birdsong while Rosie reads the letter again.

"I don't get this," Rosie says, scanning the letter. "Marguerite is writing to Collette, right? So Marguerite is Skylark—and Collette is Wallcreeper. But who's Rabbit?"

"My granny is Collette, but I don't understand this any more than you do. Henry told us that Marguerite lives up the coast, outside New York City. Maybe Marguerite can explain things because my granny has never mentioned any of this."

"What does Marguerite mean about the suitcase and the fountain?"

Henry reaches for the letter. "Last time I studied French was in high school." He traces Marguerite's signature. "This was written many years ago. It sounds like Marguerite and her family escaped after the Allies liberated the south of France."

"The Allies?" Johnny and I say together.

"The countries that fought against the Germans in World War II were called the Allies, like the British and the Americans. In the summer of 1944 there was a big battle in northern France, and an invasion in the south of France. The Allies drove the Germans out of France, and the war in Europe ended soon after that."

He turns the letter so I can see the careful handwriting. "This letter was written in 1944. It was sent to Brume, in the south of France."

I'm trying to follow this, but we haven't studied World War II yet, and it's hard to picture all of this as my granny's life. "So this woman—girl—named Marguerite was a friend of my granny's in France? I don't get why she and her family had to leave suddenly and go to Spain. It sounds like the war was over."

Rosie leans forward so that her pile of red hair shifts to the side and loose curls fall across her face. "I've lived in Paris, so I know a little bit about this. I had so many friends in France." She stares off in the distance. By the look on her face, she seems to be lost in pleasant memories. "We spent many hours in restaurants with bottles of wine and amazing food, talking about art, and literature, and history."

She refocuses on the letters. "That time in France is known as the Dark Years." She twists the strands of hair gently around her finger and tucks them behind her ear. "When the Germans took over France during the war, there was little fighting in the south, near towns like Brume. But it was still terrible. Most of the French people were starving and terrified of the Germans." Her hair falls in her face again, and she pulls a wide silver barrette out of her kimono pocket, wraps up the wayward strands, and clamps the barrette shut. "But some of the French people made friends with the Germans. Those people were called collaborators." She pauses for a moment. "They were French people who made friends with the enemy."

Henry points to a passage in the letter and stumbles through the French, reading it aloud. "It sounds like Marguerite's father *pretended* to be friends with the Germans," he says, "but was really spying on them." He taps the letter and looks up at me. "The Germans could have found out, so he was risking his life! And some people in town would've been very angry that he was treating the Germans so well. He was a very brave man."

"People in the French towns who secretly spied on the Germans," Rosie adds, "also stole German food and equipment. They were so courageous! They reported to the Allies where the Germans hid their tanks and ammunition. It was very dangerous for the spies, and many of them were caught and—" She looks over at me, suddenly solemn. "—didn't survive. Those brave people were in the French Resistance. They resisted the Germans taking over their country."

Henry continues, his voice rising with enthusiasm. "It sounds like Marguerite's father was in the French Resistance and probably reported information about the Germans to Charles de Gaulle, one of the leaders of the Resistance. That's why Marguerite says that de Gaulle should help him."

Could all of this have happened to Granny's friend Marguerite? Why didn't Granny ever tell me about it? She never said a word about Marguerite, Rabbit, or a resistance—or even the war—and we talk all the time, even when she can't remember what we were talking about. "Do you think my granny knew that Marguerite's father was in the French Resistance?"

Henry hands the letter back to Rosie, and she returns it to the envelope. "Marguerite and Collette both must have known." She taps the stack of letters. "They had to keep a very dangerous secret. Where'd you get these?"

"My granny kept them. She just turned eighty, and she's kept the letters in her favorite pocketbook." I briefly tell her why I'm at her father's store, leaving out the part that no one but Johnny knows where I am. I make it sound as if I'm in constant contact with my mom and Granny.

Johnny pitches in a few more details but doesn't

give me away. "This is all very cool, but I still don't get that part about a rabbit."

The man rubs his forehead. "I don't remember much about the war. Believe it or not, I'm not that old."

Rosie interrupts, flapping the letter in the air. "I think I can explain the Rabbit part!" She looks at me, her eyes wide, and I can see she's wearing false eyelashes. She's caught up in this mystery, but I'm getting uncomfortable with my granny's letters being opened and passed back and forth.

Rosie picks up a pen, pops off the cap, and scribbles *Collette* on a small pad of white paper. "So your grandmother is Collette, right?"

"That's right." Should I be talking to *another* stranger about Granny?

"She has a code name, so she must have been a Resistance fighter, too." Rosie writes *Wallcreeper* next to *Collette*. "Everything was very, very secret, and many resisters had secret names. Have you ever heard of Marie-Madeleine Fourcade?" She looks around at all of us and we shake our heads. "Oh—she's very famous in France. She was in charge of hundreds of people in the French Resistance. Her group of Resistance fighters were called Noah's Ark by the Nazis."

"Noah's Ark?" I ask.

Johnny chimes in, "You mean the animals, two by two?"

"Yes, that's where it came from." Rosie's voice is becoming fuller and louder as she gets caught up in her explanation. I can see how she could be on the Broadway stage. "In Noah's Ark, every Resistance fighter had a secret animal name. It looks like Rabbit was a member, Marguerite was Skylark—and your granny was Wallcreeper." She jots down *Marguerite = Skylark*.

She pulls the letter out of the envelope again, and snaps it open. "Listen to this: *Wallcreeper—we have so much we could tell, don't we?*" She looks up at me, and her eyes are bright. She has big pouty lips, and she lights up when she smiles. "Your grandmother was in the French Resistance, little one. And if she's eighty now, she was about your age. That's amazing."

"Can we read more?" Johnny looks expectantly at me. I'm just as curious and drop my backpack at my feet. My little granny? A spy?

I nod at Rosie. Henry pulls another stool over and pats it. "Climb up, Rosie, and keep reading."

Chapter 21
Letters from London

Rosie gently pulls the second letter out of its tattered envelope. This one includes a black-and-white picture of two young boys. They're standing in front of a stone wall, their raggedy, too-big pants rolled up to their knees, their sleeves pushed up around the elbows.

One of the boys is grinning and aiming a long stick at the camera, while the other is leaning forward, laughing. Their hair is cut very short, and they're both wearing giant boots.

Rosie hands the photo to me, and I study their happy faces. The sun is bright in the photo and clusters of flowers are at their feet.

I flip the photo over. Someone has scrawled *Marguerite and Collette* on the back.

"This is my granny!" I study the details more closely—the stone formation of the wall, the skinny legs, the chopped hair.

"Which one?" Rosie asks, leaning in to look.

"I don't know. They look alike." I show the picture to Henry, and he comments on how relaxed and joyful the two girls look. "It's like they were twins," he says. "And to think that these beautiful girls were up to no good." I run my finger over their faces and take another long look before I slip it back into the envelope.

"This next letter's from London," Rosie says. We all lean forward, ready for another chapter.

August 1945

Dearest Collette,

I was in such despair when I did not hear from you, but then your letter finally arrived here in London. We left Spain when Father was cleared to go to work—and, Collette, he has been awarded the Croix de Guerre! Such an honor! I am so proud of him! (You should get one, too, you know.)

It takes so long for our letters to find each other. I hope your mama is feeling better and you are not so lonely. You can always write me here—we have no plans to leave London, but I think often of home.

I am happy to hear that some of the French boys are beginning to return to Brume. Are there any handsome ones? I know there isn't much for them to do but clear the fields for next spring, but can you imagine what you will finally be able to grow again?

I have enclosed the picture that my father took after our encounter with the train, when you were still using a crutch. I am sure that your scar is not as ugly as you say. At least we can cover up our scars and no one will see them. But I agree, we will always have those reminders.

Mama insisted that I grow my hair out again. I'm actually quite pretty! She says that I have to meet a nice boy, not BE a nice boy!

She has no idea how much I miss wearing pants, especially when I ride my bicycle.

Collette, I am delaying in this letter. There is sad news—Panther is gone. Perhaps you have heard? He was part of a raid on Milice headquarters in Vichy and did not survive. You said in a letter that Rabbit and Hélène still keep up the fight to rid France of all collaborators, but they don't want you to deliver for them anymore. As they say, go to school. No more secrets.

Please write and tell me about my lovely Brume.

Marguerite (Skylark)

I pull out the picture again and point to the girl with the stick. "This must be Granny with the crutch." It dawns on me that Granny wasn't asking for a broom to clean the Armory. She was talking about the "lovely Brume" in Marguerite's letter. My heart sinks as I wish I had understood.

Rosie studies both sides of the letter again. "I wonder what they meant about being a boy and their encounter with the train?"

"Maybe they blew one up," Henry chuckles. "They did that, you know—the Resistance. Kept the supply lines shut down, killed a lot of Germans that way. Sounds like your granny tangled with a train."

Johnny and I look at each other in dismay. This time Johnny says, "Granny?"

"Lily?" Rosie leans on the counter and props her chin up with her hands so that her pink nails glow on her cheek. "Does your grandmother have a scar?" She looks at me with kind eyes, and everyone grows quiet.

I've helped Granny into her nightgown so many times. I've pulled her cotton shirts over her head, trying not to look at her thin, freckled skin and saggy underwear, and have gently eased her into tops that she didn't have to button, and pants with elastic waists. Because I didn't want to embarrass her, I always stood to the side or behind her back. But I knew she had a scar.

"Yes, I've seen it." With my finger I draw a zigzag

line on my thigh. "She has one a few inches above her knee. I've asked her about the scar a couple of times, but all she said was that it was caused by an accident when she was a little girl, but it healed quickly."

We stay silent for a moment. Then Rosie heaves a dramatic sigh and reaches out to touch my arm. I picture Granny in her red sweater and pink beret, waiting for me back at the Armory. My throat feels tight, and suddenly I want my mom. She would hug me too much and lecture me about running into danger, but that's what my mom is good at. She would feed me junk food and ask me all about my homework and basically drive me nuts. But I wouldn't mind some of her overkill right about now.

Johnny's voice interrupts my thoughts. "Maybe your granny will tell you more after you find Marguerite." I meet his sober gaze with a shrug.

Rosie opens the next envelope. "Let's see what the rest of the letters tell us." She continues reading through them all, struggling a bit as she tries to decipher Marguerite's elaborate handwriting. "It looks like it was very hard to get mail delivered after the war. Marguerite keeps begging Collette to write more often." She hands me each page as she finishes reading it. The paper is thin, and the ink has turned pale blue. "Marguerite got a job as a translator in London." She looks up and grins. "Listen to this! A little romance!"

Collette—I've met a soldier from the United States. His name is Andrew and he's stationed in London. We're planning to marry. Can you imagine? An American!

I have to interrupt. "My granny married an American, too! I never met him, but she says he was the handsomest man she ever met."

Rosie chuckles. "I think Marguerite feels the same way about her Andrew."

I think I've found the right man. He's very handsome and kind. God willing, we'll be able to have a family soon. I picture myself as the mother of a little boy who looks just like my wonderful Andy.

Rosie continues to translate two more letters. Marguerite talks about how she's learning to sew because the shops in London are so expensive. She says she works long hours translating French documents for the British. She never mentions the war in her London letters, but she always signs them "Skylark" and repeats that someday she will return to Brume.

When Rosie has finished, Henry seems to be reading my mind. "I can see by your face that you're about to travel alone on a train to meet Marguerite—brave as can be. It seems as if you and your granny are an awful lot alike."

Chapter 22
On the Train

Henry pulls out a laptop from under the counter, but Johnny's faster on his phone. "If you want to get to Marguerite, you're going to have to take Metro-North. It goes along the coast. The train leaves from Grand Central Station. What town, Henry?"

"She gave me an address in Stratford. She said she lives way up on a cliff overlooking the water." Henry pauses as he studies the schedule. "You're in luck. They just finished clearing the tracks from the storm and got that line up and running. It looks like the train takes about ninety minutes."

I gasp and Johnny looks up from scrolling on his phone. "Johnny—she's just ninety minutes away. Isn't that amazing? I wonder if Granny knows she's so close."

Johnny beams and shows me the phone. "Looks like the next Metro-North train leaves from Grand Central Station at 11:34 a.m. You'll never make that, but there's another one at 12:04."

Rosie had been quietly watching this activity when she asks, "Do you have your school ID? They won't ask but just in case."

I reach into my backpack. "Actually, I have a passport!" They all looked startled, and I don't blame them. I'm full of surprises and enjoying it. "I haven't had a chance to use it yet, but my granny insisted that I get one." I flip through the empty pages and show them the photo of my grinning face.

"Nice picture," Johnny laughs.

A notecard falls out of the passport onto Henry's counter. The front of the card is covered with tiny sketches of flowers and is torn at the crease from the many times I've opened it.

Johnny picks up the card. "What's this?"

"My granny gave that to me when my passport arrived. I like to carry it with me. It makes me feel like I can go just about anywhere."

Johnny shows Henry the note inside the card, written in loopy letters in black ink. Henry runs his fingers over the words. "She used a fountain pen—a woman after my own heart." Rosie peers over his shoulder as he reads the note aloud:

My lovely Lily has permission to travel anywhere she wants, whenever the spirit moves her, as long as she spreads peace, and stays as kind as she already is.

My granny had signed the card with our apartment address. The date is the day that we moved her to Rockaway Manor.

I picture her back at the Armory, bent over on her wobbly cot, with everything she owns in a plastic garbage bag. I want so much to brighten her day. If she can't travel, I can make the trip for her. "I need to get to Grand Central and get a train ticket."

Henry chuckles and one of the strands of greasy hair dislodges and drops down over his face. "Between you and your granny, your mother sure has her hands full! Is she going to be able to make it to the train station in time?"

I realize that Henry hasn't figured out that I'm

planning on going alone to Stratford. My mom doesn't like to explore beyond the city—she doesn't even have a passport. She says there's plenty to see in New York and she can visit other places in books and movies.

Rosie catches my eye. She understands the plan.

Johnny glances at me and raises his eyebrows. "Don't you think you should call Marguerite and let her know you're coming?"

"I'll do it at the station. I'll text my mom, too."

"So you're going alone?" Henry picks up the cloth again, and vigorously rubs a pen covered in ink stains. Teeny daisies emerge on a pale pink background.

I stuff my passport in the outside pocket of my backpack, and fling the pack over my shoulder. Johnny zips up the pocket. "Don't forget, Lily, your granny wants Marguerite to have that pen. You can't very well knock on the door and demand it back just because you don't want your granny to know you lost it."

He has a point. I'm so anxious to make Granny happy and show that nothing can stop me, I haven't really thought it through. In fact, I've been running so fast over the last few days that I've forgotten how to slow down. Maybe I should just tell Granny that Marguerite now has the pen. My granny doesn't have to know that I didn't deliver it to her.

But I won't be able to lie to my granny. She'll want to know all about Marguerite, and I'll have nothing to tell, except that I lost the special pen. "I'll figure out what to say to Marguerite, but now I better get moving."

Henry hands me a paper with Marguerite's address and phone number. "I'm not happy about this, but you're not my kid and I'm getting the impression I can't stop you anyway. Go straight to Stratford. She calls her home Maison de Falaise, or Cliff House." He pulls the shop door open and motions for us to be on our way. "At least call the poor woman—you don't want to upset her by showing up at her doorstep."

Rosie joins him, pulling her robe close. She gives a little wave before Henry gently closes the door. I can hear the lock click into place.

It's still damp and chilly as Johnny and I stand on the empty street while he unlocks the bikes. I count the cash Nicole gave me for food and add my mother's contribution. "Did you see on the website how much the ticket is?"

Johnny watches me shove the money back in the envelope. "Lily, you've never even been out of the city!"

"It's less than two hours away!"

"Maybe this Marguerite doesn't want to see you. I wish I could go with you, but I have to help out at the restaurant." He tugs on a blue streak in his hair. I don't think I've ever seen Johnny nervous before. "I'm serious, Lily. Is this a good idea?"

"What are you worried about?" I hope he doesn't answer because there's a lot to worry about. "It's just a ride on a train."

"Maybe your mother can go with you?"

"Then I'd have to tell her everything, and she'd be furious."

Johnny takes his black hat from his backpack and pulls it over his frizzy hair. "Maybe Marguerite will kidnap you and lock you in the basement. At least call her first, check her out."

For some reason, this makes me smile. Johnny's

looking out for me by painting a scary picture. I pull my phone out of my pocket and tap out the phone number that Henry had given me. A woman gruffly answers, "Maison de Falaise. Who's calling, please?" I explain who I am and that I would like to talk to a woman named Marguerite. "I'm planning on taking the Metro-North to see her today."

The woman responds with the same words my mother would've said. "Alone? You're traveling alone on the Metro-North? To see my mother? Is that safe? You sound so young! How old are you?"

I can hear rustling and what sounds like arguing in French. I put the phone on speaker so Johnny can help me figure out what's going on.

"Hello?" a strained woman's voice comes on the phone.

We can hear the woman who answered the phone talking urgently in the background. "Mother, don't let her travel by herself. It's not safe."

The woman on the phone continues. "This is Marguerite. You are Collette's granddaughter calling?"

She has a heavy French accent.

I explained again that I want to visit but don't mention the pen.

There's silence, then, "But how did you find me?" She doesn't wait for an answer and asks breathlessly, "Is Collette still living?"

"Alive and kicking," I say, and then remember that Granny hates it when people say that. "I mean, she's fine. I just spoke to her."

"Ah, my Collette! Can I speak to her?"

"It's kind of complicated. She's not here right now." I don't want to alarm her, so I add, "But she's okay. It's just not a good time for her to travel."

"I have to meet you! Please come! When can you get here?"

I look at Johnny, who's leaning in close to the phone, and he nods. "I can be there early this afternoon. Is that okay with you?"

"Wait at the train station. I'll send a car for you."

"A car?" My mom sometimes orders a car when we're in a hurry. She says they're faster than taxis and usually cleaner. There are also fancy black limousines all over the city, whisking rich people around so they won't have to take the subway.

"Don't worry, Simone will be driving. Come quick—but keep an eye out for trouble, ma chérie!"

As I slide the phone into my pocket, I can feel a rush of excitement. *I can see why Granny liked to travel,* I think as I picture a sleek limousine gliding up to the Stratford station, a uniformed Simone at the wheel.

Quickly Johnny and I make arrangements for him to get my bike back to André at the restaurant. "I hope nobody asks me where you've gone," he mutters. "You better text me every chance you get."

I scan the block, looking for the nearest subway entrance that's open. The one on the corner doesn't have a yellow tape across the steps.

"Hey, kid." Henry suddenly steps outside into the crisp air and hands me a black winter coat. "You'll need this. It'll be chillier near the ocean."

I hate to take his coat, but I'm afraid I might need it. "I'll bring it back, I promise."

"I'm sure you will," he says as he slips back inside

his store and pulls a long shade over the window.

I head toward the corner, and Johnny shouts one more time, "Text me!"

As I reach the stairs leading underground, I hear Henry's voice again. "Wait!" He rushes over, waving Granny's special notecard. "You left this, you may need it." He slides it into the coat pocket. "Rosie stamped it to make it look official. I have a lot of fancy-looking stamps." He grabs my arms and stares into my eyes through his smeared glasses. I pull back a little, startled at his sudden intensity. "Stick with a family, or a woman traveling alone. Put that note in your passport and keep it handy in case anyone asks why you are traveling alone. Better yet, pretend to be asleep."

He must have seen he was making me nervous, because he breaks out into a grin that looks forced and strange on his washed-out face. "Don't worry, you won't have any trouble," he says, waving me on. "Bon voyage!"

He turns and I hear him say to Johnny, "See what I mean? Every pen, young man, has a story!"

Chapter 23
Up the Coast

Grand Central Station to Marguerite's
November 2012—Day 8

It takes a while for a subway to show up, but getting off at Grand Central isn't so hard. I know how to ride a subway in New York—don't look at anyone, try to snare a seat near a woman but don't sit too close, and keep the backpack away from probing fingers.

I pretend to stare into space on the subway, but I'm really reading the names of the stops embedded in the tile walls. Once we empty out at the Grand Central stop, there are people swarming in all directions. We're still underground, but where are the Metro-North trains going out of the city?

I follow a group of kids past a row of turnstiles until

we enter a passage wide enough to hold two armories. I have to keep dodging the constant flow of people rushing around me, their conversations mixing with the screech of the subway trains, repeated announcements, and loud boarding calls. Newsstands and gift shops line the hall, mixed with narrow shops that have displays of pizza on rotating stands, stacks of burritos and egg rolls, and tired-looking pastries.

I press against the dirty wall to keep from being pushed aside. I don't want to hold up foot traffic while I scan the dozens of signs scattered all over the cavernous space. I might be noticed by the police, who are everywhere. My mom wouldn't let me out of her sight ever again if she got a call from the New York City police about her twelve-year-old girl, wearing a man's oversized coat, lost in Grand Central.

If I ask anyone for directions, would they ask me why I am traveling alone? I finally join a line at Adriano's pizza stand. "Metro-North?" I say to a girl with a lot of piercings who's sitting on a battered suitcase, texting. She doesn't look up but points down the hall. I order a plain slice and hand over four precious dollars, hoping I'll have enough money left over for the ticket. But I figure it will be some time before I can get food again, and now is not the time to stop and dig out one of Johnny's gooey doughnuts.

I roll up the pizza slice, grab napkins, and join the crowd moving quickly in the direction the girl had indicated. More people have luggage and briefcases, so I keep going. The pizza tastes much better than the Armory's soggy peanut butter and jelly sandwiches, but my stomach is so unsettled that I'm sorry I bought it. Maybe the Oreo doughnut from this morning wasn't such a good idea.

Some of the police officers have big guard dogs that all seem to stare right at me. I hope the dogs are just interested in the pizza, and not trained to spot girls who look lost. I pretend to be part of a large family that's pulling rolling suitcases and finally spot a tiny sign that says METRO-NORTH way above me. A list of towns, including STRATFORD, is listed under CONNECTICUT. I'm leaving the state!

The first time I took the subway alone from school to Rockaway Manor, my mom practiced the route with me over and over. I had to text at the end of the first stop, the second stop, and then when I walked through the front door and signed in. But in the last few days, no matter where I've actually been, the texts I've sent her have been about everything but me: Granny walked around the gym! McDonald's delivered! Nicole says hi!

It's been hard to think of upbeat text messages to keep my mom happy. Sometimes I delete once or twice before taking a breath and hitting send.

But I know as soon as I get on that train I'm going to have to text her to make her think I'm having a casual supper at the Armory, surrounded by people who pay attention to me—instead of the hundreds of strangers who walk right by.

She won't be able to tell how far away I really am. She'll find out the truth eventually, especially if I really do make it to Marguerite's, but once she calms down, I think she'll understand. If she ever calms down.

The echo of the crowd fades away as I enter the giant domed center of the station and stand in line to buy my ticket. Sounds seem to be muffled, even though hundreds of people are moving in all directions. The seller behind the window shouts in a small silver microphone, "One ticket?" I grip Nicole's envelope of money, staining it with pizza grease and sweat, as the seller's eyes dart behind me. I freeze until I realize she's checking the long line, not looking for an adult traveling with me.

My mind buzzes with questions. Connecticut suddenly seems like a very long way, and for what? I'm actually leaving New York to go to another state, to visit a stranger. I nod and tell her my destination. "Train leaves in ten!" the woman barks. "Next?" She slaps the ticket under the window, and the next customer pushes in front of me. I feel like I am going to throw up. I have my ticket, but I still don't know where to find the train. I don't want to be noticed, but at the same time, I hope someone will say, "Would you like some help?"

Ahead of me are many groups of travelers standing silently, staring at a billboard as big as a movie screen. It has a list of all the trains. I join them, all of us riveted to the board as destinations and gate numbers appear. Travelers dash away the minute the gate number for their train slides into view. There it is, Metro-North to Connecticut, with a list of stops—on time.

"The 12:04! Hurry!" A woman grabs the hand of a little girl and sets off for the far end of the station. Guessing it's the same 12:04 I'm taking, I follow them to the gate and copy everything they do. I stick close as they board, and slide into a seat across from them. There are no signs that I'm on the right train, but I don't dare look lost. The conductor walks up the aisle, cracking jokes and punching tickets. My stomach is still roiling, and I feel flushed as I hold back tears. I pull the coat collar up to hide my face.

As the train edges away from the city, slowly rolling through dark tunnels, I give in. The double seat is all mine, so I move over to the window and watch through tears as we emerge into overcast daylight. An announcer recites the stops ahead, and I hold my breath until he says, "Stratford," near the end of the list. Miles of city pass by, and I catch glimpses of endless apartment buildings and giant billboards as we rush away from Manhattan. I can't believe what I've done. I wipe my nose on the sleeve of Henry's coat and think about how my mom would react if she knew, and how my granny is waiting for me at the Armory.

I text my mom: Pizza tonight! Showing a movie!

It's tempting to call and say, "Guess what!" But I know the story of Granny's missing pen and finding Marguerite would not be nearly as shocking as Lilybelle alone on a train heading out of the city, up the coast.

I can feel the train pick up speed and sit up to see what we'll pass next. Crossing the Brooklyn Bridge on a bicycle is nothing compared to a train zooming along to another part of the world. I rest my head on the back of the seat, pull Henry's coat tight, and let the tears trickle down.

I must have dozed a little, until I feel someone poking my arm and a soft voice in my ear. I slowly wake up and realize it's a girl, about eight years old, sitting next to me. "Excuse me? Your backpack fell and spilled. Sorry to wake you."

I pull myself up and gradually comprehend where I am. I'd fallen asleep on a train that's barreling out of New York City and up the coast. I'm on my way to Marguerite's home, a place that Henry said is called Cliff House.

I slide off Henry's coat that I'd been using as a blanket and reach down to the floor to gather the items that had fallen out of my backpack. I scoop up Johnny's bag of doughnuts, the envelope of petty cash from Nicole, and my passport. I check my pocket for my phone and decide to wait before looking to see how many text messages my mom has sent.

"Where are we?" I ask the girl.

"We've left the city and stopped a couple of times. I hope you didn't miss your stop." She tucks her wavy brown hair behind her ears and adjusts her glasses. Her mother, across the aisle reading the *New York Times*, doesn't look up.

"Have we been to Stratford yet?" I frantically scan the scenery whizzing by for any sign of where we are. I expect to see ocean along the route, but there's nothing but houses and the occasional office building or string of stores. Piles of debris line the tracks, the stores are boarded up, and some of the roofs we pass have peeled away. Windows are smashed in some of the taller buildings, and soaked curtains hang limply in the rain outside the frames. Hurricane Sandy had roared in from the ocean and battered the coast.

"It's just a little bit farther." The girl plays with the strings of her hoodie. "We're going back home to Stratford. My dad says the storm washed mud over our front porch and some trees blew over, but we can move back in now."

It's good to hear that someone can move back home. "Where'd you stay?"

"My grandmother's apartment. It was crowded, but the food was good."

Another wave of worry hits. My granny doesn't even have a home and is eating peanut butter and jelly and cheese crackers, with bottles of water. Maybe I should have stayed in Brooklyn and tried to get more restaurants to donate food. Maybe soon Granny will be able to get her lemon meringue pie at Rockaway Manor, her favorite dessert.

"So Stratford was hit by the storm?" It hadn't occurred to me that I might be traveling to the same flooding that I'd left behind at the nursing home.

"It was pretty bad. My dad says the wind broke up some of the houses on the ocean, and the high waves took away a lot of the beach." She reaches into the pocket of her hoodie and hands me Granny's letters. "You also dropped these," she adds sheepishly. "Sorry I kept them. I was going to read the letters because I was so bored, but they're all in a foreign language."

I snatch the letters from her and clutch them to my chest. I can't be so careless. The letters remind me of why I'm on the train. Even though I can't read the French, I feel as if I know the contents by heart already. Rosie had read all of them for us. She had folded the fragile letters and slipped them back into their envelopes.

In 1950, the letters stopped. Maybe without the war, Collette and Marguerite no longer had a friendship.

I carefully place the letters in my backpack and lean back against the seat, as the girl and I watch the destruction of Hurricane Sandy go by.

Chapter 24
A Shiny Bird

Cliff House
November 2012—Day 8

The train station at Stratford is empty when we arrive. There's a long, open platform with a few benches, and I find one where I think I can be easily seen. The sun has come out in full force, and even though I need Henry's coat and André's scarf, there's heat as I turn my face to the sunshine. A few cars pull out of the parking lot. The girl waves good-bye as she climbs into her father's car. I hope their house is all cleaned up and they can really move back in.

I quickly scan a series of chatty texts from my mom and apologize for being too busy helping out at the Armory to be able to answer her right away. I tell her I'm looking forward to pizza later, even though it won't be Lombardi's, our favorite. I guess she's not mad because she sends back emojis of a pizza slice and chocolate cake, followed by a row of hearts.

Then I send a text to Johnny, Made it to Stratford, and look around.

There's a stack of large tree branches piled along the side of the parking lot, but the thick trees are still standing tall, with a few remaining rust-colored leaves. The bushes are bare, and the ground is littered with orange and yellow leaves, mostly dried out by now. A man reads a newspaper as he walks his tiny dog, but other than that there isn't much activity. I just want to sit and soak in the quiet for a little while. I'm not used to it, but it's a pleasant change. *Granny would like the peacefulness*, I think as I stretch out my legs.

There's no response from Johnny, but he's probably helping his family prep for the dinner rush at the restaurant. Maybe he's creating one of his new crazy recipes. I'll be able to taste test it when I get back. I smile to myself, picturing the weird concoctions he's come up with that have been delicious.

I begin to notice there are many different birdsongs coming from the trees and bushes, when the quiet is broken by the hum of an engine. The low drone turns into a louder rumble, and a sleek maroon convertible swerves into the parking lot and comes to an abrupt halt. I've never seen a car like it before—it's a small convertible, low to the ground, with a shiny grill that's splashed with mud, and silver trim around the edges of the doors. I can see where spots have been touched up with paint that doesn't quite match the maroon, between swaths of streaked dirt along the side of the car.

A woman with a long green scarf wrapped around her head and shoulders swings her legs around from the driver's seat and attempts to hoist herself out of the car. It takes a few tries before she manages to stand. She seems pretty wide, and I wonder how she was able to stuff herself in the car in the first place.

She tosses the scarf into the car, rearranges her matching green dress, fluffs her shortly cropped gray hair, and reaches in the car for a pair of clogs. As she slips them on her feet she looks around the station and her eyes land on me.

"You must be Lily!"

This was not the car I expected to come to pick me up. I thought Simone the driver might even be wearing a chauffeur's cap, or at least have a normal car. But instead of looking for the nearest train back to Manhattan, I think about how I will tell Granny about this part of my adventure. I spot the word PEUGEOT in a silver scroll on the side of the car and think that it's probably French, so the car must be Marguerite's. I give a small wave and make my way down the platform stairs.

Simone grabs my arms and kisses both of my cheeks with dry lips. "Can I hug you?" she asks as she squishes me. I'm a little surprised that a woman who works for Marguerite could be so affectionate, but I like the feel of the hug. It makes me relax a little.

"I'm Simone—Marguerite's daughter." She grabs my shoulders and abruptly turns me and marches me away from the car. "Look up there!" She points to a patch of sky between the station and the trees. "See that house on the top of the hill?"

I can barely see a large brick house off in the distance, at the top of a winding, unpaved road. "Is that Marguerite's house?" It looks like a castle in the clouds, sitting on the edge of a cliff.

"Maison de Falaise. Cliff House!" Simone waves for me to climb into the car. "I grew up there. Solid brick and marble, untouched by Sandy. We watched the storm blow in." She swings open the driver's door, and as I toss my pack onto the narrow back seat and jump in the front, she collapses into her seat and lifts one leg at a time under the steering wheel. She reaches down, pulls off her shoes, and hands them to me. I have to suppress a giggle when she realizes that she's sat on her scarf and has to wiggle and bend until she can pull it out and wrap it around her head. "It's still pretty windy and chilly when I get going. Better put up your hood." She turns the key, and the car lurches forward. Soon we're speeding around curves, and she's shifting gears and yelling in the wind at the same time. "My mother is beside herself with excitement. She's been trying to find your grandmother for a very long time."

The wind is bitter, and I keep my head down and clutch the handle on the door. I thought convertibles were summer cars, but apparently Simone either can't get the roof up or loves the outdoors. She's not even wearing a coat. I start to respond but give up as she keeps shouting, "What?"

In a few minutes, we're bucking up the road to the top of the hill. Up close it's clear that the road is mostly mud. This doesn't seem to bother Simone. She presses the accelerator down hard, and as the wind swirls around us, we slosh through puddles that splash the side of the car, and swerve in the mud as she avoids deep ruts. By the time we get to the front door, I've ducked down so far I can barely see over the dashboard.

I hand her the shoes and step out onto a piece of slate that's part of a path to a massive front porch. As I reach in to get my backpack, Simone makes several attempts to exit the car, muttering to herself until she's finally standing. We make our way up wide stairs to a massive front door.

A fluffy gray cat races by Simone and rubs against me, purring. I stroke her and scratch behind her ears. "Do you want the cat inside?"

"Oh, no, she's an outdoor cat. Couldn't keep her inside if I tried. That's why we call her Collette."

I stop short. "Collette? That's my granny's name."

The woman smiles and gently pulls me inside to a cramped entranceway. "I know, sweetie. Every cat we've had my mama has insisted on calling Collette. We've had five Collettes so far. Take your coat?"

She hangs my coat and scarf on a skinny coat tree in the corner. There's a tall, cracked mirror on the wall, reflecting the black-and-white tile floor. I take a quick glance, and all I see is a girl with tired-looking clothes and shadows under her eyes. I slept on the train, but sleeping in the Armory is clearly wearing me out.

If I'm this tired, I can't imagine how Granny must feel. I flash an image of her trying to get some rest on her thin cot, surrounded by constant noise and activity. I need to meet Marguerite, get to the bottom of this mystery, and get back home.

I follow the woman up a steep flight of stairs. Her black clogs have solid rubber soles that squeak at every step. She's almost as wide as the staircase, and her dress looks like a wall of green in front of me. I expect her to rest halfway up the stairs, but she manages to talk and climb at the same time.

"The tea we made is probably cold by now, but I hope you're hungry because we went to the local bakery and stocked up." She stops abruptly and turns back to talk to me, causing me to grab the wooden railing. "This is the most exciting thing that's happened to her in years. And, trust me, that woman has lived a pretty exciting life."

I'm not sure why Marguerite is so excited to see me. She urged me to come when we talked on the phone, but it seems like she'd be a lot more interested in seeing my granny instead of me.

We get to the top of the staircase and enter a huge room with a wall of windows overlooking the cliffs and an expansive view of the ocean. My first impression is that the room is crowded—stuffed with chairs and dressers and a great big cushy-looking red couch on a giant Oriental rug, plus several tables covered with lamps, china figurines, clocks, and what looks like inkwells. There's a ceiling-high statue of a giraffe in one corner, and a large wicker birdcage hanging in another. The back wall is covered floor to ceiling with books that are crammed every which way on rows and rows of bookshelves. The room is so cluttered it's hard to focus on any one thing.

But it feels nice. I want to grab a book and settle in. My mom is always redecorating our apartment with things that she buys after looking through those home design magazines. Everything is new and changing all the time. The only thing that stays steady is one wall of pictures of the two of us—and my granny.

Marguerite's house feels as if nothing has changed in years and everything in the room was chosen for a reason. Even the framed posters are a bit crooked and not exactly lined up properly, but they look as if they mean something.

I don't realize that Marguerite is sitting right in

front of me until she jumps out of a wingback chair and flings her arms around me. She's about my height, like Granny.

Her hug is tight. She seems so much stronger than my granny.

She speaks rapidly in French and I can pick up "chérie" and "belle," which I know are *dear* and *pretty*. Then she points at my eyes and switches to English. "Your grandmother's eyes were as blue as cornflowers. And yours are like the fields of Provence."

I guess she means my eyes look like dirt and grass, not flowers. I'm not sure if it's a compliment, but then she grabs my hands. "So beautiful you are! And you look so much like my Collette," she says with a heavy French accent.

I don't think I look like Granny, other than we both have very short haircuts and are not very tall. But I remember the photograph in the letter, with Granny holding her stick crutch, and I can see how we might look alike. I never really noticed it before.

It's exciting to hear from someone who knew my

granny before she got old. My mom hardly ever talks about Granny's childhood. I guess it's because she could never get Granny to tell her anything. I want to hear the whole story, beyond the hints in the letters.

Marguerite continues to talk while she serves tea and makes sure that Simone has explained that the house is safe and survived Sandy. "Simone wanted me to evacuate, but I wasn't going anywhere." I remember how Marguerite had said in her letter that she was hoping to give birth to a boy, and I wonder if Simone knows that.

A large china plate is set out on a marble-topped coffee table. The plate is loaded with bite-sized pastries. I pick up a miniature croissant. When I bite down, chocolate oozes out, and I immediately add another one to a small plate that Marguerite hands me. I'm kind of sorry I had that slice of pizza at Grand Central station, but somehow my stomach seems to have settled down.

I'm glad Marguerite's doing all the talking because I don't know where to begin. Besides, I like watching her. She's ancient like my granny and has pulled her gray hair into a tight bun at the top of her head and wrapped it in a bejeweled ribbon. She's small and wiry, and can't seem to hold still. She's wearing pink ballet slippers and a collection of scarves and necklaces over a white tunic and black tights. She looks like a shiny bird.

"So tell me about your grand-mère." Marguerite sits on the edge of the wingback chair and leans toward me. I've slumped into the couch—it's amazingly comfortable—and struggle to sit up. "No, no, sit back." She flips her hand at me. "It's been a busy day for you, and we have much to talk about." I place my empty plate on the coffee table and happily obey her. I just want to fold into the couch and study everything in the room.

"I looked for Collette, you know." I still haven't said a word, but she apparently has a lot to say. "My family left France in such a hurry in 1944, and we were able to find each other for a while. But then I married and changed my name and moved to the U.S." She pops up and retrieves a photo from a table covered with at least a hundred framed pictures. "My Andy. My sweet Andy." She pauses and strokes the picture without showing it to me.

Simone had been hovering in the background, fiddling with a camera, folding a quilt on the back of her mother's chair. "My father was an officer in the United States Army, stationed in London," Simone says. "They moved around a lot. Mama finally agreed to move to this house with him, but only if she could return to France often and keep her French roots."

Marguerite makes a *pfft!* sound and interrupts her daughter. "This is *not* the same as France! But I took my husband's name and off we went to stay in his family's home on the cliff. I replaced the CLIFF HOUSE sign with MAISON DE FALAISE and made this my new home. But with so many changes, Collette and I lost touch." She pauses and props up the photo on the table. "Collette said in a letter that she was marrying, too, but I never found out her new last name. Simone tried to find her on the internet, but we didn't even know where to begin. We didn't even know that Collette had moved to New York."

I know about this and can explain. "My grandpa was from New York. He died when my mom was three years old."

"Oh, I'm so sorry to hear that. My poor Collette. So young to lose a husband." She presses her fingers to her lips, pauses for a moment, then picks up another picture. "I can hardly believe that we ended up so near to each other." She hands me the same black-and-white photo that was in the letter—the two girls dressed as boys, grinning at the photographer. "Here's the two of us."

"I've seen this!" I tell about the evacuation and how a woman named Rosie translated the letters. I leave out how I know Rosie and don't mention that my mom has no idea where I am. "Granny's still at the Armory."

"Oh mon Dieu!" Marguerite slaps her hands on her face.

Simone stops taking pictures. "Is Collette okay?"

"Oh—she's fine!" I don't want them to get upset. "She's actually enjoying it, I think."

Marguerite drops her hands and chuckles. I give her back the photo, grab one of the couch pillows, and pull it into my lap. "I have a million questions after hearing those letters." I don't want to tell her that Granny never talked about her, but there's a lot I need to know. Were they really in the French Resistance?

Marguerite settles back in her chair. "It's incredible that we have that picture, Lily. The Germans didn't allow cameras, and we certainly couldn't take photographs if someone could see us. But my father took the risk." She gazes at the photo with a half smile and places it gently on the coffee table. Her smile widens as she looks at me. "Let me tell you what you need to know."

"Oh, here we go." Simone slides the big plate of pastries closer to me. "Better fuel up and hang on to your hat, kid. Prepare to be amazed." She walks over to the bookshelves and takes down an old, worn shoebox. As she places it on the coffee table, she looks directly at me. "Please remember that it's not all glamour. Don't get any bright ideas." She turns to her mother and says clearly, "Right, Mama? You will stress the danger?"

Marguerite waves her daughter off, mumbling a few words in French.

"Lily." Simone speaks so seriously that it sounds like she's warning me of something. "My mama has traveled all over the world telling her story. She keeps the story alive so that no one will repeat what she had to go through. So you'll excuse me if I retire to the kitchen since I've heard it a million times. But please remember that what she and your granny did was very, very dangerous."

Chapter 25
Tools of the Trade

Dangerous? I stack pillows behind my back so that I can sit up comfortably and hear every word.

When Simone leaves the room, Marguerite shakes her head and points to the doorway. "Big chicken, that one. Not like my Collette."

I realize that I'm going to have to confess how little I know. "I'm sorry, but I don't really know much about you and Granny . . . Collette. I learned a lot from the letters, and it sounds like you must have been in the French Resistance? Is that true?"

Marguerite gasps, touching her thin fingers to her lips. "Collette never told you?"

"She didn't talk about France, and now she doesn't remember much." I figure that's a better way than telling

Marguerite that my granny never mentioned her until recently. "Her memory comes and goes."

Marguerite puts her hand on her heart and murmurs a few words in French. "She is well, though?"

"She's amazing. But I don't want to leave her alone for too long. My mom will check on her, but . . . it's not the same."

Marguerite flies out of the chair and around the coffee table to land on the couch and hug me. "I feel like she's here right now," she says, squeezing me. "You came all this way by yourself, but you want to be home caring for her. So much like Collette." She kisses my cheek. "So good. You are so good."

Instantly my eyes well up, and I put my head down to hide my tears. Marguerite reaches for a tiny éclair and places it in my hand. "You eat. I will tell you our story." I chew on the sweet éclair as she gently pats my back, returns to her chair, and slides over the shoebox.

She carefully lifts the lid.

One by one she places items on the coffee table and explains the missions of the French Resistance. First, a pair of black women's shoes with thick black heels. She holds one shoe up, twists the heel, and a folding knife pops out. I slide forward to get a better look.

She shows me a small box of soap with a wrapper decorated with the Eiffel Tower. The box has a false bottom, just enough room for a tiny written note.

A man's pipe also has a secret compartment, and Marguerite shows how a hidden piece of paper in the bowl of the pipe doesn't burn when she lights the pipe. "For messages," she says, pretending to smoke the pipe.

There are lock picks, a miniature telescope, a compass covered by a belt buckle, and a cigarette lighter with a hidden camera. She picks up a coin and slides it open to reveal a swivel blade. "Tools of the trade," she says as she lines them up neatly in front of me.

She holds up a pencil from the box. "You have to be careful with this." She points to the tip. "It's actually a dagger." She pauses and smiles to herself. "Don't ever put it in your pocket. That's not a very good idea."

"Did you use all of these?" I can't resist looking through the tiny telescope, getting a close-up view of the ocean. The gray waves are still pounding over the top of a stone seawall.

"I delivered these tools to Resistance fighters." She picks up the box of soap. "I was able to bicycle around town in front of the Germans and the Milice—that's the French police—because my father knew everyone and they knew me. I was always afraid that they would confiscate my bicycle, but I would wave at German soldiers on the streets of Brume and they would wave back. They never knew that in my basket would be boxes of soap with hidden messages, to deliver to members of Noah's Ark. You know this—Noah's Ark?"

I think about what Rosie had told us, back at the Pen Emporium. "I know that people had animal names."

She claps her hands and laughs, then explains. She describes Panther, and Hélène, and my granny Collette as Wallcreeper—sneaking around the village at night collecting Xs in her notebook, climbing cliffs to drop off a dangerous chemical, counting German soldiers at a bridge outside Brume. She even shows me the small burn scar between her shoulder blades and tells me how she got it when a German soldier poked her with a hot stick. She continues at a rapid pace, describing life in Brume in 1944.

She tells me that the shoes belonged to a Resistance fighter named Rabbit who worked in their kitchen and gathered information with Marguerite's father, as they entertained German soldiers. "Rabbit made regular visits to the Marseille market on the Mediterranean Sea, and brought back tools for the resisters in Noah's Ark. She often brought someone to help with the fight, hidden in the back of her wagon. She was so brave, so beautiful—always wearing a scarf painted with flowers."

The stories keep coming. I feel as if I'm five years old, when my mom read me fairy tales and I could imagine every scene. Marguerite acts them out like she's in a play, climbing walls, riding her bike, hiding behind trees. She tells me about a British spy called "the lieutenant," who wore red lipstick. "She saved our lives."

"How?" I ask. The stories are almost impossible to believe. But Marguerite is so sure of herself as she relives the memories.

She picks up the pencil from the table. "Your granny Collette and I had to get a message to the lieutenant. She was hiding in . . . how do you say . . . outside toilet . . . ?"

"She was hiding in an outhouse?"

Marguerite nods vigorously and holds her nose. We both laugh as I join her in "Ewww!"

"We had to hide there, too. We were in a storage bin attached to the back." She drops the pencil on the table and curls into a ball on the winged chair, her knees against her chest, arms around knees, head down. She stays that way for a minute or two.

I lean forward to try to see her face. She seems lost in thought. I don't say anything, but I'm getting nervous.

She finally looks up and stretches out her legs. "I

don't like tight spaces," she says as she reaches down and grabs a book from a stack next to the chair. "I'll show you why we met the lieutenant." She hands me the slim book. *Provence* is written in fancy script across the cover, over a picture of fields of lavender and sunflowers. "Give me three numbers. The last two numbers have to be below fifteen."

I'm confused. "Three numbers?"

"We're going to decode. Go ahead—three numbers."

"Thirty-four, six, twelve."

She points to the book. "Open to page thirty-four."

I flip to a page of French text.

"Now paragraph six."

I count down. "Twelfth word?"

"Correct! What's the first letter of the twelfth word?"

"H!"

"That's the first letter of your secret message!"

We try it again, and I decode quickly. I think about sending messages to Johnny, using our social studies books. "But how did you end up in an outhouse?"

Marguerite tells me the entire story of the coded message and hiding in the storage bin. "The lieutenant distracted the Germans by offering them cigarettes. They had no idea the brass cigarette case was rigged to explode. She tossed it at them, and . . . *boom!*"

"It blew up? Was she hurt?"

"Oh, no! She took off. It was just enough noise to scare them so she could get away. We all made it to the olive grove, but she went her own way and we never saw her again."

I realized I've sucked in my breath, and I let it out slowly. I pick up the pencil. "Did you ever have to use one of these?"

Marguerite is quick to respond. "No, we never did." She reaches into the shoebox and pulls out a compact and flips it open to show the mirror. "This is just an ordinary compact that the lieutenant gave me from her rucksack, before she took off." She hands it to me, and I imagine checking my lipstick. "She gave Collette a pretty pink beret."

I almost drop the compact. "She still has it!" We

talk over each other, exclaiming about my granny and that old, worn-out beret.

Simone drifts in and out of the room, adding plates of food, sometimes stopping to listen. "She has told these stories many times," she says, shaking her head, "but you are her best audience."

I keep nibbling on the steady flow of food—chewy bread with a crisp crust, bites of weird-tasting cheese, even tangy olives. I try some café au lait served in a round, delicate cup, while Marguerite describes why the members of Noah's Ark were so determined to drive the Germans out of their country.

By this time I've settled into the cozy couch, wrapped up in a soft, worn quilt, trying to imagine the stories that she's telling me. The more she talks the more I can see my granny, her hair exactly like mine in a pixie cut, wearing her brother's big boots, brave enough to be a Resistance fighter. I wonder why didn't she want to talk about it.

She was my age. I wonder if I could be as brave.

I want to get back to Brooklyn and ask Granny so

many questions—if she can remember the answers. Right now Marguerite is my best source.

I pull the packet of letters out of my backpack and hand them to her. She holds them to her chest while looking at me with delight, even though there are tears in her eyes. She takes a pair of half-glasses from her pocket and slides them on. As she reads through the letters, commenting on what she wrote to my granny so long ago, she fills in the details. "I was called Skylark because I could sing . . . and sing . . . and sing. That's what skylarks do. They even sing when they are hovering in the air." She stares out the window for a moment. "I still love to sing, but not in German. Never in German." She points to a small desk with spindly legs hidden in the corner near the windows. "Look in the bottom drawer. The key is in the inkwell on top of the desk."

I find a tiny skeleton key inside a cut glass jar and wiggle it in the keyhole until the drawer pops open. Postcards, old letters, and folded sheets of yellowed paper are stacked neatly, filling the narrow drawer. At the top is a newspaper clipping with a picture of a younger Marguerite. "You were in the *New York Times*?"

"We can look at all of that later. Dig around in the bottom."

My heart races as I pull out a thin stack of letters and postcards tied together with a pink ribbon and place them on Marguerite's lap. "Are these from Granny?"

Marguerite strokes the pile. "The only mail I ever received from her. It was impossible to get letters out of France after the war. The post offices had been destroyed and the postal vans were stolen by the Germans."

She fusses with the ribbon, and I help her untie the knot. The top envelope has red-and-blue postage stamps across the top and markings in black ink, long faded. Granny has simply written *Brume, France* in the corner, and a Madrid address in bold letters in the center. "This one is my favorite because Collette filled the pages."

I settle down at her feet and she begins to read, translating the French:

March 1945

Dear Marguerite—

It took so long to hear from you! I have to write quickly because Hélène knows someone who is taking mail to Spain. We have no other way to send mail, and I have so much to tell.

Marguerite pauses and looks out the window at the sea. "After the Germans left France, the Americans found thousands of letters piled up in German head-quarters, never delivered. Everyone was writing to try to find lost relatives. Soon only postal cards were allowed—no more letters—but Collette slipped this through by getting it to Spain."

I urge her to go on. What would my granny Collette, a little older than me, write about after the war?

It's lonely here in Brume. Sometimes it seems as if the war isn't over because we're still not sure about our neighbors and what they did during the war. Papa saw a woman pelted with stones because she was friends with a German officer. It was wise for your family to leave Brume, even though your father was braver than any of them.

Hélène and Rabbit are still very busy. I'm sure you know what I mean. They want every collaborator out of France. But they want me to go to school. No more deliveries.

Marguerite again looks up from the letter. "Do you know who collaborators were?"

"Yes!" I'm pleased I remember what Rosie had explained. "They were French people who made friends with the enemy."

Marguerite starts to say more, but she thinks for a moment and returns to the letter. "Collette writes about the liberation of Brume when the Americans arrived."

Marguerite—I got to see the American soldiers when they came through town! They were marching beside jeeps and trucks and huge tanks. They shouted "bonjour" and "liberation" in terrible French. Once we realized they were truly friendly, most of the village came to greet them. One of the soldiers gave me an American flag on a stick, to wave in the air. We are a small town, but we cheered so loud! I haven't seen so many smiles in years.

One soldier gave Papa a pack of cigarettes called Lucky Strikes. Mama hugged the soldier so hard we thought she would never let him go. Now she can't stop crying. I think she wishes she'd been hugging my brother.

We still don't have much food, so Papa traded the pack for four eggs. The American soldier promised that sugar would be coming soon.

Please write and tell me about your life away from Brume. Your house is still empty, but I picked a few of the forget-me-nots and snowdrops that are coming up near your back porch and brought them home to Mama.

The train tracks near Brume have been repaired, and whenever I hear a train whistle, I think of my brave friend Skylark. Maybe someday I'll go back to where we counted soldiers at the bridge, but not yet. Our scars are ugly reminders, aren't they?

Very few people have returned to Brume. Some of the boys released from German labor camps have come back to work in the fields. I am hoping your family might decide to come home.

Your lonely friend,
Collette (Wallcreeper)

"She sounds so sad." The letter reminds me of Granny's first day at Rockaway Manor. "It's lonely here," she had whispered to me. After that, I was determined to visit her as often as I could.

Marguerite selects a plain postcard and holds it up for me to see. "I could send letters through the embassy, but Collette had to write on these postal cards. You were allowed to write only about personal or family matters—nothing about the war."

"But the war was over!"

"It took a few years to finish the war completely and to figure out who to trust. Would you like to hear about Collette's life in Brume?" She doesn't wait for my response. "She couldn't fit much on a postal card, but she mentions Madame Monette and her stone cottage in the country, and that stinky outhouse!" She giggles. I join her, eager to hear more.

June 1946

Dear Marguerite—

I never know if my mail can find you. I bicycle to Madame Monette's, and together we write postal cards to you because letters in envelopes are no longer allowed. The cards go in a sack to be taken to Marseille or Paris, but do they reach you?

Madame and I pick lavender and sunflowers and make jars of berry jam, and olives soaked in oil and herbs. We sell at the market on the Rue d'Azur. I'm saving to go to Paris someday.

Please write back. I miss my friend.

Wallcreeper

P.S. Madame still has the same outhouse, and now she has a cow! Papa buys butter from her and made our first clafoutis in many years, with hot batter folded over dark, sweet cherries. We were in heaven.

Marguerite shows me the postcard. My granny's words are in tiny print, crammed onto the postcard. She'd sketched a bouquet of flowers in the center, two cherries with stems in one of the corners, and a string of blossoms all around the edges. Even then she was drawing pictures of flowers.

"And then in 1948," Marguerite continues, "I finally got another letter, not a card."

I was still looking at Granny's tiny illustrations. "So much time between letters!"

"She says in this letter that she was writing me, but

letters got lost so easily. Don't forget—we didn't have internet back then, and even a phone call to another country was extremely difficult and very expensive."

Her words remind me of how I have a phone in my pocket that can connect me right away to anyone in the world. But sometimes it's better if it's not so easy. I'm not ready to use my phone yet. "Read the letter, please."

"She seemed to be in a hurry for this one. Wait until you hear Collette's plans!"

Chapter 26
Les Belles Fleurs

Marguerite adjusts her glasses and squints at the tiny print.

June 1948

Dearest Marguerite—

I hope you have been getting my letters. You sound like you have such a busy life in London! Someday I will meet your Andy. I'm sure he's very handsome. Does he call you Skylark?

This time my news is not about cows and olives. I'm going to Montpellier to see the Tour de France in July! In case you haven't heard, the bicycle race is bigger than ever, now that the war is over. There will be teams from Belgium and Italy, and even a rider from Poland! They will circle the entire country.

My friends and I are going in a truck so we can stand in the back and watch the race and see the ocean. Who knows—maybe I'll go to Paris next, and then I'll find you in London.

Mama wants me to marry a farm boy and take over the bakery. But Hélène says I was born to explore the world. Besides, there are no handsome boys in Brume.

Please write to me and tell me about the world. Maybe soon I'll see your face because I want to travel to you!

Always Wallcreeper,
Collette

"The Tour de France! She never mentioned that!" I'm beginning to think that Granny's memory may be worse than I thought. Why wouldn't she tell me about seeing a famous bicycle race? "But she never did find you, did she? I guess the letters stopped in 1950. What happened?"

"Wait—there are two more postcards. The first one is soon after she went to the race."

October 1949
My M—

I'm sending another postal card and refuse to give up, even though the mail is terrible. They are now using old German warplanes to deliver the mail, and we still duck and hide when they fly over our heads. Maybe THIS card will make it to London.

IF YOU ARE THE POSTMAN AND YOU ARE READING THIS CARD, STOP HERE. THIS IS NONE OF YOUR BUSINESS!

We both laugh. "That sounds like my granny! Keep reading!"

Skylark, I met a boy! His name is Marcel

and he's from Arles. (He actually looks like Vincent van Gogh!) He's staying in Brume to repair the bridges. He thinks I'm pretty but wants me to grow my hair longer. I don't want to do that—I think there's a little Jean-Pierre still left in me. Besides, he dreams of settling in Brume and opening a tool shop, but I feel that the world is waiting for me.

I haven't even seen Italy or Spain, and they're just a few hours away. No more room on this card! Please write back

—Wallcreeper

I'm still giggling at Granny yelling at the postman. "Sounds like Marcel didn't have a chance." I try to picture my granny with long hair. "My mom has pictures of my granny in our apartment, and I don't think her hair was ever very long. It's short, like mine."

Marguerite smooths her hair around her bun and plays with her necklaces. "I had long, beautiful hair during the war. Rabbit saved the fat from cooking, and we made horrible-smelling soap. Once a week, she'd scrub my neck and wash my hair in the kitchen sink."

That sounds awful to me, but Marguerite is smiling at the memory. I pick up the photo of Granny and Marguerite grinning in their pixie cuts. "But you have very short hair in this picture."

Marguerite's expression changes instantly. "I cut it off right before that picture was taken, and gave myself a boy's name, just like Collette."

This is startling new information. "A boy's name?"

"The only way Collette could wander Brume, especially on a bicycle, was if she pretended to be a boy. It was not acceptable for a girl to explore alone." She taps the photo. "Your granny was Jean-Pierre, dressed in her brother's old clothes."

I must look confused because she continues to explain. "I was busy entertaining Germans at our home, all dressed up. People in town recognized me when I made deliveries, and I waved at them like an innocent young girl." She gives me a little finger wave and a phony sweet smile. "But Collette had to be in disguise."

I'm struggling to picture my granny wearing her

brother's clothes when she's so careful about her appearance, even when she's in her pink bathrobe. "Why did you cut your hair?"

Marguerite thinks over her answer before she responds. "It was close to the end of the war, and it was important for me to go on missions and not be recognized. I cut my hair and called myself Léo."

"So Wallcreeper and Skylark were also Jean-Pierre and Léo?"

"And also Collette and Marguerite!" She places her finger on her lips, and her eyes seem to light up. "Lots of necessary secrets."

I repeat the names. "Jean-Pierre and Léo." If I had to choose a boy's name, I wonder what it would be.

"Léo was a common name at the time. I liked it because it means *lion*." She tosses her head and roars, and we laugh when I roar back. "I felt like a lion, even without my mane."

"I've always kept my hair short, even when my mom has begged me to try it longer."

"You look just like Collette. Did she ever get to travel?"

I tell her all about Granny's gardens and the

drawings on the wall of her room at Rockaway Manor. I wish I'd brought them with us, but we had to leave in such a hurry. I hope they're still there. "She's talking about taking a trip to Morocco." I stop because I know Granny will never get there.

"North Africa! A few years ago, I took a ferry to Morocco from France, across the Mediterranean Sea. The same sea the Americans crossed to set us free from the Germans."

"I wish she could have gone with you." It's easy to picture Granny in her pink beret, standing at the bow of the ferry, heading for the coast of Africa.

Marguerite must be able to tell what I'm imagining because she says, "Collette would have pointed the way for the ferry captain." She rests her hand on the top of my head. For a moment, I think it's Granny's hand. "You'll have to go instead," she says quietly. She hands me the last postcard. It has a drawing on one side, filled in with soft colors. "What do you see?"

"It looks like a picture of a flower shop." There's a narrow stone building with a blue door. *Les Belles Fleurs* is etched in gold in a large display window. Iron benches, wooden ladders, and metal plant stands fill the sidewalk, stacked with pots that overflow with every color of flower. Hundreds of tiny pink blossoms climb a rickety trellis that leans against the building.

"That's the flower shop where your granny worked in Paris. Simply called 'Beautiful Flowers.'"

"She got to Paris!" I study the window in the drawing to see if I can see my granny inside the store.

Marguerite takes the card from me and translates:

May 1950

My dearest Marguerite—

I've made it to Paris! I saved money from selling flowers and am working for a florist at the Rue des Saints-Pères. I've met a wonderful man stationed here, and believe it or not, Wallcreeper is getting married soon!

Please, please, please write me, Skylark. It's been so long.

Your friend, Collette

P.S. You can send letters to the shop.
Everyone knows me here because I deliver
flowers on my bicycle.

"I did send a letter right away." Marguerite sighs.
"But it was returned—the shop had closed. I married
and moved here to Stratford, and it looks like Collette
married, too, and changed her name. I had no idea
that she had also moved to the United States, just a
couple of hours away." She stacks the mail into a neat
pile. "So many memories. It seems like yesterday." She
reties the ribbon. "Before you put these letters back in
the drawer, I have something else to show you."

She reaches into the shoebox, dramatically lifts
out a fountain pen, and places it on the table. The red
velveteen box is missing, but the pen is the same blue
marble, engraved with an F. I slide over to get a closer
look. She pulls off the cap to reveal the gold nib with
the tiny **4810**.

"That's the pen!" I blurt out, and without thinking,
confess the real reason I took the train to Stratford. I'm

worried that Marguerite will be disappointed that I didn't travel just to visit her, and explain that I wanted to retrieve something I'd lost.

She doesn't seem at all concerned. "You had a mission," she says, shrugging her shoulders. She pops the cap back on the pen and hands it to me. "It's yours to keep, my dear."

I stroke the smooth side and inspect the engraving. Even though it was just a missing pen before, now it seems precious and I know I'll never lose it again.

Marguerite points to the **F**. "I stole that pen."

She waits for a moment for a reaction, but at this point, nothing surprises me. "You stole it?"

"From a German officer. He was at our home often, eating all our food, drinking my father's wine, bragging about how the Germans were going to take over the world. My father would smile and pour more wine. The more drinking, the more information."

"How'd you get his pen?"

"Easy. It was in his coat. Rabbit and I were both responsible for collecting the winter coats and hanging

330

them up when guests arrived. We always checked the pockets for letters, notes, maps—anything that could be shared with Resistance fighters. He had this blue fountain pen, but he never kept it in the same place. Sometimes deep in the side pocket, sometimes in the little pocket inside the lining, sometimes not at all. I figured he would think he lost it, so I lifted it."

"But why?"

"Because he stole so much from us." Marguerite's face changes for a moment. Her eyes narrow, and she looks like one of my teachers when they're annoyed with the class. She stands abruptly and walks to the big windows. The sky is steel gray, and a few sprinkles tap the glass. As she continues, her voice sounds tight and gravelly and her accent is heavy. "These are not adventures I'm telling you, my Lily. We knew we could be killed at any time. There were firing squads always on duty, and they executed so many. We were actors, all of us."

Simone appears from the kitchen carrying a glass pitcher of ice water and a plate of baby cream puffs.

She watches her mother closely. Marguerite's voice makes me feel a little bit afraid. She sounds so cold. I crawl back onto the couch and watch her closely, too.

Simone places the pitcher and plate on the table, then leads her mother over to the wingback chair. Marguerite rearranges her many necklaces, takes a deep breath, and gives me a weak smile. "It wasn't the notebook, you know."

"The notebook?"

"Collette was supposed to have everyone sign a notebook." She explains how my granny would say *sign here* or *initial here* to let members of Noah's Ark know if there would be a mission that night. I think about Granny muttering, "sign here," and picture the notebook filled with **XXXXX**. I wonder what happened to it. "But," Marguerite says softly, "it was the pen that really mattered."

She pauses as Simone touches her shoulder and then clears the plates, leaving a full plate in front of her mother.

"You mean this pen? The one you stole from the German officer?"

"That pen was the signal that Collette could be trusted. Everyone in Noah's Ark knew that the pen was a Montblanc, a fancy one made in Germany, stolen from a German officer. They knew that if Collette made them sign with that specific pen—she always made sure they could see the **F** on the side—that she, too, was working for the Resistance."

"What did the **F** mean?"

"That was the officer's initial. His name was Franz." She shudders. "That's what made it unique, that engraved letter on the side."

"What's the meaning of the number on the nib?"

Marguerite giggles, back to her exuberant self. "That's proof that it was made by Montblanc. The mountain Mont Blanc is 4,810 meters high. That's always engraved on the nib of the finest Montblanc pens. It was another sign for the Resistance fighters that it was the actual stolen pen."

"If you stole it, how did my granny get it?" I inspect the nib again and think about how Johnny and I thought the **4810** was a secret code. I want to call Johnny right now and tell him everything. I want to go back to the Pen Emporium and tell Henry about how one of his special pens was used on secret missions.

"I hadn't met Collette at the time I stole the pen. Rabbit gave it to Hélène for forging documents, but Hélène wanted Collette to use the pen when she asked for signatures in the notebook. Collette found out later, when we did missions together, that I was the one who stole the pen."

"Why do you think my granny's so worried about getting it back to you now?"

"I'm not really sure, Lily. But I am so pleased you found me." She's quiet for a while as I uncap the pen and write **XXX** in the air. "Collette had the pen when my family left Brume. Later, when I lost touch with her, I had a strong feeling that if I could find that pen, I would find Collette. That's why I left instructions with stores that sold fountain pens—all over the world. I just knew that was the way to find out what happened to her even if it was too late and she was gone." She gazes out the window at the sea.

I carefully slide the cap back on the pen and weigh

334

it in my hand like Henry would do. "Granny was using this pen to find you, too."

"Your grandmother knows what that pen meant to us—to everyone in the Resistance. She took that pen everywhere she went." Marguerite rips off a chunk of bread and swirls it in the olive oil that Simone has dripped on plates decorated with tiny pictures of fruit. "Even when we crashed the train."

She calmly chews on the bread and smirks as I sit up quickly. "You crashed a train?"

Simone, who had been so quiet up to now, bursts out laughing. "Oh, here she goes again!" She pops a cream puff into her mouth. "Yes, Lily, my mother and your granny were hellions. I'm surprised she lived to tell about it, but they did, indeed, crash a train."

Chapter 27
Le Roi

Collette and Marguerite bicycle all day in the countryside in the warm sun. Marguerite's basket is filled with a picnic lunch, wrapped by Rabbit in a white linen cloth. Collette has a fishing pole strapped to her bike. Now that summer has arrived, the people in the village are desperate to eat the trout from the melted streams in the countryside. Collette can practically taste the fish, but today there will be no time to stand by the waters and wait to catch supper.

The morning fog of Brume burned off long ago. After biking several miles, they find the barn that Panther had described to them, close to the town of Avignon. It's caved in on one side from years of neglect, but the stone cottage nearby is solid and has scrubbed white window frames and a blue glass vase catching light in the window. Collette points to the vase, and they know they've found the right place. They wheel their bicycles behind a rolled bale of rotting hay.

A farmer is sitting on the porch steps. They've been told that he's a Resistance sympathizer, but he doesn't want any trouble. "You're overdressed for this heat," he growls at them. They don't respond. They know that their disguise as boys is hardly working anymore. They both have grown over the winter and can no longer cover up with sweaters and coats.

Marguerite's new pixie cut has caused her pretty face and full eyelashes to emerge even more than before. A plain navy cap does little to hide who she really is.

The farmer persists. "They'll notice if you're overdressed. They'll wonder what you're hiding."

Collette looks down at her soiled, torn wool pants

and battered boots. Her homespun, long-sleeved shirt is already soaked in sweat.

Marguerite is wearing raggedy, patched pants and an oversized shirt that Rabbit has given her, since everything Marguerite owns is new and freshly pressed. Marguerite has bicycled just as hard as Collette, yet she somehow manages to look fresh and dry. She flashes a smile at the farmer. He looks away, shaking his head.

He looks so sad, Collette thinks. *Victory is so close, but everyone looks so sad.*

"Get in the cart." The old man stands up, hikes up his loose pants that are held together by frayed rope, and points at the bikes. "No one said anything about those. Throw them in."

They haul the bicycles into a small wooden cart pulled by a bony horse covered with scabs. The horse's breathing is labored as it slowly drags them forward. The farmer speaks gently to the horse, and it picks up the pace. "We will eat you for supper, Le Roi," he threatens mildly as the girls chuckle.

It's unusual to see a horse on a farm in southern

France during the war. Horses were one of the first things the Germans requisitioned, along with the chickens and pigs, and even run-down farm equipment. "I have a permit for Le Roi," the farmer says, as if they had asked.

For miles they rock along dirt paths off the main roads, the sun beating down. They eat Rabbit's bread and cheese, and the man shares his portion with the listless horse. They pass another farmer walking along the path carrying an empty bucket, but the only other activity is birds and butterflies flitting around the fields. "Getting too hot for potatoes," the farmer mutters at one point, waving his hand over a field with dry dirt. "Soil parched," he says another time.

They cross wider roads, but none of them are marked. Most of the fields are empty except for scattered weeds and wildflowers. Loose mounds of grass and hay dot some of the open fields, the twine to bind them long confiscated by the Germans. Some wheat fields have abandoned tractors, useless without fuel.

"There's where the Germans had rifle and mortar

practice." The farmer points to a wide, pock-marked pasture. Most of the Germans had been called to the northern front recently, but enough soldiers remain, and Collette knows to stay vigilant. She scans the land, ever alert.

They pass by acres of lavender still cultivated by a handful of farmers working steadfastly in the heat. Twisted trunks of silvery green olive trees are lined up in groves, marked with crumbling low stone walls. Collette concentrates on the directions, making sure she knows how they can get back to Brume. Occasionally, off in the distance, she spots a stone house to serve as a landmark—a sunflower in front of one, a row of rickety sheds behind another. They turn slowly onto a road that meanders through a tunnel of tall evergreens.

It seems to be a long way to the train tracks where Panther has sent them for their mission.

"We could walk faster than this." Marguerite shoves a bicycle over to make more room in the cart just as the horse wheezes loudly and stumbles forward. The man pulls the reins, and they come to a sudden halt. He jumps out and pats Le Roi's rump, murmuring words of encouragement in the horse's ear. "You can do this, Le Roi. We'll both rest later. Let's get them on their way."

Just as the horse vigorously shakes its head and neighs in despair, they hear a truck whining behind them. "That's German," the farmer snaps. "Get out— go ahead on your bikes. We can't be seen together."

The girls jump off the cart and pull out the bikes as the truck gets louder. They're able to round a bend on the thin road and stop behind a row of pines, just as the truck screeches and is suddenly silent.

"Go!" Collette mouths to Marguerite, and they pedal the bikes as hard as they can on the uneven road, frantically looking for a better place to hide. They can hear yelling in German, a shout from the farmer, then a high-pitched whinny.

A shot is fired, and Le Roi sounds like he's screaming. Germans are shouting all at once. The girls frantically pump, making little progress as the bicycle wheels catch in the ruts and slide in the dirt. Collette can feel her heart racing, and she can't seem to control her legs. Her face is covered in sweat, and she can hear Marguerite gasping behind her.

As the road begins to climb, she jumps off her bike and drags it behind a pile of giant limestone boulders. Marguerite joins her, and they duck down, shaking. Their eyes lock in fear until Marguerite looks away. "We'll be fine," Collette insists as she pulls the bicycles in closer, to make sure they can't be seen from the road. They huddle close, pressed against the back of the rocks.

The truck starts up, and the rumble of the engine gets louder as it approaches their hiding place, roars past them, and charges up the hill. Collette catches a glimpse of German soldiers hanging off the sides. Dust scatters as the truck disappears.

"I'll go back," Collette says, peering around the rocks. "Stay here." She's gone before Marguerite can object.

The horse is in the middle of the road, lying on its

side, as if sleeping. The farmer is sitting on the ground, leaning against the emaciated horse. "I wouldn't let them have him. They were not going to take Le Roi," he repeats angrily without looking at Collette.

She steps closer to the horse and is relieved to see he's panting, and there's no sign of blood. As if to reassure her, he snorts and tries to lift his head.

She squats down to inspect the farmer. "Are you hurt?" He shakes his head. "Stupid German, he tried to shoot me because I wouldn't let him have this poor, tired horse." He pats Le Roi's sweaty neck. "But Le Roi reared up when that German aimed at me, and the gun went off in the sky." He points up at the cornflower blue sky with wispy white clouds, then drops his hand and strokes the horse's side. "He was protecting me. I didn't know he had it in him."

Marguerite appears and leans over Le Roi. "You saved him," she says to the horse, and pats his nose. Le Roi stares up at Marguerite, his eyes bloodshot and wide with fear. He gives a feeble kick with his back legs. One rubber-coated horseshoe, replacing iron shoes no longer available, dangles loosely from a hind foot.

"And they let you go?"

"They're in a hurry. They know their time in France is ending." The farmer struggles to stand up, and Collette reaches for his hand. "Go," he says firmly, giving her a slight push. "We'll be fine." He stands as Le Roi jerks in an attempt to rise. "Maybe those Germans will be on that train. Get it done."

He rattles off directions, describing an abandoned hut where they'll be able to hide their bicycles and see the train tracks. They don't have to hurry; they're close. Their mission must be done at dusk, right when a loaded German supply train will be roaring toward them.

Still unsteady, the girls walk their bicycles for a while before they feel they can ride again, dodging large stones in the dirt road. Without rubber available for extra bicycle tires, a flat tire would be disastrous. But soon they see the dilapidated hut by the side of the road, its door hanging loose, the crossbar dangling.

"We're here." Collette removes the fishing pole from her bicycle and props the pole against the side of the hut. She rolls her bicycle inside, leaving room in the cramped space for Marguerite's. They lean both their bicycles against the rickety walls and slump to the ground. The dark hut is shaded by tall plane trees that protect them from the hot sun, but the hut is still warm and musty. Marguerite takes a canteen from her bicycle basket and shares it with Collette.

"It's not much longer, but I don't think we should wait here. If another truck goes by, we'll be trapped. Leave the bikes." Collette passes back the canteen, carefully opens the door to the hut and peers out to check the road. She dashes into the surrounding woods, Marguerite at her heels. They clear out a cool, mossy spot under low juniper trees to wait until dusk when the train is due so they won't be seen as easily.

Collette plucks wild rosemary and rubs it between her fingers, smelling it. A rush of hunger for her mama's long forgotten roast lamb helps her forget the night's mission for a moment.

Panther had described their task as "quick and simple," but they both know they're an important link in a chain of Resistance missions. Tonight, the Resistance fighters will guide a British plane so that spies can parachute into a field nearby. "The British will stay in France to gather intelligence on the ground," Panther explained to both of them. "It looks like soon there will be an attack on the Germans from the south, and we need to help."

Collette had overheard conversations in her father's shop about an invasion from the north that would destroy the Germans and finally force them out of her country. The stories had given the townspeople hope and motivated Noah's Ark to step up their secret resistance.

But Collette had heard nothing about an attack from the south.

Panther continued to describe how the British paratroopers were going to bring gas and radios, more guns, and better maps. Members of Noah's Ark were prepared to turn on flashlights to guide the men floating down onto the field.

"Your mission is to create a distraction to take attention away from the landing field." He spoke urgently to Skylark and Wallcreeper, his voice rising. "Liberation is near!"

Hélène interrupted, her voice steady and calm. "You're going to crash a train."

Marguerite reached for Collette's hand and squeezed tightly.

"But not with explosives," Hélène continued. "The American Army has figured out a way to derail a train without blowing up the tracks."

Panther grunted. "You're removing pieces of the track. That's all. The pieces are already cut. You just have to pull them out."

"Just slide them out," Hélène added. "At the right time."

"When the train comes?" Marguerite asked. Her voice sounded unusually high-pitched. "We'll be on the tracks?"

Collette could picture it. "Before the train approaches, we'll slide out pieces of track and disappear. By the time the train derails, we'll be gone, right?"

"You'll be gone," Panther said, sounding pleased that Collette was following. "And while the plane is dropping British spies two miles away, the Germans will be busy pulling soldiers out of the train wreck and scrambling to clean up a mess."

Collette and Marguerite understood what they had to do.

And now they had to get it done.

Chapter 28
Thunderclaps

Collette and Marguerite crawl in the gravel and dirt along the side of the railroad track until they reach the spot that has been marked with a small pyramid of pebbles. This is where the rails had been cut.

Collette scrambles across the track to the other side. It may be getting dark, but they both lie flat to make sure that the locomotive engineer won't see them. Collette presses her chin to the rough ground and thinks about the warning that Hélène gave the girls before they left for the mission. "Be very careful. Don't get caught. Every day another Resistance fighter is killed or sent away."

"I know that," Marguerite had responded

impatiently. "I've heard the German officers and Milice talking in my home. They brag about torturing and killing anyone who gives them trouble. *Anyone* they don't like."

Hélène hushed her. "Don't talk about that. Not even to me. You put everyone in danger if you reveal anything at all." Her piercing eyes bore into Marguerite. "Remember that we are the people of the underground. You must be sure you want to do this."

As Collette stretches along the side of the tracks, she can feel determination strengthen her body. She will not quit until every German is gone from France. Her brother started the fight, and she will finish it.

She can't see Marguerite's face on the other side of the tracks, but she knows that Marguerite's just as determined. Collette can count on her. As soon as Collette signals, they will complete their task, dash back to the hut where their bicycles are hidden, and follow the dirt roads through the countryside, back to Brume. It will be a long way back to Panther, but they must only report that the mission was a success. They can't fail.

She studies the rail next to her and spots the cuts that have been made, marking off a piece of iron almost two meters long. The cuts are barely visible. It must have taken a long time to get through the solid rail. The bolts connecting the rail to the cross ties have already been removed by someone from Noah's Ark.

The other rail will have cuts, too, a little farther up from Marguerite. Panther explained that the cuts in the tracks were staggered, as that would better trip up the wheels of the train. But since the Germans send scouts to check the tracks for explosives, the rails have to be lifted out at the last minute.

Collette starts to tell Marguerite to crawl forward and look for slices in the other rail, when Marguerite raises her head slightly. "I see the train," she shouts, "but there's no whistle!"

Collette doesn't hesitate. "Now! Hurry!" She grabs the cut piece of rail with both hands, but it's thick and much too heavy to lift. How is she ever going to pull it out?

"Marguerite! Help me!" She pulls on the piece with both hands and can feel it vibrating from the approaching train that is still miles away. Her hands barely fit around the rail. She tries to get a strong grip and pull hard, but the piece won't budge.

Marguerite is quickly at her side and they pull together. The piece of rail wobbles, but rests heavily on the railroad ties and can't be lifted. Collette desperately digs with her hands between the ties and tries again. No movement.

She tries pushing forward to see if she can dislodge it, while Marguerite searches the ground for something to use as leverage. While Collette pushes, throwing her entire body into it, Marguerite grabs a flat rock and jams the rock into the dirt, working to lift up the rail. The rail gives a little, just as the train whistle blows. They both glance up to see in the distance the train moving over the top of a hill, in their direction. The headlamp on the front casts a wide arc over the tracks. The engineer, hanging on to a bar on the side of the locomotive, leans out, shades his eyes, and peers down the tracks.

"Can't we just slide it over instead of lifting it out?" Collette pushes on the side of one end and the rail moves another inch. Marguerite drops the rock and pushes with her so that the piece begins to slide at a wide angle and is finally free from the main track.

"Grab the end and slide it out!" Marguerite yells.

Panther had demonstrated lifting the rail as if it were made out of straw. But the rail is at least six inches thick and solid iron. Together they stand, grab the end of the long piece, and pull hard, using any strength they have left. The piece slides slowly away, leaving a gap in the rail. The rhythmic pounding of the train can now be heard, and the whistle blows again, continuously.

"That's good enough!" Collette pushes Marguerite toward the other side of the track.

"We're halfway there!" Marguerite can barely be heard as she crawls over the tracks, Collette right behind her.

The second piece of rail is half the size of the first, and about three feet up the track. Although shorter, it's tougher to remove. They pull and push together as the screaming train rapidly approaches. But the rail doesn't move.

Collette spots one bolt that has been loosened, but not removed. She grabs the nut, gives one more twist, and yanks the bolt out of the tie. The clatter of the oncoming train is deafening. Together, they pull hard and slide the piece of rail away as the train continues to bear down on them. Collette, aware that they are visible, glances up to see the engineer in the front of the locomotive peering out into the night. Can he see them? He makes no attempt to slow down.

As the train barrels toward them, the girls roll away from the track and tumble on top of each other. They scramble to get up and run fast toward the protection of the trees, just as the locomotive and first three boxcars fly by, speeding along easily over the broken track.

But the fourth car wobbles, and the fifth car shakes even more. The sixth car starts to drift and suddenly topples and plunges off the track, twisting in a heap, pulling the remaining cars with it. On both sides of the track, the cars roll, smashing into each other as they skid onto the fields. The brakes shriek as the engineer tries to control the engine and the attached cars that made it over the dismantled rails.

Dirt and rocks fly around Collette and Marguerite as they race away from the crash, away from train cars that slide behind them on the dirt. They keep running, heat blowing at their backs, sudden booms and long, high screeches filling the air. It's hard to tell how close they are to the tumbling cars, and they don't dare look back.

Collette wants to leap out of her heavy boots and leave them behind, but the broken train is at their heels and she needs to move fast. She focuses on Marguerite's pale shirt ahead of her. She feels a thrill of pride as the outline of the trees appears, and she can still hear the train cars smash into one another like thunderclaps, tossing crates, heavy boxes, and metal barrels in all directions. Quick blasts explode, filling the air with thick black smoke and chunks of splintered wood.

Suddenly Collette feels a sharp pain, as if she's been stabbed by a hot poker in her thigh. She rolls onto the ground clutching her leg and slams into the side of a metal box that has tumbled far from the tracks and broken open. Guns and ammunition have spilled on the ground. She lies disoriented in the dirt, staring in shock at a Nazi swastika painted on the side of the box.

The train cars nearby have stopped rolling, but the wheels are still spinning and squealing. Men are shouting in German amid loud popping sounds. Flames flicker along the tracks. Cargo is scattered everywhere.

Collette can't see Marguerite. *I've got to get away,* she thinks as she presses her hand on the box and pushes to help herself up. A sharp pain shoots up her leg, and she groans in surprise and falls back to the ground. She can see that her pants are torn and burned. She carefully pulls the cloth away to reveal a ripped cut on her thigh, globs of blood congealing in the cut and lines of red running down her leg. Her eyes blur as she registers the pain, and she realizes that she's in terrible danger. She has to be able to walk. She has to find Marguerite.

Two German soldiers run by, yelling orders. Collette manages to roll over and press against the box, but it's hard to figure out where she is. Can she possibly get out of there if she can stand and run?

"Collette!"

Is that Marguerite? Collette whips her head around but can't see her.

"Collette. Over here." Collette can hardly see in the dark and the smoke. There, peeking around an overturned railroad car is a girl with baggy clothes and a crooked beret. Marguerite.

Collette points to where the soldiers went. Marguerite stands on her toes and looks around, then sneaks over to Collette. In an instant, she pulls off her cotton shirt and wraps it around Collette's leg. Her loose gray undershirt is covered in soot and sweat. "Can you walk if I help you?"

"Was ist das?" A German soldier looms over them and kicks Marguerite's leg with his high leather boot. As he continues to shout, he grabs Marguerite's chin and glares into eyes that are wide with fright. She jerks her head away and slides closer to Collette. He squats down, unwraps the shirt around Collette's leg, studies the wound, and uses the shirtsleeves to tie a makeshift bandage over the cut. Collette winces as he roughly tightens the cloth, and she shudders in dread as he leans so close she can smell cigarettes on his breath. She can't help the tears as her leg throbs.

Steam and sooty smoke are still rising from the rubble. The noise from the crash has quieted down so that the voices of running, shouting soldiers can be clearly heard.

"Steh en sie auf!" the man orders, gesturing for them to stand. He grabs the back of their shirts and lifts the girls up. Collette leans on the metal box trying not to cry out, and Marguerite wraps her arm around Collette's waist. They exchange a look of dismay as they take in the pileup of train cars and German war supplies strewn along the tracks and into the fields. They hadn't expected to see the damage they'd done. They thought they would be on their bicycles by now. Collette wants to shout, "We did that!"

"Was machen sie denn hier?" the soldier asks harshly as he pushes them toward a tipped boxcar that's lying on its side. Every step sends a sharp pain up Collette's leg, but Marguerite holds tight.

He shoves them roughly into the boxcar and slides the heavy door shut, leaving them alone in the pitch-dark. Collette waits to hear the clang of the lock, but there's just the distant sound of yelling soldiers.

"We have to get out of here before he comes back!" Marguerite tugs on the metal door handle. "They'll never think we could have crashed their train, but they're going to want to know why we were so close to the tracks—if they don't shoot us first." She grabs the handle with both hands and shifts her weight, and the wide door opens slightly, revealing shadows of train cars in pale moonlight. "Do you think you can walk if you lean on me?"

Collette grits her teeth and leans back against the warm metal wall of the boxcar. "I'll *have* to. We have to get back to Panther."

Marguerite carefully slides the boxcar door open

a few more inches. The Germans have set up torches, and the soldiers have flashlights. They're still running around shouting as they drag boxes of supplies into one giant pile.

"We have to go right now." Marguerite reaches behind for Collette.

A wave of nausea suddenly hits Collette. As she looks out over the scene of the wreckage, it seems to be spinning. "You go. I'll slow you down."

"Collette—get up!" Marguerite barks, just like the German soldier. "Think about what we'll tell Panther. Think about those British paratroopers who'll give us chocolate and maybe even a medal. We did it, Collette. Skylark and Wallcreeper destroyed a German train! Now let's get out of here."

Then she smiles. Collette cannot believe that in the middle of the enemy, shoved into a toppled boxcar, Marguerite can manage a smile. "I am Wallcreeper," she says wearily, and heaves herself up, reaching for Marguerite's hand.

"Yes, you are. And I am Skylark, and I'm not

leaving you. We're in this together, my friend. Now hold on, and let's go."

They gingerly climb down from the boxcar, scanning the area to make sure that all the soldiers are busy elsewhere. Protected by train cars lying on their sides, piles of debris, and coal smoke, Marguerite half drags Collette away from the havoc they created. She moves them into dark corners, flattens them against the sides of the cars, and keeps them low when they might be visible. She never lets go, even as Collette falters.

Soon they leave the broken railroad tracks behind and make it across the fields to the woods, and finally to the hut. Collette collapses on the ground next to the hidden bicycles.

Marguerite rolls her bicycle out onto the road and flicks on the light mounted on the handlebars. "Climb in the basket." She motions to Collette. "Tonight *you* are the delivery."

Chapter 29
Chocolate Croissants

Cliff House

November 2012—Day 8

I don't interrupt once.

Marguerite moves around the cluttered room like a ballerina, waving her arms, rising on her toes, acting out the crashing of the train. She shows how they tossed their bicycles, stroked Le Roi's sweaty neck, and sneaked out of the woods toward the railroad tracks.

She demonstrates pushing the sliced railroad tracks with such strength that I almost jump up to help her.

I am there with her in southern France, frightened as the train pounds down the tracks, shaking in fear as she and my granny hide in the boxcar. I believe every word and can see it all.

The second she finishes telling about how she helped the injured Collette climb into the bicycle basket, Simone appears behind Marguerite's chair and gently places her hands on her mother's shoulders. "Time for a little rest now." She points at me. "Let's get you situated in the guest room. How long can you stay?"

But Marguerite isn't finished. "Let me tell Lily one more thing."

"Of course, Mama." Simone rests her elbows on the top of the wingback chair. "But you know how you like your nap before supper."

I hadn't noticed that Simone must have turned on a few of the lamps. In October, it starts to get dark earlier, and the day is already overcast and gloomy. A soft yellow glow highlights the collection of objects laid out carefully on the tables and bureaus crowding the room. I notice for the first time that the fabric of Marguerite's chair looks like antique maps.

I want to stay and explore the house, and hear more stories about Marguerite and my granny. But Simone's question also makes me realize that I have no plan. I was going to get the pen, hop on the train, and be back in Brooklyn before anyone missed me.

But it's so tempting to stay here longer. New York City, especially the Armory and Rockaway Manor, seem so far away. Was it only a few days ago I was watching the ocean rise?

I better check to make sure I haven't been declared a missing person. "Can I charge my phone?" I pull my phone out of my backpack. The battery is low, but it's still alive. There's a long list of texts, missed calls, and voice mails. I scan quickly and see that they are from my mom (every ten or fifteen minutes), Nicole, and Johnny.

While I had been engrossed in tales of a world war, comfortable in an old house overlooking the ocean, everyone else had been going nuts trying to reach me. Had something happened to Granny?

Simone points to an outlet located next to a small round table that seems to have dozens of postcards glued to the top of it. "I've made up a room for you. But you've called home, right?"

"I have a lot of messages. I'll call as soon as the phone's charged. I think I better let everyone know I'm okay." I dread hearing what my mom will say, but know I have to check in soon. I want to tell her about Granny and Marguerite, but I'm not so sure she'll listen.

Marguerite stands unsteadily, and Simone reaches out to help her. "Mama, you've worn yourself out. Let's have a little lie-down."

"We are not doing anything." Marguerite winks at me. "But I will indulge in a little nap now. And then at supper I'll tell Lily all about how soon after we derailed the train, the south of France was liberated from the Germans. It was glorious! But also so sad because that's when I had to leave Collette and my beloved Brume."

She shuffles across the room toward the back of the house, suddenly appearing much older than the Marguerite who acted out her days as a Resistance fighter.

I need to check on Granny.

I scroll through the texts but don't bother to listen to the voice mails. They're all from my mom and I have a pretty good idea what she's said.

Johnny's texts start with:

Everyone freaking out.

Call your mom

And, after a series of additional warnings, follows with his admission that he finally had to tell everyone where I am.

Had to show your mom your last text to prove u r alive.

I guess I haven't handled this part of my mission very well. So far I managed to keep everyone distracted, but this time I am definitely in trouble.

I listen to Nicole's message. She explains that my mom wouldn't leave the Armory and at first had Granny all upset—until Granny realized where I am and is thrilled. "Miss Collette wants you to tell her all about it and keeps talking about someone named Marguerite. I'm getting concerned because she seems more confused than ever. Who's Marguerite?"

I have to smile at that message. Poor Granny is making sense to me but probably appears to be deep in a period of dementia.

Simone comes back from settling Marguerite and grabs my boots and backpack. I unplug my phone, and she leads the way to the guest room up another flight of stairs. It's surprisingly plain, with a single bed piled with quilts and patchwork pillows, a rocking chair draped with a woven shawl, and a bedside table with a china lamp. Two fat books are stacked on the table.

A window overlooks a small courtyard with bushes stripped of leaves, and chairs like the ones outside the restaurant in Brooklyn.

"You can come help me in the kitchen after you make your calls, if you want." Simone barely fits through the doorway of the small room. She straightens a small braided rug with the toe of her shoe and drops my backpack and boots on the rocker. "Or you can take some time to look at everything in the living room."

I can tell by her smile that she knows exactly what I'll do after I make my calls. She pulls out of her apron pocket a sample bottle of shampoo, a toothbrush, and mini toothpaste. "I still haven't seen everything she has in that room, and I've lived here all my life. She keeps hauling things out of the attic and moving things around."

"Where'd she get all that stuff?" I sink onto the edge of the bed. Everything in the house seems so comfortable.

"Well, as I said, she traveled everywhere, talking about the war, sharing her stories. She's made friends around the world and saved everything they gave her. She must have more in her collection than some museums—postcards, maps, compasses . . ."

"Fountain pens?"

"She only wanted one fountain pen. She has very little from her childhood in France. Everyone was so scattered—she had no one who could tell her what happened to her friend. She went back to Brume a few times, but there was no one left who remembered her as a child. Years ago she decided not to go back until she found out about Collette. You have no idea what joy you've brought my mama."

Simone straightens the shawl on the back of the chair, and as she leaves the room, she says, "Thank you for coming here, Lily. You are braver than I'll ever be. I don't even have a passport." She points to the books on the bedside table: *The Wonders of Argentina* and *View from the Great Wall*. "That's how I travel."

I scoot back on the bed and lean on fat pillows stacked against the wide, carved wooden headboard.

I decide I'd better call Johnny and find out what's going on, before I talk to my mom. He's at the restaurant and can't talk much but basically warns me that my mom, Nicole, and Maria are freaked out, and now even he's seriously worried. "You better call your mom right away. Be prepared to catch hell. Why didn't you text me after you got to Marguerite's, Lily?"

I'm not used to Johnny showing that much concern. He's usually pretty relaxed. I pull my legs up and drag a quilt over them. I really screwed up, but hasn't it been worth it? I try to explain about Marguerite and Collette, Skylark and Wallcreeper, but he cuts me off. "There's a Metro-North train tonight. You better be on it. I can't cover for you anymore." He hangs up, and I hold the phone in front of me, shocked. Johnny has never even been this mad at me before. He must be catching it hard from my mom.

Just as I start to call my mom, Johnny texts, Sorry. Come home. I grip the phone and want to call him back and keep him on the phone as I explore Marguerite's house. I want to describe everything, even bring him there to see it with his own eyes. He should meet Marguerite and hear her tell the stories in person.

My mom answers without a hello. "You are so grounded. No phone, no friends, no . . . no . . . no anything," she sputters. "What in the *world* were you thinking?"

I start to answer, but she just picks up speed. "Obviously, you were *not* thinking! Seriously, did you consider anyone else at all?"

"I was thinking about Granny," I say softly.

That stops her for a moment, but she starts up again. "I can't believe you lied to me, Lily. How am I ever going to trust you again?" Her voice is shaky, and she blows her nose loudly into the phone.

I clutch a soft pillow to my chest and think about Simone's words about how brave I am. If you are brave, do you feel this awful and make people cry? Maybe this is how Granny used to make Mom feel when she traveled. "I'm sorry, Mom. I really am. But everything turned out fine."

"Lily, if you say everything is fine to me one more time, I'll . . ." She blows her nose again and is finally quiet on the other end of the phone.

"Mom—are you still there?"

"Of course I am," she says. "I'm trying to absorb all of this, Lily." She asks me if I'm okay. "Did anyone bother you on the train? Did you get anything to eat? Does Marguerite live in a safe neighborhood?" I tell her all about Marguerite's intriguing Cliff House, and about Henry and the Fountain Pen Emporium, the letters, and the ride on the Metro-North. I repeat the adventures of Collette and Marguerite as secret members of Noah's Ark, and she actually listens. She's completely surprised and doesn't interrupt with questions, just exclaims and gasps, amazed at the story. When I finish, she bursts out, "You have to write this down!"

Then it's my turn to ask questions about Granny. For once, my mom doesn't avoid talking about anything that makes her nervous. She explains how Granny traveled a lot when my mom was growing up, and when Granny came home, she tried to share the details of her adventures, but my mom didn't want to hear the stories. She didn't beg to go along on the trips. My mom just wanted to keep Granny home.

"One time, Lily, I heard on the radio that a hotel had been bombed in the Middle East somewhere. It was the hotel that your grandmother was staying at—we'd talked briefly on the phone the night before. I was staying with a friend."

"What happened? Was it her hotel?"

"She'd left for the airport just before the bombing but didn't try to reach me because she didn't think I knew about it. It was a terrible night. When she got home, I didn't speak to her for days."

There's silence as I realize why my mom seems to worry a lot. "Well, we have cell phones now, Mom."

"Not much good if you don't use them."

"I'm sorry, Mom. It's just that everything happened so fast. And I *did* text you." I don't want to tell her that I didn't call because she wouldn't let me go. I want her to know that there were times that I missed her, but the words won't come.

"Texting about pizza and movies at the Armory when you're really at Grand Central Station? Never again, Lily. You really pushed the limit this time, and I am *not pleased.*"

I can hear her anger through the phone, but all I want is one of her crushing hugs. I whisper, "I'm sorry," but it doesn't feel like enough.

"We have a lot to talk about." I can tell it's going to take a long time before she'll trust me again.

She seems to be winding down, but she's using her I-mean-business voice. "You have my mother's genes, and I guess there's nothing I can do about that. But, Lily, you're only twelve, and I'm going to have to watch you a lot more closely." She sighs so loudly I'm sure the entire Armory can hear her.

I think about my granny saying that my dad was fearless. Maybe I have his genes, too.

"Mom, Granny never told you about Marguerite?"

My mom hesitates. "She mentioned her once or twice, said she was an old friend in France. She made a lot of friends during her life, so I didn't pursue it."

"But Marguerite is special."

"Yes, she most certainly is."

I describe Simone. "You'd like her, Mom. She doesn't have a passport, either!"

"And you carry yours wherever you go." She pauses, and I prepare for another lecture. Surprisingly, she adds, "But you uncovered so much information that I didn't know!" She goes on to tell me that Granny never once mentioned anything about the French Resistance. "I knew that she lived in France as a child, but she moved to New York and never talked about it again. She worked on perfecting her English. It's as if she deliberately left it all behind." I could hear the dismay in my mom's voice. "Well, it's certainly understandable, considering what she experienced during the war."

"There's so much more I want to know."

"I'm sorry, Lily, I've never heard the details about Marguerite, never saw the pen, and certainly never knew that she was doing such treacherous heroic things like scaling mountains, hiding from German soldiers, and crashing trains at twelve years old. Do you think it's all true?"

I picture Marguerite deep in memory as she told her stories. "Oh, Marguerite was definitely there with Granny. But why didn't Granny tell you about it?"

"It must have been too horrible to remember." Her voice softens. "She only told me that she lost her big brother in the war and saw terrible, frightening things. She just wanted to forget. It happens to a lot of people who survive wars, Lilybelle."

My granny always calls me Lilybelle, but not my

mom. I slide down so that I'm buried in pillows and the warm quilt. "Mom, isn't Granny amazing?"

I think she's crying because she has trouble answering me. "You both are, sweetie. Now get your butt on that morning train. I just wish Simone could travel with you, but you say she doesn't travel, so make sure she gets you safely on the train." She starts rambling. "Please be careful, don't talk to strangers, and I'll be at Grand Central when you arrive." I think about all the strangers I've met since I was checking the floodwaters for Nicole at Rockaway Manor.

I don't want my mom to go, but the bed is pulling me in for a nap. "Mom, have you ever had crème brûlée? Or a chocolate croissant?"

She chuckles. "Your granny's from France, Lily. Of course I have. I guess we'll have to put those on the list for Johnny to learn how to make. Now get some rest." She waits for me to hang up first. As I start to call Nicole, the phone beeps: HUG HUG HUG. I send her back a heart.

Chapter 30
Evacuation

As it turns out, I do get a chaperone for my train ride back to Manhattan. Marguerite insisted on traveling to New York so she could finally see my granny. "I'm just going to be sitting and sleeping," Marguerite tried to reassure Simone.

"But you hate trains! Do you want me to go with you?" Marguerite made her *pfft* sound again, and Simone fussed and lectured. Finally they agreed that Simone would drive us to the station and Marguerite and I would take the Metro-North train to Manhattan.

By late morning, we settle next to each other on the Metro-North, equipped with a basket of goodies prepared by Simone. A loaf of French bread pokes out of the basket. Apparently Simone thought that we would be starving in the ninety-minute ride back.

Marguerite naps for a bit, but she's so excited she can't stay quiet for long. She keeps asking me all about my granny, and I realize that I don't know much about Granny's life. "Granny doesn't talk much about herself, except to describe the gardens she planted all over the world. Of course, I never really asked." I'm going to ask now, that's for sure. I hope it's not too late and Granny can still remember.

To pass the time, Marguerite teaches me some questions in French that she thinks everyone should know if they travel: *Where does this bus go? How much does this cost? Where are the restrooms?* She must think that my mission to Cliff House is just the beginning of my travels. She's right because now I want to go everywhere.

She also teaches me sentences that crack me up. *Do you know any cute boys? This meal is disgusting.* The people across the aisle look up from their iPads and smile at the two of us. We must be an odd pair, twelve-year-old me with my pirate boots and Henry's black coat, and eighty-year-old Marguerite in her "traveling outfit" of leggings tucked into UGGs. Her long tunic is a swirl of blues and greens, and she's loaded on several shiny necklaces. This time she's wearing a series of silver bracelets that jangle at her wrist.

She has a fur cape that she's assured me is fake fur, but she's brought along a fuzzy pink fur hat that ties under her chin. It's kind of ratty-looking, and she places it over the seat in front of us "to air out."

We're both so anxious to see Granny again. It's hard to believe I've only been gone for little more than a day.

We go through the letters again, and Marguerite tells me more about her life after Brume. "I've been almost everywhere in the world, but the most special place was Germany."

"Germany?" After what she'd told me about her experiences with German soldiers in France, I'm surprised that she even wanted to go there. "Don't you hate the Germans?"

She pauses for a moment and gently folds the

letters and replaces the rubber band. "I did when I was a child. It took many years for me to even think of the Germans as real people. The memories were too horrible."

"So why did you go?"

"I was invited." She points to her tapestry bag above the seats across the aisle, and I struggle to pull it down. As I place it on the space between us, it pops open to reveal the shoebox filled with the tools of the Resistance. I wonder what else she's brought along to share with Granny.

She rummages around in the side pockets and pulls out a flyer that announces her as a speaker at the United Nations. "You spoke at the United Nations? In New York City? That's so cool!"

"I gave speeches at a lot of places in the world, but speaking in New York was a real honor. If only I'd known that Collette was so close." She flattens the flyer and reads aloud the heading "Let There Be Peace on Earth." She points at her name highlighted under the title. "My speech was about what it feels like to be living in constant danger, terrified that your family will be taken away and killed."

"But how could you talk about that in Germany? They were the ones who made your life so miserable!"

"It was extremely hard, but I discovered it was possible." She folds up the flyer and tucks it back into the bag. She reaches into another pocket and pulls out two candy sticks. "Root beer," she says, and winks as she hands one of them to me. "I tell Simone my mouth gets dry, but I just like candy." She giggles.

"My granny likes chocolate." That causes her to beam a wide smile. She reaches into the bottom of the bag and displays two Hershey bars. "One for us to share, and one for Collette. I have them stashed all over the house. You never know when you might need some chocolate."

I ask her to tell me the story of the bridge again and how she gave candy bars to the German soldiers. "I know it sounds exciting, Lily. But we were always afraid." She slips all the candy into a side pocket of the bag so that it's handy. "At some point, I realized that someone needed to speak up so that children like you won't have to go through the same thing."

"And that meant talking to the Germans?" I try to understand, but it's confusing. There are some kids at school that I stay far away from because they've done things that are mean. I can't imagine even bothering to talk to them. "How could you forget what they'd done?"

As I shove the tapestry bag back onto the rack above us and grab the basket of food, she responds, choosing her words carefully. Her accent seems especially heavy, and her voice fades as she speaks. I glance over to see if she's all right. "Oh, I don't forget," she says with a sigh. "I don't even forgive. But we do have to make sure that history doesn't repeat itself." She points to her lap, and I place the square basket on her thin legs.

She pulls out overloaded sandwiches, hard-boiled eggs, a thermos filled with cold soup that she calls "vichyssoise," and bottles of Snapple. "No wonder this was so heavy!" We laugh as she keeps adding food to my lap and the opened tray table. She holds

382

up a box of different kinds of pastries. "Simone must think we'll be on this train for days!"

Stuck in the corner of the basket is a cluster of silk flowers. I carefully lift the bouquet, and Marguerite pats my hand. "Daisies are still one of her favorites?" I nod and gently put them back where they won't get crushed.

I watch as we speed by some of the sites that I missed when I slept on the train going up the coast. I think about how scared and lonely I was. Now I text back and forth with Johnny and my mom and finally get a chance to talk to Nicole. My mom has told everyone at the Armory the entire story, from the beginning. She visited Granny after work and tells me every detail about the complicated route she had to take because some subways are still closed.

Johnny stopped by the Armory to check on Granny, too. He provided the details about Henry and the Pen Emporium, and Granny seems to be following it all, although she's still not sharing any information about her childhood in France.

Nicole gets on the phone and tells me that Granny is so overwhelmed about seeing Marguerite that they have to keep checking her blood pressure. Granny's laid out her favorite dress with the tiny blue flowers and her red sweater, and is planning on wearing her blue silk wedding shoes. "She can't even stand in them, but she insists. This is a very special occasion!"

I tell this to Marguerite and she again describes how Collette became Jean-Pierre and the two of them kept their hair short and dressed as boys. "We weren't going to get away with our disguise too much longer, but I sure did like riding around on a bicycle wearing pants. You can do that now, but back then it was highly unusual. You're a lucky girl." We reload the basket, and she reaches for the thermos as the train begins to slow down. "Are we there already?"

The Metro-North train jerks ahead for a few moments, jostling the basket of food so that it almost falls off Marguerite's lap. She closes the top of the basket, and we both lean to look out the window. There's nothing but a crumbling wall marked with graffiti a few feet from the train.

"We're getting close to Manhattan, but this doesn't look like a stop." I stretch to peer out the window on the other side of the train. There's more wall on that side, with piles of discarded tires and lumber scattered on the ground. Passengers look around in confusion. A murmur starts to build.

A low train whistle is heard in the distance, and the train screeches to a sudden halt, throwing us both forward. Marguerite flings out her arm to stop me from crashing into the seat in front of us. I reach for the basket, but it falls to the floor, spilling out the loaf of French bread and bottles of Snapple.

We slam back into our seats. For a moment, there's silence in the car, then everyone begins talking at once. Voices are low at first, but as people rise to peer out the windows, the noise level builds.

"Are you okay?" we both say at once. Marguerite mutters something in French and straightens the silver combs in her hair. "Qu'est-ce qui se passe?" She fusses with her bracelets and smooths her shirt. I watch her to see if I should be worried. "Find out what's happening, Lily."

A crackling noise comes over a loudspeaker, followed by a muffled announcement. "Can't hear you!" someone yells, while others push the buttons on the doors to move to other cars. A red light near the ceiling comes on and starts to flash.

The announcement is repeated, this time by a robotic voice repeating, "Stay seated. Do not evacuate. Stay seated. Do not evacuate."

"We need to get off this train." Marguerite grabs the seat in front of her and tries to stand up. She stumbles over the basket of food on the floor but manages to step over me to the aisle and wrap her fur cape around her shoulders, closing the toggle at the top. She snatches the pink fur hat and reaches for her tapestry bag, but it's too high. "Come, Lily. Hurry."

"They're telling us to stay here." Marguerite's already moving toward the back of the train. Passengers fill the aisle so that she disappears from view.

"Do not evacuate," the announcement keeps repeating as the train car begins to empty. I can see people outside, stepping over piles of debris.

I immediately think of downtown Manhattan and wonder if it was Sandy that dumped the garbage.

"Marguerite!" She doesn't answer, but then I spot her pressed against the back wall of the train near the exit, as if she's trying to hide. "I don't think we're supposed to leave the train, Marguerite. Come back to the seat with me." I try to pull gently on her arm, but she pulls away roughly and goes out the door to the gangway that connects the cars. As a man helps her down the stairs, I squirm between people blocking the doorway and scramble down the steps to get to her.

There's smoke pouring out from the engine of the train way down the line, and it's blowing toward us, irritating my eyes. It's chilly, and I take the pink fur hat from Marguerite's hand and place it on her head, tying the pom-poms. She adjusts her fur cape, and as I hold her arm, we make our way down the side of the tracks. It's eerily quiet, even though we're surrounded by people who were nervous enough to quickly evacuate.

"Get away from the train," Marguerite says

urgently, tightening her elbow around my arm. I guide her around a crushed wooden box. "Go close to the wall." As we approach the cement wall a group of kids about my age gather near us, chattering and laughing. They all have their phones out and are filming or taking pictures as they pose against the colorful graffiti.

The urge to join them is strong. I feel like I haven't seen anyone my age in weeks, except for the kids who came to the Armory and then left again. I understand how these kids, dressed in shirts and jeans but ignoring the cold, can joke around while the adults worry. I want to be silly with them. But I understand how things can go wrong.

Marguerite hasn't said a word. She's still clinging to me and I can feel her shaking. She leans against the hard wall, closes her eyes, takes in deep breaths, slowly letting them out. "I hate trains," she says, "but I'll do anything for Collette."

A conductor comes by, waving a flashlight. "Back on board, folks. It's just kids on the tracks. Started a fire." He ushers our huddled group back on the train.

Marguerite seems steadier now, and when we reach our seat, she calmly hands me her cape and hat. I reload the food basket, checking to make sure that the daisies are still protected. I set aside the box of pastries and shove the basket back into the overhead bin next to the tapestry bag. As the conductor walks up the aisle answering questions, Marguerite opens up the pastry box and offers one to him.

"So sorry about the inconvenience, ma'am." He eyes the desserts briefly but refuses. "We have a team working on the problem and we'll be on our way in a little while."

Marguerite adjusts her seat so that she's leaning back. "Just kids on the tracks," she says softly to herself.

Chapter 31
Huzzah!

Brooklyn
November 2012—Day 9

Marguerite hands me the pastry box and points to the group of kids who have now gathered in the back of the train. "Give them this. They'll love you."

As I approach them, they're taking silly pictures and playing a game on an iPad. I offer them the box of desserts and am immediately absorbed into the group. Soon I'm in the pictures and sending them to Johnny. They climb on the seats, jump in the air, and flop on top of each other to get a better photo. No one tells them to stop. Passengers are on their phones or complaining to each other about the delay.

One boy stands on his head, his feet resting on the

doorway under the exit sign so we can take a picture. It's nice not to worry if he'll fall and get hurt.

"That old lady's waving at you." A girl with sleek blond hair points to Marguerite, who's waiting in a line for the restroom at the other end of the aisle. We both wave back. I want to say, "That's not an old lady; that's Marguerite," but that wouldn't make much sense if you hadn't spent time in a nursing home. Instead I say, "Her name is Skylark."

"Sweet." The girl flashes a picture of Marguerite and takes another one of herself. She shows me a video on her phone that makes us both giggle as if it were the funniest video ever made.

When we finally pull into Grand Central, there's Johnny waiting with my mom. Marguerite looks worn out, but she walks briskly up to my mom and grips her with a hug. I can't look my mom in the eye, and expect her to put her hand out for my phone. But she turns to me and smushes me with a long welcome hug. Maybe she realizes that if I'm going to keep in touch, then I need to keep my phone.

Johnny is standing by with a wheelchair. "Hey," he says to me, and that's all he needs to say. I wave good-bye to my new friends. The blond girl checks out Johnny as she waves back.

Marguerite refuses the wheelchair, but in the long cab ride to the Armory, Johnny and I squish her between us so she won't get tossed around in the back seat. Johnny plows through the food basket, inspecting uneaten cheeses and asking about the leftovers. As we pull up to the Armory, Marguerite is sharing the recipe for vichyssoise as Johnny records it on his phone.

The welcome at the Armory is ridiculous. We are immediately surrounded by residents. I hadn't been gone long at all, but some of them have no sense of time anymore, so I guess they think I've been gone for weeks. Everyone seems to know why I left for the coast and brought back the long-lost Marguerite.

My granny is wobbly in her blue shoes, and Maria has to hold her up. I pull Granny in gently. We don't speak, just wrap our arms around each other. Then I step back and turn my cheek so she can kiss it and say,

"Such a good girl, my Lilybelle." I feel like I'm home.

Marguerite watches and waits. Her skin is pale so that her freckles stand out more than ever. There are dark circles under her eyes, but she still looks strong and cheerful.

My granny is obviously frail next to Marguerite, and she's pale under the pink powder that someone has brushed on her cheeks. But her blue eyes are gleaming when Marguerite steps forward. Nurses and volunteers hover in the background, eager to witness the reunion.

At first the two old friends engage in a fast conversation in French that no one understands. Granny is stuck in place in her high heel shoes, so Marguerite reaches out her arms, bracelets jangling, and steps forward to embrace her Collette. I worry that the hug is too hard for Granny and will hurt her. But they're laughing and crying and rocking back and forth, so I guess she's all right. Johnny gives me a thumbs-up, and WM, free of her neck brace, raises her arms and shouts, "Huzzah!"

"Quite a stunt you pulled there, kiddo," a deep voice says behind me. "Can I have my coat back now?" I turn to see Henry, his hair neatly slicked over his head and his glasses just as smeared. He flashes his uneven yellow teeth. I'm glad to see him. "Your friend came back to get your bicycle, and he filled me in."

I hand him his coat. "Thanks. For more than the coat." He nods and steps aside to make room for André, who's pushing the restaurant bicycle with the big basket.

"André!" shouts Johnny, working his way through the crowd to shake André's hand. I must look confused because Johnny quickly explains. "Remember when you asked me to return the bike to the restaurant? Well, André was making desserts when I got there, and he's taught me how to make crème brûlée!"

I tell them about the food that Simone served while Marguerite told her stories. "I promised Simone I'd come back to Cliff House. Next time, Johnny, you can come with me." Johnny gives me that smile that I know is only meant for me. I grin back.

Marguerite and Granny sit on Granny's cot, furiously speaking French. Granny's kicked off her fancy shoes, and her bare feet look so tiny. They're poring through the shoebox and inspecting the blue marble pen. "Brume!" I hear Granny say a few times. They appear to be two elderly ladies sitting on a cot in a temporary nursing home, but to me they are two young girls, Skylark and Wallcreeper, plotting their next mission. I want to join them.

"Let's get a picture!" Henry pulls out a camera from his fanny pack and gestures for everyone to gather together. Marguerite pulls her fluffy pink hat out of the tapestry bag. Johnny ties it under her chin as I help Granny put on her pink beret. We help them off the cot, and my mom and I bunch together with the two brave Resistance fighters.

"Wait!" Marguerite's commanding voice penetrates the constant talking. She signals for Johnny and gives him instructions, her hands flying around. He turns and talks to André, and they roll the bicycle into the middle of the group. Marguerite stands proudly next to the bike while I hold it firmly in place. She rearranges the plastic flowers on the basket, then grasps the handlebars. Granny joins Marguerite, holds the fountain pen in the air, and orders Henry, "Take the picture!"

As Henry takes several shots, I notice a National Guardsman saunter into the Armory. He's dressed in full camouflage and strides over to Nicole, who's been trying to keep Mr. Tennenbaum out of the pictures. "Are you in charge here?" He looks serious.

"I suppose you'd say so," she says warily. We all quiet down. "Now what?"

"Well, I'm happy to tell you that Rockaway Manor is solid." He grins so that it looks like his entire face is a smile. "Give us a few more days to finish the paint job, and you're all going home!" A cheer goes up throughout the Armory. The Guardsman tries to keep speaking to Nicole, but he can't be heard. We're still posed for the next picture, chattering about the news. Nicole motions for everyone to settle down.

The Guardsman gives Nicole a clipboard with a

sheet of paper attached. "You have to authorize the move back to Rockaway Manor." He reaches over to Granny. "Can I borrow your pen?" She hands over the fountain pen with a flourish.

He points to the paper on the clipboard. "Sign here."

He jumps in surprise as we all laugh and exclaim, "Sign here!"

Maria calls us over to sit at a table set up under the basketball hoop that has paper-towel place mats held down by small cartons of chocolate milk. In the center of the table there are peanut butter and jelly sandwiches and pudding cups stacked around an extra-large sheet cake decorated in glow sticks: *S & W!*

The group gathers around the table to feast on Armory food, but Granny and Marguerite walk arm in arm to a set of aluminum beach chairs arranged in the corner near Granny's cot.

"Would you like some cake?" I ask them, but they're deep in conversation. I'm not sure if I should join them. Granny looks up and points to the shoebox on her cot. "Can you bring that to me, Lily?" Marguerite pulls over an empty chair, and they sit down next to each other.

I carefully place the heavy shoebox on Granny's lap. I guess they want to be alone with their memories, but as I turn away, they both call out, "Lilybelle?" Marguerite motions for me to sit across from them.

Granny reaches into the shoebox, and she pulls out one of the small boxes of soap that's decorated with the Eiffel Tower and has a false bottom for hiding secret messages. She gives Marguerite a long look and Marguerite nods. Granny places the box of soap in the palm of my hand. There's still a faint whiff of lavender.

"Lilybelle," Granny says as they both lean forward, "we need you to go to Brume."

Author's Note

Although this book is fiction, the story is based on actual events. There really was a nursing home evacuated during Superstorm Sandy, in 2012, in Queens, New York, and the residents and nurses stayed for three weeks in an armory. There really was a French Resistance group called the Alliance that the Germans referred to as Noah's Ark because its members had animal code names. The leader, Marie-Madeleine Fourcade, was code-named Hedgehog.

There were many different resistance groups in France that performed various types of sabotage and espionage. It was extremely hazardous work and took great determination, especially because of the risk of torture, death, and deportation, and the possibility of reprisals against French citizens. The resistance workers blew up bridges, trains, and supply dumps; kidnapped and killed German Army officers; passed along vital intelligence information; hid families trying to escape; ambushed German troops; decoded secret messages; and assisted Allied soldiers and intelligence operatives who landed in southern France to deliver supplies and carry out spy missions.

Children also participated in the French Resistance. One example is that boys (or maybe they were really girls?) threw fake lumps of coal onto the open coal cars of German supply trains. Hidden in the coal was plastic explosive. When the coal was shoveled into the boiler of the locomotive, trains exploded and crashed.

It is also true that the American Office of Strategic Services in 1944 experimented in derailing trains without explosives. After several tries, they figured out that if a piece of rail sixty inches long was removed from one side of the track, and a piece thirty inches long removed from the other side of the track, offset by thirty inches, the train would derail. The locomotive and first few cars would hang together, but the rest of the loaded cars would drift and crash.

Collette and Marguerite's Brume could be any

village in southern France during World War II in 1944. The author would like to thank the International Museum of World War II in Natick, Massachusetts (https://museumofworldwarii.org); the World War II veterans who gave the author detailed personal accounts of liberating the south of France; and the real Nicole for her unbelievable dedication to her elderly residents.

Special thanks to Barbara Kelly, Carrie Pestritto, and Charlie Ilgunas for their encouraging words and remarkable attention to detail.

DEC - - 2018